Rosemary Friedman

We All Fall Down

This edition published in 2001 by House of Stratus, an imprint of Stratus Holdings plc, 24c Old Burlington Street,.London, W1X 1RL, UK.

www.houseofstratus.com

Typeset, printed and bound by House of Stratus.

A catalogue record for this book is available from the British Library.

ISBN 0-7551-0113-8

Rosemary Friedman's writing career was launched with great success by her first novel *No White Coat*, published in *Best*

BY THE SAME AUTHOR
ALL PUBLISHED BY HOUSE OF STRATUS

No White Coat
Love on My List
Patients of a Saint
The Fraternity
The Commonplace Day
The General Practice
Practice Makes Perfect
The Life Situation
The Long Hot Summer
Proofs of Affection
A Loving Mistress
Rose of Jericho
A Second Wife
To Live in Peace
An Eligible Man
Golden Boy
Vintage
Intensive Care

To D.

One

Had it not been for the fact that steel king William Boothroyd, familiar face on the City page of every daily newspaper and always good for half a column of gossip, dropped dead in the street one April afternoon, the treadmill might never have slowed down long enough for Arthur Dexter to step off. As it was, it stopped turning for a moment in time not only long enough to let Arthur off, dragging his wife and children behind him, but, as it gathered momentum, to send Honey and Basil and Howard and the Gurneys and Louise and her old mother sprawling at his feet. No one was more surprised than Arthur to find himself, standing on unfamiliar ground, watching the great wheel turn without him. When it happened he shrugged his shoulders and walked, not a very big man, away from its inevitable roll.

The day, as usually happens with days that are to prove different, began as any other. From the April sun which found its way through the chink in his heavy satin bedroom curtains, to the April sun on the yellow bricks and the sooted cowls of the city, Arthur Dexter made the customary daily, unextraordinary transition. From his large desk with its basket of letters to be dealt with and ashtray full of paper clips, elastic bands and keys with which to wind mechanical toys, to his secretary with her permanently red nose, the inevitable packet of Kleenex on her lap, all was as usual. Against a background of yapping City dogs in the yard below and delivery lorries with clanking chains, Arthur Dexter went about his business. Briskly, methodically, interrupted constantly by the buzz of the telephones, he began on the day's correspondence. Miss Walsh, the soft sliding of her pencil across her notebook accompanied by the regular sniffing which Arthur after fifteen years no longer noticed, took letters to the Customs and Excise Office re importation of pottery, book-ends from Japan, another to enquire whether glass marbles such as the one Arthur rolled towards her across the desk, and which she caught expertly, might be imported under open general licence, and one to the Chinese Toy Merchandising Company, Foochow, China, concerning an order for binoculars, tom-tom sets and compendiums of jokes. In between his dictation, allowing time for Miss Walsh to deal with her nose and to speculate about the various men she imagined, poor soul, to be in love with her, Arthur spoke to a clerk about a confirmation he had not yet received for a thousand guitars, another about some samples from South America, and to a supplier to complain about the faulty mechanism in a consignment of walking elephants. He dealt also with a cable from Warsaw put on his desk by a high-heeled typist with blue eye-shadow, an artist's agent who arrived with a new design for a snakes and ladder box, an inefficient invoice clerk who received short shrift, letters from Sweden, China, Japan, Poland, Italy and Russia, and a sales note about a strolling duck family. Because it was Monday and he wished to clear his desk, he had a sandwich brought to his office and continued working, at undiminished pace but with rising temper, on into the afternoon.

By the time Miss Walsh came softly into the office and handed him the evening paper the pall of smoke was grey outside his window, the sun had completely disappeared, and the sooty buildings were almost one with the sky. As on every other evening, Arthur took the newspaper from her and turned, as he always did, straight to the closing prices. Wall Street was firm, he noted, and many equities were up. There was also a column to the effect that exports were being hit by a fall in commodity prices. Although this last item affected the affairs of Arthur Dexter directly, he was not too worried. One could not, he thought, take too seriously the rumblings from the Far East. Satisfied that all was reasonably well as far as his investments were concerned, he closed the paper, laid it on his blotter, and picking up the receivers of both the telephones on his desk he held one to each ear. Into one he said: "Ask Mr Beesley if he's found out yet about the chenille dolls from Italy. I asked him half an hour ago to make enquiries," and into the other: "Johnson, I haven't had a single stock card; will you bring them in immediately, please!" It was then that he noticed the headline in the newspaper, 'Millionaire drops dead in street', and underneath a bad picture of Willie Boothroyd in evening dress arriving at a film première. For a moment there was a vacuum in Arthur Dexter's mind. Mentally and physically he froze. It was a full minute before he laid the telephone receivers on the desk and picked up the newspaper. He stared at it, then took off his glasses and stared again. It was, of course, ridiculous, completely fantastic. Last night the Dexters had sat next to the Boothroyds at a dinner given at the Dorchester in aid of an invalid Children's Association, and Arthur and his close friend Willie Boothroyd had spent most of the evening in conversation. Willie had been in a particularly jolly mood, and bursting with vitality as always. He had, in fact, been dancing the cha-cha-cha at midnight, and Arthur remembered wondering where he got the energy from, knowing, as he did, that he was at his desk every morning at eight o'clock. They had been discussing, he recalled, Willie's forthcoming cruise to South America, and he had asked Arthur why he and Vera didn't come along, too, and Arthur had said he couldn't afford to leave his business for so long. Then Willie had asked about Victor and if he still refused to go into his father's business, and Arthur said that he was still set on going up to Cambridge and that he was going to read history. History! Willie's reaction had been the same as his own.

What would happen to the business? What *would* happen to the business...?

There was a buzzing noise from the telephone receiver. "Mr Beesley here, sir, about the chenille dolls..."

Arthur held the paper closer. It was a bad picture of Willie anyway. It made him look older than he was. How old was he? Fifty? Fifty-one? Not more. They had been at school together in the same class, and Arthur was fifty.

"Mr Dexter, sir, about the chenille dolls..."

Perhaps they had made a mistake. Arthur unfolded the paper and spread it flat on the desk. He put on his glasses again in order to read the small print. 'Mr William Boothroyd,' he read, 'President of English Steel Holdings, collapsed and died outside his office building at lunchtime today. Mr Boothroyd, well known financier and philanthropist, was, as far as was known, in good health. He is survived by his wife Mrs Margaret Boothroyd formerly Miss Margaret Lubbock... There were no children... An inquest will be held.' On page four there were other paragraphs. Arthur wondered where they dug them up from so quickly. William Boothroyd's charitable work, his house in Nassau, his enormous steel organisation, his friends (famous, of course), his race-horses, speculations as to how much he was worth. Last night William Boothroyd had left his soup and joked about his diet, pierced his cigar with Arthur's gadget, stood on the pavement outside the Dorchester for a breather, danced jovially with Arthur's daughter. Now William Boothroyd was no longer in existence. Arthur put down the newspaper. It was no good. It was too sudden. Too much of a shock. He could not be expected to believe it.

There was a knock at his door which he didn't answer. Miss Walsh came in pulling at her cardigan, already shapeless from her nervous habit, and sucking a throat pastille. She picked up the telephone receiver and handed it to him. "I thought perhaps you'd gone out. It's Mr Beesley about the chenille dolls."

"What does he want?"

"I'll enquire." Miss Walsh spoke into the telephone, then with her hand over the mouthpiece turned to Arthur. "He says the chenille dolls with wooden stands *do* need stronger packing."

Arthur stared at her.

"What shall I tell him, Mr Dexter?"

"Tell him it doesn't matter."

A young man in his shirtsleeves came into the office.

"You wanted the stock cards, Mr Dexter."

"Not now, Johnson." Arthur stood up.

"But you particularly said..."

Arthur had his hat on. "I'm going now."

"What about the Japanese coffee sets?" Miss Walsh said.

"I don't know." He opened the door.

"Mr Dexter!"

"What is it, Miss Walsh?"

"You've forgotten your paper."

Arthur held out his hand for the newsprint which was all that remained of his friend Willie Boothroyd.

In the street outside his office, Arthur stopped. His first thought had been to get out of the office, to go home. Now he knew that for the moment he was unable to face Vera, the normalcy of his house and the drinks on the tray as if nothing had happened to Willie. It had hit him too close and too hard. It was he who had dropped dead in the street outside his office. He was the same age, same build. If not still young men, he and Willie had considered themselves barely middle-aged. School even seemed such a short time ago. What had poor Willie done to have such a mean trick played upon him? Standing on the pavement, Arthur thought: I am William Boothroyd. One moment I am here, outside my office, the next I am lying dead, right here at my feet. No chance to say anything, do anything, not even to round anything off. Just 'phht', like a candle... 'in the midst of our days'. Arthur looked down at the pavement half expecting to see himself lying there.

"Why'nt yer look where yer going?" Arthur looked up at the two girls, arm in arm, who had bumped into him.

"Sorry." He walked along, the way the crowds were going. No, he certainly didn't feel like facing Vera yet. She would understand, of course, that he was upset, but not quite the feeling he had that it was as though he, not Willie, had died, or at least might equally well have died. As he walked along, the newspaper under his arm, he felt almost as if he were cheating by breathing the stale city air, touching arms with his neighbours, hearing their voices when he should be lying lifeless on the pavement, waiting for the ambulance to take him to some ice-cold City mortuary. He found himself shivering at the thought, and wished he had stopped to have a whisky in the office. It was twenty minutes later, when he had wandered unseeingly as far as Fleet Street, that it occurred to him he might go into a pub. That it had not occurred to him before was due mainly to the fact that Arthur Dexters are not familiar with public houses. They drink, if and when they wish to drink, in their offices, their friends' offices, their clubs, their homes, their friends' homes, or, if they go out to dine, in the bar while waiting for a table. They are not in the habit, on leaving their offices, of dropping in for a 'quick one'.

The pub that Arthur Dexter chose, the first one in fact that he passed having made his decision, was large and friendly. Its clientele consisted mainly of those concerned with newspapers of the Law, who by day inhabited the surrounding district. Standing at the bar, awaiting the moment when he could catch the eye of the flitting bartender, he found himself next to a group of pink-faced, very young men in stiff white collars and vent-backed, dark suits. They each held a beer tankard, and appeared to be discussing crankshafts. Each had his spare hand in his trouser pocket and laughed, frequently, freely and heartily, at what seemed to Arthur nothing at all. From time to time they were joined by new equally pink-faced young men who, having hung their bowler hats and rolled umbrellas on the stand by the door, slapped one or two of their fellows on the back, guffawed merrily once or twice, laid their evening papers on the counter, jingled the change in their pockets, and accepted responsibility for the next round.

Arthur looked miserably along the counter at the inverted green-glass bottles of gin, the fruit juices, bottled beers and Lea & Perrins Worcester sauce. The bartender stuck a pound note into the glass tankard by the till, already full of pound notes, and danced up to where Arthur stood.

"Yessir?" One hand was wiping the counter, the other handing a packet of cigarettes to someone from the shelf behind him.

"Double Scotch." Poor Willie had drunk his last one last night.

At the back of the large room, with its black and white tiled floor, were some green covered chairs and tables. Arthur needed to sit down. One table with six seats was empty. He was glad, not wanting to be too close to humanity. A stout, dark, kindly-looking lady with comfortable looking bosom and shoes came up with a cloth. She said, "Good-evening, dear," to Arthur, and having mopped up the small puddles of spilled beer and emptied the ashtray, said, "Nothing worse than a dirty table," and moved on. He became lost in thoughts of Willie, and was surprised to find when he next looked up that he was no longer alone at the table, and that he had not touched his drink. A young man in a green jersey, a slightly older man in black jacket and striped trousers, and a girl, very pretty, with long black hair, were sharing the table with him. They all had drinks before them. The man in the black jacket was looking at Willie's picture on the front page of his newspaper.

"He was my friend," Arthur said, surprised at himself for addressing a strange man in a pub.

The young man in the jersey glanced at the headline.

"The lolly doesn't help," he said. Arthur wasn't quite sure what he meant.

The man in the black jacket, obviously a barrister, Arthur thought, had a beautiful, Cambridge voice. "And the dust returneth to the earth as it was," he said piously, "but the Spirit returneth unto God who gave it."

"Is that what you believe?" Arthur asked.

"One must believe. How else could one go on living?"

Arthur was silent. He had never considered the problem of an after-life.

Green jersey ran his fingers through the long hair that flopped over his forehead.

"I don't believe all that bunk," he said. "When you're dead, you're dead, and that's that. It's all a huge bloody joke and sometimes it isn't very funny."

"Then what's the point in living, working, carrying on?" the Cambridge accents said.

"I'll tell you," green jersey said, leaning forward confidentially. "It's because we're all on a bloody treadmill and we can't get off. We have so much to do, and so little time in which to do it. With every year that the world gets older, the treadmill turns a little faster, and there's so much that is exciting and new, almost, almost within our reach and we don't know where to grab first. New plays, a little more shocking — my God, we're not even in the social swim unless we've seen them — new speeds across the world, ten minutes off the journey to Karachi; ten minutes, I ask you! Larger and larger cinema screens with stupider and less artistic films than we have ever had, colour television, stereophonic gramophones - but how many people damn well care about the quality of the recording? New clothes washers, dish washers, brain washers, suffocating heat from the walls and the floors, atomic lighting, the Japanese influence in interiors — contemporary simply won't any longer do — new names, stars born overnight; stars! Babes with mascara hurled to the lions by their publicity agents; new this, new that, new worlds even to conquer, and if we lived to be a hundred it's doubtful whether we should be using the right toothpaste or the right soap. And we're scared, too. We're scared of war; not nice, comprehensible wars like those we've known in the past, where the worst that could happen was that you'd be killed by a bayonet or a bomb or tortured until you became a gibbering idiot, or herded into a gas oven – we knew where we were then. Now we don't even know what we're afraid of – cold wars, nerve wars, trade wars even; war with Russia, war with China, the slow drowning democracy in the muddy bogs of communism – where can we look and not be afraid? But we don't stop to look because we have to run, faster and faster and faster. We run so fast we leave our souls behind in the company of our honesty, our integrity and our peace of mind. We go on and on and on, step after step after step, to make the treadmill turn faster and faster until 'Wham!'" he slapped Willie's picture in the newspaper so hard he made them all jump, "You've had it! You're off all right but what good is it to you?"

Black jacket pointed to the headline. "He had the money to get off the treadmill if he'd wanted," he said.

"Ah! But did he? Of course not! And you know why? Because money wasn't enough. He wanted more money. What for? Don't ask me. He probably could have retired years ago if he'd wanted to. But he liked being a tycoon; the power and the glory! He was mad with it, drunk with it, enslaved by it, and he trod the steps of his own particular treadmill harder, faster, more urgently than most of us who have more need to. He was afraid to get off. And now he has simply been removed, like a fly picked off the jam."

"Our days are as a hand-breadth," striped trousers said.

"Then why don't we bloody well do something about it?"

"I don't know," striped trousers said, slowly, beautifully, "I really don't know."

"Because we can't," his hair flopped into his eyes again. "We're just pawns in this great bloody game that somebody's playing, generation after generation. We feel sorry for prisoners, but aren't we all in prison, except perhaps that we haven't any bars? Are we free? Of course we aren't. If we didn't work day after day we'd starve and if we starved we'd die. We've no choice except to keep on and on and on. And if we have the choice, like Boothroyd must have had, what do we do about it? Nothing. And why? Because we're prisoners. Our own, if nobody else's."

"You're drunk," Arthur said.

The young man pushed the hair out of his eyes.

"I know," he said. "My wife's just left me."

"I'm sorry," Arthur said.

"There's no need to be." He denied the misery in his bloodshot eyes.

There was a moment's embarrassed silence for green jersey's errant wife, then Cambridge said: "You're too cynical. Life is worth living to some. Don't you find life worth living?" he said, addressing the black-haired girl who sat with both hands round her drink.

The girl raised her long dark lashes from large blue eyes. She smiled and was quite fabulously pretty.

"I'm sorry," she said, "did you say something to me?"

Black jacket said: "I asked you if you felt that life was worth living."

"Why not?" The blue eyes grew larger. She did not appear to have given the matter a great deal of thought. She drank the last of her drink. "I think I've a cold coming on. I thought that this might help." Her mouth was pursed prettily round the rim of the glass.

"Won't you have another?" black jacket asked politely.

"No thank you. I have to go now or I shall be late for work."

"You see!" green jersey said triumphantly. "The treadmill again. She daren't even be late. And what an odd time to start work. What is it you do?"

The girl hesitated for a moment, than said: "I'm a singer. The show starts in twenty minutes." She stood up.

"How can you sing with a cold?" black jacket said.

She gave him a curious look. "It won't make any difference."

She was very pretty.

"I'd better go. Goodbye."

They watched her go, straight-backed, long-legged, hair round her shoulders. She was followed to the door by the eyes of the pink-faced young men. Afterwards they snickered into their drinks.

"I'd better be going, too," Arthur said. He felt more himself, able to face Vera. The shock had been blunted by the drink and the talk. He was glad he had come into the pub. He stood up.

"Your newspaper!" black jacket said, holding it out. It seemed that Willie was reluctant to leave him.

At home Arthur closed the front door gently behind him hoping to have a few moments to himself.

"Arthur! Is that you, Arthur?" Vera's voice sounded shrill, irritated.

He went slowly into the lounge.

"Arthur, I asked you particularly to be early; you know the Fergusons are coming to dinner and they're always punctual and you have to change, and I managed to get seats for 'Cry not the Angels', it had the most wonderful write-up in the *Telegraph* this morning and there wasn't a single seat to be had but my man in Webster's... Arthur, what's the matter? Are you all right?"

"Willie Boothroyd's dead."

"Willie! Dead? You can't be serious. He was all right last night." She took the newspaper Arthur held out. "Dropped dead in the street! I can't understand it. I must sit down for a moment. Poor Polly, what a terrible, terrible shock. I must go round. Perhaps I'd better ring her first. What could have been the matter with him?"

Arthur shrugged. "Overwork perhaps."

"Lord knows he had no need to work as he did."

Arthur thought of the drunk young man in the pub. "Willie enjoyed working," he said. "I don't think he could have stopped.

There was something in him that made him keep on and on and on… What are we going to do about the Fergusons? I don't feel much like listening to that wretched woman's cackle all the evening, or to Leonard's pointless stories."

"It's too late to get in touch. She was meeting him in town."

"I don't know why we had to ask them. We don't even like them."

"They asked us."

"And we ask them, then they ask us again, so we have to ask them again, and we still don't care if we never saw each other again after all that, so I don't quite see the point. I'm not going to the theatre anyway. You can take them. They'll understand."

"All right." Vera got up. "I must go and phone Polly."

When she came back, Arthur, who had been sitting staring at the same spot on the carpet, said: "Well?"

"The doctor's given poor Polly something for the shock and she's in bed," Vera said, dabbing at her eyes. "All the family's round there and there's nothing we can do for the moment. The inquest's tomorrow. It's so dreadful. I keep seeing him last night, dancing with Vanessa."

"It might have been me. We were the same age."

"Don't be morbid. Doctor Gurney says that you're as fit as many men half your age."

"Perhaps I should retire… Ease up a bit."

Vera straightened the cushions that were already straight and shook the waiting dish of salted almonds. "There's Victor, going up to Cambridge. And Vanessa's coming-out dance, and I suppose before we know where we are her wedding and trousseau…"

"I hope I can manage all that before they find me dead on the pavement."

"Arthur, dear, you seem awfully upset. Would you like me to ring Doctor Gurney? He could give you something for the shock."

"It'll pass. It was so sudden...just picking up the newspaper and reading it like that. I'd better go and change if we really can't do anything about the Fergusons."

After he'd gone Vera straightened the cushion on which he'd been sitting and took his empty whisky glass into the kitchen.

When the bell rang at eleven o'clock Arthur, who had been asleep in the armchair in front of the fire, thought it must be Vera back from the theatre. He crossed the large, parquet-floored, oak-panelled hall, buttoning his waistcoat as he went, and opened the front door. On the step stood Doctor Francis Gurney with his case and stethoscope.

"What's the matter?" Arthur said.

"Your wife asked me to call in when I'd finished. She said you'd had a bit of a shaking this afternoon and she was worried about you. I'm not supposed to tell you she telephoned. I'm just passing by as it were."

"Women!" Arthur said, and held the front door wide.

"What do you think Willie died of?" Arthur said, when Doctor Gurney had listened to his heart and taken his blood pressure and they were sitting opposite each other in the deep, tapestry covered armchairs.

"Difficult to say. Coronary thrombosis most likely, or cerebral haemorrhage. I suppose there'll be an inquest?"

Arthur nodded. "What about overwork?" he said. "Willie always went at it like a madman."

"As an indirect cause of death?"

"Yes."

"I don't know. There are schools of thought on both sides."

"It would be nice to know something other than work before it was your turn. This has shaken me a bit. I suppose when one's own generation starts disappearing..."

"Why don't you retire?" Doctor Gurney said, looking round the room at the expensive furnishings, the money spent freely.

"Why? Do you think I may be next on the list?"

"Not at all. But if you're fed up with working. You could afford to, couldn't you?"

Arthur looked into the fire. "I could," he said, "if we were content to live differently. I would be willing to try, but Vera and the children…you get used to things. Victor and Vanessa are eighteen. There's Cambridge and coming-out dances, and clothes, and riding, and parties, and Vera wants Vanessa to have a fur coat and a small car for Victor, and these curtains," he waved his arm towards the windows, "are too old or too gold, I can't remember… So you see it's not quite so easy. Mine's not a public company, remember, there's only me."

"Of course, I think you work too hard though…"

"We all do. Look at you, wasting time with me when you should be at home in bed. My wife should be ashamed of herself for bringing you out at nearly midnight. I suppose you haven't sat down yet this evening?"

"No. I had four visits after evening surgery. It was just one of those nights."

"It means nothing to Vera. 'I'll phone Doctor Gurney. That's what we pay him for.' The women don't care. They expect us to keep on and on and on until they have to scrape us up off the pavement."

Doctor Gurney smiled. "And then our widows will go romping off on sightseeing tours of Europe on the life insurance like the American women."

"It's not so funny. But why is it happening? Why has life suddenly become so hard, so fast and so earnest? Where are all the old men, puffing at their pipes, sitting on village seats?"

"The old men who were always on the village seats are still there. For the rest of us, I suppose we're too greedy. We want it all and we want it quickly. I don't know why. Perhaps the not so ludicrous thought of possible annihilation; perhaps because more things are within the reach of more people. We are a nasty, predatory lot."

So it wasn't only Green Jersey, Arthur thought.

"But why?" he said, "Why are we like this?"

Doctor Gurney shrugged. "Perhaps we're trying to run too fast to keep up with all that has happened in the last ten years. Most probably, in a generation or two, things will settle down again."

"We run so fast we leave our souls behind." His mind was back in the pub with the young man in the green jersey.

Doctor Gurney stood up. "Maybe. Fortunately, I'm only responsible for the bodies. And I suggest you take yours to bed."

Arthur said: "I shouldn't have kept you talking." He put his arm round the young man's shoulders as they walked to the door. "It was good of you to come. I'm sorry it was unnecessary. Don't work too hard."

Doctor Gurney grinned. "*Facile dictu, difficile factu*," he said, "which is about all I remember of my Latin."

Upstairs in his dressing-room Arthur wearily and mechanically removed the things from his pockets and laid them neatly on the top of the chest. Coppers in one pile, silver in another; keys, nail-file, diary, wallet, breast-pocket handkerchief, pen, pencil, cigar piercer, watch...a folded paper. This last should not have been in that particular pocket. He opened it out and remembered that he had intended to show it to his accountant. It was from Parker & Parker, estate agents, and contained the details of a property in Whitecliffs-by-the-Sea. '...a new block of six flats...one, two, and three beds...pleasant aspect...five minutes sea and shops...rents...suitable investment...' Arthur put it down on the glass top then picked it up again. He stared at the paper, groping for the idea that flashed elusively through his mind. Suitable investment! But suppose, just suppose... They had spent holidays at Whitecliffs when the children were little, and he had always had a soft spot for it. No; of course it was impossible. Vera would say it was impossible. Thoughtfully, the paper still in his hand, Arthur left his dressing-room and crossed the landing. He opened his son's bedroom door and peered into the darkness. "You in bed, Victor?"

Victor switched on the lamp by the bed. His face was rumpled with sleep. "What is it, Dad?"

"What does 'Fackilly dicter diffickilly facter' mean? It's Latin."

Victor smiled at his father's pronunciation.

" 'Easy to say, difficult to do', why?"

"Nothing. Thanks, Vic. Sorry for waking you. Good night."

"Night, Dad."

Arthur went back across the landing. "Easy to say, difficult to do," he repeated as he removed his cuff-links. He put the paper from Parker & Parker into the pocket of his pyjamas ready to show Vera in the morning.

Two

Even in sleep Arthur and Vera Dexter bespoke their lack of nothing.

The curtains, weighty with lining and inter-lining that protected them from the cool April light, were satin; so were their eiderdowns, the facings of Arthur's pyjamas and the pale blue dressing-gown that lay across the end of his wife's bed. From Vera's blue-rinsed beautifully shaped grey hair tidily in place on the embroidered pillow, to the dressing-table with its costly pots of anti-wrinkle oil and hormone creams, all was in order and of the very best. As far as Vera Dexter was concerned the money which had bought the top quality, rose Wilton carpet, the ormolu light fittings and the avant-garde collection of clothes in the built-in cupboards, was plucked effortlessly and frequently from trees. For Arthur it was not so simple. He had paid for the good things surrounding both himself and his wife, not only with pound notes, of which he had a fair number at his disposal, but with the deepening lines that creased his forehead, his inability to attain a state of unconsciousness unaided by the pills he swallowed nightly in varying quantities, and above all with the total exclusion from his mind of anything that was sweet and light and free. He was a man in chains, and the links were endless; his business, his home, his wife, his son, his daughter, their futures, his future, his wife's (hysterectomy pending), his brother's heart, worse of late and of course it would fall to Arthur to…the maids, the lack of maids, the subsidence of the house, the Rent Act, his case against Popular Plastics Ltd., his car, his income tax, his surtax, Schedule A, did he carry enough life insurance?… What would happen to the business if he dropped down dead?… His face even in sleep was harassed. For Arthur Dexter the ravelled sleeve of care was nothing like knit up. When he opened his eyes to the morning he was as tired as if he had not slept.

There was something about this day, he remembered, that was different. What it was he was unable to recall until he turned to look at the clock by his bedside and heard the crackle of paper in his pyjama pocket. He took out the letter from the estate agents and glanced towards his wife.

"Vera," he said softly. And then again, "Vera."

Vera stirred, moaned, yawned, and finally opened her eyes. When she realised that it was morning and that her husband had deliberately woken her up, a thing he never did, she said: "What is it, Arthur?" and listened to the astonishing things her husband had to say. When he had finished, Arthur, leaning towards her in his enthusiasm, propped up on one elbow, waited for her response.

"It's quite out of the question, Arthur," Vera said firmly, pulling the bedclothes up to her chin. And had it not been less than twenty-four hours ago that Willie Boothroyd had died, that might very well have been that.

Vera was unable all day to forget the strangeness that had come over her husband, whose every move she could usually accurately prophesy, with the sudden death of his friend.

"Can you imagine," she said later as she paid her bill in the hairdresser's, "my husband wants us to live, actually live, in some horrid little flat in a tiny, draughty little seaside town where there's nothing; absolutely nothing at all but some sort of potty little village High Street."

"Shampoo and set, trim, rinse, manicure, thirty-five-and-six, if you please, madame. I can't think of anything nicer," Louise

Crosland said, sighing as she took the money with her elegant hands and thought how lucky her clients were even to be able to think of moving hither and thither while she remained stuck, year after year, in the semi-detached she shared with her mother in Cedars Avenue.

"For a weekend perhaps," Vera said, picking up her change. "But to live! One would die of boredom. Now if it were Nassau or Jamaica...but an *English* seaside! My hair wouldn't last five minutes in all that wind and wet. We had enough of it when the children were little." She shuddered.

"It can be quite pleasant in the summer, Mrs Dexter."

"Both days! No. I can't understand what's got into Arthur." Vera put half-a-crown on the desk. "Would you give this to Alphonse," she said. "I have to run."

Louise picked it up. "With pleasure, madame. Goodbye, madame." She watched the elegant head, above the elegant mink tie, above the elegant suit, leave the salon.

But if Vera was shocked at her husband's outrageous early morning proposal, she was to be even more vexed with him before the day was out. At six o'clock he phoned home to say that he wouldn't be home for dinner. He had gone to a club, he said. A sort of a show. Vera looked at the telephone receiver as if it had gone mad.

"Arthur, what on earth are you talking about?" she said. "You know perfectly well you never go to shows by yourself. What sort of a show anyway?"

"Well, it's a sort of striptease show. Cabaret – you know the idea..."

"Arthur!" Vera's voice was shrill. "Arthur, please come home. You aren't well..."

"Vera, I'm perfectly all right and I've got to rush. Sorry about the dinner. Keep it hot. I'll explain when I get home."

"Explain! Arthur... Arthur?" But he had rung off. Vera replaced the receiver slowly. She went into the kitchen upstairs to put on her coat and ring for a taxi.

All day in his office Arthur had been thinking. His thoughts ran back and forth across the same small field. He had a good, flourishing business whose profits were up fifteen per cent on the previous year, he was not a poor man, and yet it looked as if he would have to keep on and on, following the same routine until the day came when they would pick him up off the floor as they had Willie Boothroyd. His wife would mourn, his children would mourn and that would be that. When his friends remembered him it would be as 'poor old Arthur Dexter, you remember poor Arthur?' The more he thought about it the more he realised that it wasn't good enough. He wanted to know something else before he died. That he was a great deal luckier than many people he appreciated. He was able to take a good holiday each year, and he and Vera had seen a fair bit of the world. But even their holidays were simply an extension of the never-changing round they followed at home. In Monte Carlo or in Cannes they 'bumped into' the Westburys or the Ridgeways and spent their days on the beach with them, their evenings together at the Casino. When they got home they'd get together again and discuss what a wonderful time they'd had. But had they? True it was a rest from the office, but why go to Monte Carlo or Cannes to meet no one but the Westburys or the Ridgeways who lived practically round the corner? Sometimes it was a cruise, with hot, day-excursions to Athens, Pompeii and Istanbul when Vera would be more preoccupied with her swollen feet than the ancient temples, the lava-covered survivals, the mosques and minarets; and he, the cine-camera heavy round his neck, his stomach protesting at the unfamiliar food, too worried that the dark-skinned taxi-driver had got the better of him, that the heat would be too much for Vera, to spare more than a cursory, uncomprehending glance at the marvels that surrounded them. They were always glad to get back to the ship and the couple they had met, who lived not far away from them at home and, wasn't it a coincidence, he was in the same business as Arthur and she went to the same chiropodist as

Vera! And it all sounded wonderful on the postcards they wrote home, and even more wonderful when, back in the comfort of their own surroundings, they unpacked the gifts they had brought for Victor and Vanessa and the maids, and remembered the Attic skies, the golden days, the white sands, and forgot the heat and the flies and the suspicious-looking natives, the shopkeepers who diddled them and the greasy food. True, they were holidays, but where was the repose? Vera, he knew, was in a perpetual turmoil. Had she bought the right clothes, did he think those dreadful people in the sausage business would collar them after dinner again, should she have brought a fur wrap, all the other women seemed to have brought more jewellery… It was no better for him. He seemed to be constantly changing from his shorts to his lightweight tropical slacks, from his slacks to his white dinner-jacket, and shaving, his beard grew so quickly in the tropics, and arguing with the purser and getting a different table because Vera was in a draught, and wishing he was back in the office. There must be something else, and the death of Willie Boothroyd had made him determined to find it.

The paper from Parker & Parker had been in front of him all day. He had nostalgic memories of Whitecliffs, where they had gone year after year to rented houses when the twins were small. He remembered the wind and the smell of the seaweed and being huddled in an overcoat on the beach watching the children paddle or catch shrimps; the brisk walks along the front, when the tide was up and the sea spray drenching the promenade; the children on stuffed photographers' donkeys saying 'cheese'; visits to the fun-fair, rolling pennies, candy floss and long empty evenings when there was nothing to do except perhaps go to the pictures. Vera, of course, had hated it. Year after year she sat uncomfortably on the beach trying to keep the sand out of the picnic tea, and talked about how wonderful it would be when the children were old enough to take abroad. She hated the rented houses full of someone else's possessions, the bracing, spray-damp air, the cups in the beach cafés. But there was something about Whitecliffs, and Arthur wondered if there he might find time to think. There were many things he wanted to think about, and yesterday, which had begun as ordinarily as any other, had brought home to him the realisation that unless he took active steps to do something about it he would simply never have the time. His days were mapped out. With his morning cup of tea he thought about the French in Algeria, the Russians in Hungary, the Arabs in the Lebanon, depending on the headlines; with his bath and shave he wondered whether he should have the car serviced or wait till next week, or whether he should change it, he had had it a year but it was running fairly well, of course the new model had the automatic gear change... At the office there was more than enough to keep him occupied; the morning post, the orders, the deliveries, the staff, the travellers, the designs, the factory, the imports, the exports, the eternal battle with HM Customs...the day soon went. Then home. At home a man could relax, but not at his home. The Lawrences were coming to dinner, to bridge, to sell him tickets for the Spastics Dance; the maid had given notice, Victor couldn't manage on his allowance and there was that new tape-recorder he wanted, Vanessa, out with a new boy-friend, had not come back at midnight. There must be something else. There must. Arthur picked up the white sheets of paper whose contents had burned into his memory all morning. He pulled the telephone receiver smartly off its rest and leaned back in his swivel chair.

"Get me Parker & Parker," he said, and already he was sitting on the beach at Whitecliffs.

It wasn't often that he held out against Vera. Usually they felt more or less the same way about things, and if they didn't it was simpler to drift in her direction as she was nicer when she had her own way. That she would hate living in Whitecliffs Arthur knew. She had already said so in no uncertain terms. That this was something he was going to insist upon he also knew. There are things a man must do, he said to himself as he left the office, and looking again at the pavement where he himself might so easily have died, he knew that this was one of them.

When he found himself walking towards Fleet Street he was only a little surprised. Tonight he was not in need of a drink, nor reluctant to go home, but he knew that he was making for the pub. It was stupid, he realised, they probably wouldn't be there, mightn't remember him if they were, but he had to go and look, open the door, if he could, a little wider. All night, in his fitful sleep, he had dreamed of the young man in the green jersey, the barrister and the girl; the conversation, the argument about the treadmill which had, after all, started him on the track of Whitecliffs, had gone round and round in his head. He had never talked to people like that. Ordinary people, the people who jostled each other in the streets and earned their living at different interesting things. That they existed he knew, for they were brought into his own home by his children. He was, though, scarcely allowed to speak to them, and he knew that it was in case he disgraced himself. There was that boy, who had called one night for Vanessa, who had been studying art in Italy and wore pointed suede shoes and a duffle coat. He would obviously have been most interesting to talk to if he hadn't been primed by Vanessa. He said 'Yes, sir' and 'No, sir,' and how was business? And didn't Arthur think there would be a war in the Middle East? And what a lovely house they had, when Arthur had wanted to hear about how it was in Italy and with young people, because he never heard from his children. He was a man of commerce, a philistine, and they kept him in his cage where he could continue to make the money so that they could roam freely in the world of art and music and books and history and religion; a world unbounded by the office and the telephones, and nine till five, and worry, and the income tax.

Possibly last night, for the first time, he had realised what he was missing. The young men in the pub had treated him like an equal, a man capable of thought about matters which did not earn money. He had enjoyed their unfamiliar company, and looked forward to meeting them again. Yesterday had been quite a day.

As he opened the door the stuffy welcome of the place enveloped him. Like an habitué he hung his hat and his umbrella on the stand and looked quickly round the room. There was no familiar face, and by the depth of his disappointment he realised how much he had been banking on meeting them. At the bar a group of pink-faced young men laughed and drank beer. He could not tell whether they were the same young men as yesterday or not. Today they were discussing England's chances in the Test. He ordered whisky from the indifferent bartender and, pretending to read the evening paper, but actually watching the door, he made it last as long as possible. By the time the glass was empty there was still no sign of his friends. He could not stand there drinking all night. Disappointed he unhooked his umbrella and bowler from the stand.

In the street he walked along behind a tall girl whose long black hair swung over her shoulders. She was carrying a small square make-up case and had long, slim legs. There was something about the way she walked. Arthur walked faster. When he was level with her he looked into her face.

"Excuse me," he didn't know whether or not to say 'miss'. A few people who had seen him accost her stared.

She looked at him, and he recognised the wide blue eyes, the lashes, the tip-tilted nose. She didn't stop walking.

Arthur kept in step with her. "I thought I recognised you. How is your cold? The pub last night. The same table, we were talking, don't you remember?"

She stopped and, looking at him, laughed. "Oh, of course," she said. "I was thinking you had seen me in the show. It's always happening. It's a nuisance. I feel all right today, thank you."

They walked along together, Arthur pushing past the people as it was nearing rush hour time and not easy to walk two abreast. "I was wondering about the others," he said, "the young chap in the green jersey and the other one. I looked for them in the 'Journeyman' but they weren't there. I'd like to find them. I was interested in what they said, about keeping on until we drop and all that."

The girl turned suddenly down a small side turning and he followed her. After a few paces she stopped.

"This is where I work."

Arthur looked at the small entrance hung each side with pictures of nude girls. At the box office was a queue of men.

"I'd like to talk to you." He was reluctant to let her disappear again, feeling she was the link that might lead him to the two young men.

"Why don't you come and see the show?" She seemed neither interested nor particularly disinterested. "We could talk afterwards."

Some of the men in the queue had turned round and were staring at them.

"All right," Arthur said rashly. "We can talk afterwards."

"I'll meet you in the bar," she said, and disappeared through a side door.

Standing in the queue, Arthur realised just how rash he had been. In front of him and behind him were men of all descriptions. Some carried raincoats, some brief cases, some looked sheepish, all eager; middle-aged schoolboys on an outing. Outside, men walked by, examined the photographs, looked at the queue, joined it or walked on. The tiny foyer was hung with notices. 'Amateur Striptease contest. £2,000 prizes.' 'The Paris Striptease Show' (First Edition). 'English and Continental Star Artists.' He thought the girl had said she was a singer. He couldn't see anything about singers.

At the box office a sharp-faced woman said: "Are you a member, sir?"

Arthur said he wasn't.

"This is a club, sir, and you have to join the club if you wish to see the show."

It was too late to back out. He gave the woman five pounds for a year's subscription, the minimum, and received his membership card. He wondered if he had gone a little mad. Upstairs he walked through the bar which was full of men waiting for the show to begin, and into the theatre. It wasn't exactly a theatre. It was a large room, about the size of a very small ballroom, and it was filled with a semi-circle of small tables covered with white cloths. At one end was a curtained stage, and an apron stage came out into the midst of the tables. The tables immediately surrounding the apron stage were already occupied. Men with glasses before them on the tables held the vanguard positions they had obtained. Arthur sat down nearer the back and beckoned a waiter.

"I can get you nearer the front, if you wish, sir," the white-coated man who looked as if he was capable of chucking-out, as well as waiting, said. He looked surprised when Arthur said he was quite all right where he was, and ordered a Scotch and soda.

Arthur opened his programme and looked at it in the dim light. There were twenty items in the show. The names varied: item one was, 'Welcome to the Paris Striptease', Item three, 'Nudes on the Town', Item eight, 'Striptease Teasers', Item twelve, 'Ladies Only', Item fifteen, 'The Girl with the Swinging Derrière'... The rest of the programme was filled with artistic studies of the Nudes. He recognized the girl with the long black hair. Her name was Honey DuPont, and her figure was as good as her face. There were ten minutes still before the show began. Suddenly Arthur remembered Vera and got up to look for a telephone.

When he got back the lights were lowered, the tables nearly all occupied, and the spotlight bright upon the stage. As he sat down the music started, the curtains opened and the six chorines appeared with the opening number. They wore only gloves and hats.

Three

The taxi dropped Vera outside Doctor Gurney's. It was the first time she had been to the house, as she and Arthur were private patients of the doctor's and when they called him he came to visit them. It was a large house, set down amongst rows and rows of smaller houses in a working-class district. She hadn't imagined that Doctor Gurney had so far to come when he visited them. She hadn't imagined anything about him at all, in fact. When she needed him she just lifted the phone and rang, and sooner or later he would appear. She hadn't realised that it was twenty minutes' drive. Perhaps they ought to find somebody nearer in case of emergency, although Arthur seemed quite fond of Doctor Gurney who had looked after them all for the ten years they had lived at 'The Yarrow', and she had always found him very pleasant.

The red step was not very clean. Vera pressed the bell marked 'Day' and waited. The door was opened by a cross-looking, untidy young woman who was wiping her hands on her apron.

"The surgery's round the other side of the house," she said before Vera had a chance to say anything.

"I don't want the surgery. I must have a word with Doctor Gurney. It's extremely urgent."

"Can I give him a message for you?"

"No, you can't," Vera said. "I must see him at once. I'm a patient of his. A private patient."

The young woman sighed. “You’d better come in,” she said, and held the door open wide.

The room in which she asked Vera to wait had the remains of tea on the long table, half of which was covered with a plastic tablecloth. There were partly eaten sandwiches on plates, spilled milk, a sliced loaf still in its wrapper.

“I’m sorry,” the young woman said, “I’ve no help and the baby’s got whooping cough and the other room’s being painted… I’ll tell my husband you’re here. What name shall I say?”

When she came back she had tidied her hair a little and taken her apron off. Vera saw that she would probably be quite attractive if she wasn’t so weary-looking and had some make-up on.

“He’ll come as soon as he can,” she said. “He’s with a patient at the moment.” Vera smiled and the young woman smiled back. She had nice teeth.

Alone, Vera brushed the crumbs off a chair and waited for Doctor Gurney. When he came, bursting almost into the room, he looked anxious and harassed, not like when he visited her at home.

“My wife said it was something urgent,” he said, prescription pad, stethoscope and pen in his hand. “Sorry you had to wait but I’ve a packed waiting-room.”

Vera said: “It’s Arthur. I’m worried about him. This morning he said he wanted to live in some God-forsaken seaside place, and not half an hour ago he rang me to say he’d gone to a show, a *striptease* show, and would be late home for dinner. It’s Willie Boothroyd dying that’s done it. It’s made Arthur go all peculiar.”

Doctor Gurney tapped his pen on his prescription pad. “Look, Mrs Dexter,” he said, “I’m frightfully rushed just now and I haven’t time to sort this problem out. It doesn’t seem all that urgent. If, when your husband comes home, he still seems strange give me a ring and I'll come along and talk it over with you. I'm just in the middle of surgery."

"I can't do that," Vera said. "He was cross with me for calling you last night. I came over here so that he wouldn't know I had consulted you about it behind his back. Can't you tell me what to do? I'm terribly worried. It's not a bit like Arthur. A striptease show! I've never ever had any trouble like that."

Doctor Gurney thought of the roomful of people waiting patiently for him while this middle-aged matron complained of the husband who was kicking up his heels. He remembered his conversation with Arthur Dexter last night and thought he understood about going to live at the seaside. He couldn't quite see where the striptease show came in, though. It struck an odd note.

"Can't you tell me what I should do?" Vera pleaded.

Doctor Gurney said: "My advice is to let your husband do exactly as he wants. I think he's upset by the death of his friend. But apart from that he seemed perfectly normal to me. Don't worry too much about the striptease show, and if he wants to live at the seaside let him. I wish it were me. You must excuse me now, Mrs Dexter; you can ring me later if you're still worried."

After he'd gone Vera let herself out into the hall. There were two small girls sitting on the stairs. One had a fairy dress with sequins over her school tunic, and the other high-heeled shoes and a hat with a feather.

"We're waiting for our husbands to come home," the one with the fairy dress said. She had no teeth in the front and she pronounced it 'huthbanth'.

"Are you really?" Vera said. They both looked like Doctor Gurney. "Where's Mummy?" She wanted to apologise for intruding.

"Seeing to the baby; he keeps being sick."

"How many of you are there?"

"Four. We shan't be having any more."

"Not unless there's an accident." The smallest of the two adjusted the feather in her hat.

"Really!" Vera said. "I must be going now. Will you tell Mummy I've gone?"

"All right. Did you come by car?"

"Taxi," Vera said. "It's waiting."

They stood, unself-conscious in their fancy dress, waving at the door until her taxi was out of sight.

They sat in the bar of the club at a small glass-topped table. Honey drank whisky, and the men gave Arthur envious glances as they passed.

"Did you enjoy the show?" Honey said, giving him the full load of her blue eyes in enquiry.

She asked the question, Arthur thought, as though she had been playing principal boy in a pantomime.

He flushed. In actual fact he had enjoyed the show very much. Halfway through, when it had suddenly come to him that he was sitting in the semi-dark watching a dozen naked women pirouette to music in company with a lot of other pleasure-seeking business men when he should have been at home with Vera, he had felt thoroughly ashamed of himself. The downright provocativeness of the thing, and the fact that he had been enjoying it, had filled him with guilty feelings, and he had slunk further and further into his chair as the show progressed, in case he should be recognised in the half-light by anyone he knew.

"It was a very good show," he said to Honey, not wishing to upset her. Actually the production itself had been tatty, and although fast-moving and noisy, amateurish. Even from where he had been sitting he had been able to see the glisten of sweat on the girls' bodies and the marks where their knicker elastics had been. The show lacked polish.

"I think it's good," Honey said innocently. "We've a very good producer. We do three shows a day and we're always packed."

Arthur had the impression that Honey thought the audience came to see the talent in the show rather than the bodies of the show girls. There had been, it was true, one or two legitimate turns. A conjuror to whom the audience gave scant attention and minimal applause; a balancing act which received the same treatment. Honey herself had sung a few lines in an exceedingly wobbly voice, but, as she was walking round the stage dressed only in one or two feathers at the same time, her reception had been a great deal better.

"Do you always do…er…this sort of thing?" Arthur said.

"You mean nude?"

Arthur nodded.

"No. Actually it's my first time. I was working over at the Ambassador Luncheon club, two shows a day, but I had a friend here and she got me in when one of the girls had an appendix. Mr Hamblin, our producer, liked my voice."

Arthur wondered if she really thought she had been engaged because of her singing ability.

"I want to be a pop singer really," Honey said, answering his unspoken question. "You know, on the radio."

It all seemed so simple. Arthur could see that in her mind's eye Honey was already a famous radio star pulling in the big money. He wanted to talk to her more. It was his first contact with a person of Honey's kind, and he was fascinated. He was worried though about Vera, and knew he should be getting home.

"Look," he said. "How do you think I can find those two young men? The ones that were in the pub. It's awfully important." And suddenly he realised how important it had become.

"They'll probably go back there sometime," Honey said. "I'll look in when I pass for the six o'clock show if you like."

"Would you really?"

"I have to go right by every night."

"You see," Arthur said, "I'm going to do as they said. I'm going to live at the seaside."

"Retire, you mean?"

"I don't know exactly, yet. I just want to get off the treadmill while I have a look round."

"What shall I do if I find them?"

"I'll give you my card. Will you ring me?"

Honey put the card in the purse in her make-up box. The conjuror in the show walked by their table towards the door with a blonde girl on his arm. He winked at Honey as they passed.

"My husband," Honey said in explanation.

Arthur stared. "But shouldn't you be…don't you want…?" He pointed to the door.

"No, that's all right," Honey said, drinking the last of her whisky. "We have an arrangement."

Arthur was flabbergasted. After thirty years of a world in which his main concern had been buying and marketing of various toys, and the everyday concerns of his conventional, if demanding, family, he had knocked a tiny peep-hole into a different continent. He was anxious to see more. Reluctantly he stood up.

"It's been terribly good of you to spare the time, Miss DuPont," he said. Honey lifted her lovely face. "Honey," she said.

"You will get in touch… Honey?"

"Certainly. I'll pop in every night and ring you when I find them."

Arthur made his way to the door. Turning when he got there to wave goodbye to Honey he saw a man, who had been propping up the bar, walk towards her, glass in hand. Honey was smiling at him.

Vera was distraught.

"But, Arthur," she said for the umpteenth time when he had eaten his dinner, "a *striptease* show! It's absolutely disgusting, a man of your age. Suppose someone had seen you, or the children?"

Arthur sounded weary. "Oh, it wasn't the show, Vera, I've already told you. I went because of this girl..."

"That's even worse! You've made me feel positively ill, Arthur, I just don't know what to do."

"You'd better ring up Doctor Gurney then," Arthur said unsympathetically, and picked up the evening paper.

"I have been to see him. About you," Vera said, her voice hysterical, not caring now what she said.

"Mmm. What did he say?"

"He's got no sense. When I told him you wanted to go and live at that potty Whitecliffs he said he wished he could do it! Did you know he had four children? His poor wife looks absolutely all in. One of them's got whooping cough..."

"Vera!" Arthur shouted, standing up and letting the paper drop sheet by sheet to the floor.

Vera sat on the settee and closed her eyes in martyrdom.

"What is it now, Arthur? If it's anything peculiar I don't think I can stand it."

"Whitecliffs!" Arthur said excitedly. "I've had the most wonderful idea. It came to me when you said about Doctor Gurney and how he'd go if he had the chance."

"Well?" Vera's voice was dull.

"We'll take them all! Look, there are six flats in that block. One for us, one for Honey, one for Doctor Gurney, one for the man in the green jersey, one for the barrister, after all it was their idea...and you can find somebody else if you like for the sixth one." He looked at Vera. She was sitting absolutely still, her mouth in a hard, straight line.

Vanessa Dexter walked incredibly slowly down the moon lit road towards her house hand in hand with Cliff Stafford. They walked in silence past three of the large houses, their shadows long and thin upon the pavement. When they were within sight of 'The Yarrow' Cliff said: "But do you have to go, Van? Can't you stay with an aunt or something?"

Vanessa shook her head. "Daddy's been carrying on all the evening. That's why I rang you. He's absolutely determined about this Whitecliffs idea, and Mummy says we have to do as he says. It'll only be over the summer."

"But, Van," Cliff said miserably, "it's only April."

"I suppose it'll take a while to get things fixed up."

"What about your secretarial course?"

"Daddy says I can find something to do at Whitecliffs."

"What about me?"

"Oh! Cliff," Vanessa said, and stood still on the pavement, "that's the trouble. You'll come for weekends, won't you, sometimes? It isn't very far."

"Van, you know that if I take whole days off I shall never pass my Anatomy. If I don't pass this time I'll get chucked out."

They walked on. "I don't know if I can live without you," Cliff said.

"I'll write."

"You're a rotten letter writer. Look at that time you went to stay with your uncle in Manchester. I believe you're quite glad to be going."

Vanessa stopped again. "You don't really believe that?"

"No."

In the drive of 'The Yarrow' they stopped by the laurel bushes. Cliff kissed her and traced the outline of her face in the moonlight with a gentle finger.

"I'd better go in now," Vanessa said reluctantly. "I said I was only going to post a letter."

They kissed again.

"Good night," Vanessa said.

"Good night," Cliff said, "darling."

Vanessa walked on air across the drive. It was the first time he had called her darling.

Upstairs she knocked on the door of Victor's room. Through a noisy passage of a Beethoven Symphony she could not be heard. She opened the door. Victor was lying on the bed, his eyes closed, his shirt open at the neck. Across his stomach lay an American magazine; it was called 'Moon' and on the coloured cover was a fearsome-looking rocket.

"Vic?"

He opened his eyes. "Tum-te-tum. Te-tum-te-tum-te-*tum*," he said, conducting in time to the music. "I love this bit; it's the Liszt arrangement."

Vanessa removed the pick-up from the record-player. "I want to talk to you."

"What about?"

"This seaside business. Do you want to go?"

"Suits me," Victor said. "I've nothing to do till Cambridge, and I seem to have used up nearly all the girls round here. I expect there'll be some local talent."

"It's all very well for you," Vanessa said.

"You mean Cliff?"

"Mm."

"It's only calf-love. You'll get over it."

"Don't be so superior. Just because I don't chop and change like you."

"It wouldn't hurt you if you did. You get to know what's what. You've hardly been out with anyone except that boy with the pimples and Cliff."

"I love Cliff."

"You'll get over it. Anyway he won't be qualified for about a hundred years so what's the use?"

"I don't care."

"The parents will."

"You don't understand."

"Maybe. Turn the Beethoven on again, there's a good girl. About halfway through, and for heaven's sake put the head down gently."

Vanessa left him with his music and went across to her own room.

"It isn't fair," she said to the pink and white striped curtains. "It jolly well isn't fair." She flung herself on to the bed and, taking the photo of Cliff from her bedside table, let the tears slide down on to her pillow.

Four

In a court of law, a semi-detached and a coffee-bar, three of the Dexters' surprising new acquaintances announced their decisions on the question of giving up (although in Basil's case it was an overstatement) their respective jobs and coming away from it all to Whitecliffs.

As far as black jacket and green jersey were concerned, Honey had done her work well. She had waited dutifully in the 'Journeyman' each night on the way to work, and at the end of the week had delivered them both, completely mystified, to Arthur. For herself Honey had already decided; it was not a decision that required a great deal of thought. Completely incapable of understanding the talk, of which she had heard so much in the past week, of life in general and treadmills in particular, Honey knew only that she was always game for a change. The only things that had worried her were that she would lose her job and her very adequate salary. Since Arthur had not only arranged with Mr Hamblin to give her her job back should she return, but also to provide all of them with free board and lodging until, as he put it, they had decided whether or not they were satisfied with their lives, there seemed no decision to make. Wherever there was new ground to be broken, Honey, with little more than an overnight bag, was always ready to break it.

For black jacket, or Howard Pennington-Dalby, barrister-at-law, the problem had entailed a great deal more thought. When he did finally speak his intention aloud, it surprised no one as much as himself. Whether he was influenced by the tedious morning, by his opposing counsel, or by the sun-filtered smog of Southwark, he would never know.

At five past ten on Monday morning, Howard Pennington-Dalby, in the inevitable black jacket and striped trousers, bowler hat set well over his nose, rolled umbrella over his arm and zippered bag in his hand, strode purposefully into the dank, mosaiced vestibule of Southwark County Court. He stopped before a fat pillar on which was hung a printed list attached to a grimy piece of cardboard.

"What a damned nuisance!" he said, after a moment.

An elderly man, similarly dressed but much thinner, his black jacket glistening rather at the elbows, said:

"What is it, Dalby? I've only just arrived."

"Mornin', Benson," Howard said to his opposing counsel whom he had never cared for. "Look what they've done to us."

Mr Benson took the spectacles from his top pocket and put them on his thin nose down which they immediately slipped.

He looked to where Howard was pointing.

'Judge's court postponed until twelve noon' a hastily handwritten notice said.

He took off his glasses again.

"Well, well; that's not very good, is it?"

"My dear fellow, look!" Howard said. "There's *one* Application, twenty-four judgement summonses, and *one* possession action before us."

Benson put on his glasses again and looked down the list.

" 'Harrow Motors/Buckingham; LCC/Twist; Greenboam/Mutual Loan…' What are you going to do?"

"Well, I haven't the slightest intention of remaining in Southwark for the entire day," Howard said. "I shall make an application for the registrar to hear us when his own list is finished."

"Good idea," Benson said, "good idea." But Howard had already gone.

The registrar, red-faced because of his weekend's golf and irritable because it was Monday morning, sat slumped in his chair. He had bags under his bright blue eyes, blonde moustache and eyebrows, and was in his middle forties.

At eleven thirty Howard stood up in the almost empty court whose oak pews were gleaming lightly in the sunlight, to open the case for Hemingway against Complex Securities Limited. At twelve thirty the registrar, listening to the arguments going back and forth concerning discount charges, bills of exchange, and interest per annum calculated on a day to day basis, drooped further in his chair and yawned. By one thirty, having ignored the constant references to the clock on the wall by counsel, solicitors, plaintiff, defendant and witnesses, he appeared to have sunk into a deep sleep. At ten to three he aroused himself sufficiently to wind up the case, finding for the Finance Company, and at three o'clock he bowed courteously to Howard who made a neat if pompous little speech of thanks to the 'learned registrar' for allowing them to be heard before him, and left the court.

In the counsel's robing room, Mr Benson carefully removed his wig which had become dark grey with the years, and laid it in its black tin box.

"You'd think he'd have adjourned for lunch," he grumbled. "I didn't even bring my peppermints."

Howard was sitting at the table putting in order the papers which had dealt with the case: back sheet, with seven giant pages; instructions (three pages); pleadings (five pages); correspondence (thirty-two pages); notices to produce and admit documents (eight pages); affidavit of documents, proof of evidence. He laid them neatly one inside the other and, folding them, tied the resulting bulky oblong in its length of pink tape.

"I'm rather glad he didn't adjourn," he said, "I have an urgent appointment in chambers at four."

Benson, who had nothing to do for the rest of the day, glanced at him enviously. He removed his gown and straightening his shiny jacket wished that he was half the age he was.

Outside in the car-lined street of Southwark, Howard found the defendant's solicitor, a fussy little man with a drooping moustache, waiting for him.

"I'd like to congratulate you, Mr Dalby," he said to Howard, "on the way you conducted your case."

"We hadn't a leg to stand on," Howard said.

"That's just it. You put up a jolly good show."

"Kind of you," Howard said. "Most kind."

"Not at all. I wondered if we might send you a brief or two."

Howard wondered exactly how foolish he was being and said: "I do appreciate it. I really do, but I'm taking a vacation, a long vacation. Until after the summer at least."

"Going abroad?"

Howard looked up and down the dingy street in which the dirty buildings cut out much of the light. Already he could smell the clean sea air of Whitecliffs.

"As a matter of fact, no. I'm going to a little place called Whitecliffs. It's on the south-east coast. I don't suppose you've heard of it."

"I haven't," the solicitor said. He drew himself up to his full height which wasn't very great. "We handle some very big stuff, Mr Dalby." The bait was tempting.

Howard could see the briefs arriving on his desk, marked one hundred guineas, two hundred guineas. The vision faded. He had been at the Bar too long. They were more likely to be marked two guineas only or three, that was if they materialised at all.

He put his bowler hat on his head. "Man does not live by bread alone," he said courteously. "Good day to you, sir, and thank you."

At four o'clock, still in his bowler hat, he was feeding the ducks in Regent's Park, watched by a group of small children. He was embarrassed when he looked up to find Benson standing beside him.

Benson looked ostentatiously at his watch.

"What happened to our urgent appointment?" he said. "Or aren't we as busy as we make out?"

Howard aimed a large crust far out into the water.

"My dear fellow," he said, "my client couldn't manage it. We're dining at Claridge's instead."

Louise Crosland made her decision quite quickly, but said nothing about it until Friday.

It was to Louise, the receptionist at the hairdressers, that Vera Dexter had emptied her heart whilst waiting for her appointment, and to Louise, on the spur of the moment, more to teach Arthur a lesson than anything else, that she had offered the sixth flat in the little block at Whitecliffs. To Louise the shattering invitation was opportunity knocking, the tide taken at the flood, and everything else rolled up together. The decision was easy. There was only one obstacle to overcome, and she decided to leave that until Friday.

On Friday night, Louise, tall, smart, the wrong side of forty and just a little hefty, buttoned her black coat over her thirty-eight inch bosom as she came out of the cinema. She stood for a moment on the broad steps, bathed in a glow of pink neon light, until her eyes behind the glasses with the red fly-away frames became accustomed to the darkness of the street. When she had smoothed on her kid gloves and adjusted her handbag and her umbrella firmly over her arm she stepped, in her medium heeled courts, out into the crowd which swarmed to form a patient, lengthy queue at the bus-stop. She did not mind the wait and was oblivious of the keen wind cutting along the street. She stood with head erect on swan-like neck, feet in third position, elbowless arms curved gently over stomach, waiting for the curtain to rise. Tonight she was Giselle; just as, in the film of the Russian Ballet she had just seen, Ulanova had been Giselle. She was fluid, boneless, purged, graceful, ethereal, beautiful. The orchestra was playing the overture and she was about to meet her lover.

Friday, spring, autumn, winter and summer, was cinema night. Week after week, Friday night would find her, gloves in pocket, handkerchief ready in her hand, sitting expectantly in her seat in the centre stalls. By the time the programme — the entire programme, travelogue, cartoon, adverts, news, second feature, first feature — was finished, Louise Crosland had disappeared. Buttoning her black, face-cloth coat, or in winter, huddling into the bulky beaver-lamb she had been careful not to sit on, she was a provocative, pocket-sized gangster's moll, a firm-chinned resistance heroine who had suffered all and still not told, a Poor Little Rich Girl seeking someone who loved her for herself, a Dying Swan.

Tonight she was Giselle, and the long wait in the queue, the bus journey to the request stop at Cedars Avenue, the hike to the top of the lamp-lit road where the semi-detacheds grew smaller, passed in a crescendo of soul-stirring music to which she pirouetted, arabesqued and leaped to lie limply airborne in the strong arms of her prince.

Airily, on the blocked toes of her pink satin shoes she glided, running steps infinitesimally tiny, up the garden path. Her key came effortlessly to hand and the front door swung easily, grandly open.

"That you, Louise?" Her mother's voice was croaky, querulous. "I've been waiting for my Ovaltine."

As the front door clicked shut behind her, Louise sank slowly from her toes. The satin shoes, the undulating dress, the stage-white, the garland in her hair melted whisperingly away. A glance in the oval, oak-framed mirror confirmed the suspicion that her eyes were no longer heavily shadowed into alluring butterflies, her lashes inch-long and black, and that her nose was red and needed powder. Her court shoes trod reluctantly along the threadbare line of the passage. In the front room her mother, lilac woolen shawl over her black dress, sat disconsolately before the television screen whose picture was practically obliterated by a sea of undulating light.

"It's had those wavy lines all evening," she complained. "It went funny halfway through Eamonn Andrews and I've missed TV Tune Time and Amateur Boxing. I do wish you wouldn't stay away the whole evening when I've not a soul to do anything for me. I've been gasping for my drink, the electricity makes my throat dry, and I thought I heard someone out at the back. It's no joke when you get old and nobody cares and there's nobody to do anything, and I felt that pain right across my back again and I've no more of those white tablets..."

Louise adjusted the contrast switch on the back of the television set until the picture became clear. In the kitchen she put a saucepan of milk on the gas for the Ovaltine, opened the back door to make sure there were no intruders lurking about, and went upstairs to hang up her coat and put on her slippers.

When she came back into the front room with the Ovaltine her mother said: "You may as well switch it off, it's finished. Not that I've seen much this evening."

Louise switched off the set and settled her mother with her other glasses and her drink.

"Did you put sugar in?"

"Yes, Mother."

"It doesn't taste like it. You let the milk boil. I can always taste when the milk's boiled."

Louise knew better than to argue. She sat in the small, moquette-covered armchair opposite her mother.

"Mother, I've some news."

The old lady examined the biscuit she was eating. "Is this a Marie biscuit?"

"Yes, Mother. Did you hear what I said?"

"I may be getting on a bit, but I'm not hard of hearing, Louise. What news? Not that it'll be anything that'll do me any good. If this is a Marie biscuit I'd be most surprised."

Louise said: "Mother, we're going to live at the seaside."

"The crumbs are irritating my throat and you never get crumbs with Marie biscuits. You'd better take them back in the morning."

"Did you hear what I said?"

"Yes. Ridiculous!"

"A client of ours has bought a block of flats by the sea; a little place called Whitecliffs. She's offered us a flat, rent-free. It's a sort of experiment to see if we like it. We wouldn't sell up here or anything."

"Have you been to the cinema, Louise?"

"You know perfectly well I have, Mother."

"You're always a bit odd when you come back from the cinema. You'll have forgotten all about it by tomorrow."

"I've made up my mind."

"What about me?" There was a whine in her mother's voice. "I am an old lady not a piece of furniture. You can't move me about from pillar to post."

"The sea air will do you good."

"And what about my friends and Mrs Cole and the television?"

"You'd make friends there, and I'd find someone to come in during the day and look after you, and they have television at Whitecliffs just the same."

The old lady tried a new tack. "What about your job?" she said. "You've been there ever since the war. How long is it?"

Louise thought of the seemingly endless time that she had sat behind the desk of the hairdressing salon. "Shampoo? Set? Perm? Bleach? Trim? Facial? Mr Alphonse, your client. Take madame through, Miss Joan. A taxi, madame? Certainly. You wish to pay by cheque? But of course, madame. Manicure? Eyebrow shaping? Re-styling and a bottle of our exclusive hair conditioner? Your change, madame. A brush for your suit, madame. What a charming poodle, madame, and hasn't he been exceptionally good? With Mr Maurice, madame? Today, madame? We'll try to fit you in. Your gloves, madame. You're forgetting your gloves; Miss Irene, madame's gloves. Your fur, madame; yes it is for the time of the year. The Bahamas? Naturally, madame. One wouldn't dream of a winter in this climate. Monte Carlo? But of course. Here, we have no summer to speak of at all. To Rome? To Kitzbuhel? To Paris? New York? Do have a lovely, lovely time, madame. We look forward to seeing you in a month, in two months, in a year. Your daughter? How charming. For her coming-out dance? How delightful. To Switzerland? How necessary. Where else *could* one be finished?"

"It must be nearly thirteen years, isn't it?" the old lady said.

"Whatever it is," Louise said, seeing herself as the years rolled inevitably on growing nearer the lilac shawl over the shapeless black dress, the gnarled hands and the two pairs of glasses for distance and near, "it's time we had a change!"

The young man in the green jersey jumped at it.

"But don't you see?" Basil said excitedly, "it's exactly what I've always wanted."

"It sounds incredible," Fiona said, wiping the top of the coffee bar and rearranging the tray of Danish pastries. "I wish someone would ask me. How did it happen?"

Basil put his lips to the froth on top of the coffee. "I hardly know myself. I was sitting in a pub in Fleet Street the night after Elisabeth walked out, and this bloke was sitting at the same table. I was feeling frightfully down and pretty drunk and was saying some absolutely inane things."

"What about?" Fiona said.

"Well, that's the whole point. You see this bloke's best friend had just dropped down dead outside his office, and I was saying how ghastly it is that we have to keep on and on and on..."

"You must excuse me a moment," Fiona said. "Somebody wants a capuccino."

When she came back to face him from behind the counter at which he sat on a high, red stool, Basil said: "Anyway I had completely forgotten about all that, and wouldn't have recognised this chap if I'd met him in the street. But he remembered me all right, and he sent this girl to look out for me and asked me to call and see him. He'd been thinking, you see, about what I'd apparently been shooting my mouth off about, life being a treadmill and all that crap, and he'd taken it to heart and decided to do something about it. Anyway he not only bought this block of flats at the seaside and decided to live there himself, but he wants me to come, too, because it was all my idea in the first place, and a whole lot of other people. It's a sort of experiment, you see."

"What about Elisabeth?"

"That's the only snag. I've told her, you see, but she won't come back. She says it doesn't make any difference where we live, things will be just the same again. But for me it's marvellous. I forgot to tell you we'll all be living rent free, so there won't be a thing to worry about. It's what I've always wanted and never had. The peace and the time to get cracking on something good. I feel that at Whitecliffs I shall write something really worth while. I don't think Elisabeth thinks I'm capable of it, but I know I am. I know it. Perhaps if I have something to show her, something to make her believe in me, she'd... Oh, what the hell!"

"I must say you led her a song and dance," Fiona said.

"I'm an author!" Basil said. "And we're artists. Sensitive artists. There must be allowances. We can't be treated the same as other people."

"But you expect to eat like other people, and your wife has to run the home on something."

"You have no soul," Basil said. "You're just as bad as Elisabeth." He got down from the stool. "Will you chalk it up?"

Fiona sighed and nodded.

"And if Elisabeth should drop in, tell her…tell her… Oh hell, don't tell her anything at all."

Fiona watched him, tousled hair, corduroy trousers and thick, beige jumper, go out into the Hampstead Street. She reached for her handbag and taking ninepence from it put it in the till.

Five

Doctor Gurney alone refused the offer at first. It was only at the last moment that he agreed to come at all.

Arthur, excited still by his new interest in people rather than in matters of business, called, by appointment, at Doctor Gurney's house. Informed, at some length by Vera, about the mess and the muddle she had found on her single visit to the Gurneys, Arthur was surprised, when he arrived, to see the front step gleaming redly. He was shown into a large, tidy, book-lined sitting-room by Mrs Gurney, an attractive, too thin redhead, smartly dressed in black. There was a coal fire burning softly in the grate. With his back to it Arthur thought that Vera, upset as she had been at the time, must have been imagining things.

"I'm so sorry everything was so chaotic the day your wife came round," Mrs Gurney said, pouring him a glass of sherry as they waited for her husband. "It was just one of those days. We were having this room painted, a patient of Francis' did it, and it took six endless weeks, evenings and weekends only, and the *au pair* had just gone back to Switzerland because her father was ill, or so she said, and Jonathan had whooping cough and screamed every time I went out of the room."

"Please don't worry," Arthur said. Then lied: "I'm sure that Vera didn't even notice. You must have a very busy household."

"It is, of course," Mrs Gurney said, "but the funny thing is that when everything, absolutely everything, goes wrong, when we are having one of our really slummy days, somebody's sure to call and needs to wait somewhere when there isn't anywhere at all. But when we're all properly organised, the children fit, help, and Francis not too busy so that I've time to keep things as they should be, nobody comes at all!"

Arthur smiled at her youth. She did not look as though she had had four children.

When Doctor Gurney came, apologising for his lateness, and his wife left them alone together, Arthur outlined his scheme.

Doctor Gurney said nothing for a while, looking into the fire, then he said:

"Do you know when my children last had a summer holiday?"

Arthur shook his head. He had presumed that, like most other children he knew, they went to the seaside for a month every August.

"Eight years ago," Doctor Gurney said, "when we just had Simon and Amanda. This summer Simon's going to camp with his Scout troop. The two little ones have never seen the sea at all."

Arthur said nothing.

"I've a fair-sized practice," Doctor Gurney said, "but it's a single-handed one, and there's plenty of competition round here. Simon is away at school, and you know what fees are these days, and then there's the mortgage on this house and food and clothes for all of us, and if we do go away we have to pay a locum a very large sum to look after the practice. Not only that, but the house has to be kept open for the locum, and that means a housekeeper, so you see..."

"I thought there were rota systems and things," Arthur said.

"Yes, for the odd days. But not for summer holidays. One has to have someone on the premises in a single-handed practice."

"Well, what about coming to Whitecliffs? There'd be no rent to pay and there is one reasonably large flat. You'd still get paid by the Health Service, wouldn't you?"

"I would. If I provided a competent locum who wouldn't lose all my patients for me. But I've just told you. I can't even afford one for the holidays."

"I'll pay for a locum," Arthur said, "for three months."

Doctor Gurney refilled Arthur's glass with sherry.

"Tell me, Mr Dexter, why are you doing all this? I can understand you going to Whitecliffs yourself. I think it's a very sensible decision. But why take the responsibility for all these other people you've been telling me about? Why offer to pay a locum for me? Why spend all this money on people you hardly know?"

"It's the treadmill," Arthur said. "I not only want to get off myself. I want to help you all get off. It's something that since Willie's death I want passionately to do. It'll cost me very little really, you know I'm not a poor man, but I must know, if we had the choice, if we'd still go on and on and on till we dropped."

"I can't see where the choice comes in," Doctor Gurney said, "in my case, at any rate. Suppose I agreed to your suggestion, which of course I never would, but just suppose that I did, for argument's sake. Well, after the two months or the three months for which you paid my locum, I would have no choice but to get back on my own particular treadmill. I would have had an extremely nice rest and holiday, as would Mary and the children, but after that it would be back to work, if there was to be any bread and butter."

"Ah! That's just the point," Arthur said. "You see at Whitecliffs you might discover that you would be far happier and able to earn a living doing something else. You might find you were more temperamentally suited to being a house-painter or a farmer or an insurance broker."

"It would still be a treadmill, though. Whatever it was, you would have to keep on and on doing it. Unless you wanted to starve."

"Perhaps," Arthur said. "But you must get off for a while and look at yourself. You must take time to consider whether you want to continue to do what you are doing, for the rest of your life. I want to make that possible not only for myself but you. It's not charity, or philanthropy or anything else. It's just that I don't want to die, or you, or any of these other people who are coming with us, before we've had a chance to slow down, to discover what it is that makes us turn and turn, step after step after step."

"LSD mainly," Doctor Gurney said.

"No. You're wrong! Willie had all the money he could use."

"Greed, avarice?"

"Willie was a simple man."

"Then I don't know. Probably sheer laziness. When you've taken one step the easiest thing in the world is to put your foot on the next as it comes round."

"Exactly," Arthur said. "Once you're on you stay on. But I am going to get off, much, I must say, to the disgust of my family who are afraid, not for their bread and butter, but for their cake, and I want to make it possible for you and the others to do the same. Call it an experiment if you like. It may very well be that none of us would be happy without those steps coming round and round monotonously to be trodden on. But I must find out before I end up like Willie. I must."

"It's a very generous offer," Doctor Gurney said, "and I'd very much like to accept it. You must see, though, that I can't. I can't let somebody pay for my locum while I sit on the beach. Not to mention the rent of the flat."

"I suppose," Arthur said, "that in a way, work is different for doctors. I mean it's a vocation, isn't it? Something you feel in your blood you have to do?"

Doctor Gurney looked at him, and appeared to be weighing up whether or not he should say what he was about to.

"It's work like any other," he finally said. "We are trained to take histories, examine, diagnose and prescribe, as you are trained to buy and sell toys. We are both paid for what we do."

"But you are doing something for humanity."

"Only because we do our work *to* humanity."

"Sometimes you give your services for nothing?"

Doctor Gurney shrugged. "It's a tradition."

"You give more than medical advice. You give hope, encouragement, sympathy, understanding."

"It's all part of the same thing."

"What made you take up medicine?"

"Like most boys, although they don't always admit it, my father. I would probably have been equally happy in industry or the civil service."

"What about the doctor-patient relationship?" Arthur asked. "Why do I have confidence in what you tell me and none at all in the advice of Doctor X of Doctor Y?"

"There's nothing very mysterious about that. We all give much the same advice. You just like my personality and I get on with yours. It's like choosing a chauffeur or a gardener or a secretary."

"Don't you worry about your patients in the night, whether what you have done is right? Whether they will live or die?"

"I do my best and then I go to sleep. I have to be fresh for work the next day."

"You feel no sense of vocation, no calling?"

"None at all. Being a doctor is my job as business is yours, and plumbing the next man's. I like to do my job well, but that is all. This vocation business is for the cinema, for books, for the general public, if you like. I don't believe it exists. Perhaps there was a time when it did, but not today when everyone has to scratch a living, quickly, desperately, urgently."

Arthur stood up. “I hope you’ll think over my offer,” he said.“I have the feeling that perhaps you need to take advantage of it more than any of us.”

It was a few weeks later that Doctor Gurney phoned him at his office. “Look,” he said, “our baby, the one who had whooping cough, has remained a little chesty and I’d like to take him away. Is the offer by any chance still open?”

The Dexters were dining. There were no flowers, the silver had been removed from the sideboard, the drawing-room was already shrouded in dust sheets. Arthur and Victor placidly ate their lamb chops. Vanessa and her mother played with the food on their plates, then laid down their knives and forks.

“Arthur, are you sure you know what you’re doing?” Vera said. There were desperation and tears in her voice.

“Mother, for God’s sake not again,” Victor said. “I can’t stand it. Anyway isn’t it a bit late now? All our stuff’s already in Whitecliffs and the flat furnished and what not…”

“Be quiet, Victor,” Vera said. “I’m talking to your father.”

Arthur looked up from his chop. “What is it, Vera?”

Vera clenched her napkin. “You see, you’re so busy with your idiotic, childish ideas you don’t even listen to what I’m saying. For the last time I asked you if you’re absolutely sure about this. Sure that you want to go to that idiotic, dreary place with all those idiotic, dreary people, half of whom I haven’t even met. I suppose you’re ashamed of them or something.”

“No,” Arthur said. “I just didn’t think there was any point. They are all separate flats. We shan’t be mixed up in any way. Howard, now, Howard Pennington-Dalby, he’s a nice enough chap…”

“Which one’s Howard?”

“The barrister…?”

“Barrister,” Vera said. “Well, if he’s anything like your cousin Henry…”

"He's nothing like my cousin Henry," Arthur said patiently. "My cousin Henry happens to be a crook."

"That's just what I said." Vera was triumphant. Arthur sighed.

"And Basil's harmless enough," he said. "He writes. Books or something."

"Typewriter going all night," Vera said. "And isn't there something about his wife?"

"She's left him," Arthur said. "Walked out. I don't know why."

"He's probably quite unsuitable." She suddenly thought of something. "What about references?" she said. "Have you taken up references from someone who knows all these peculiar people? I mean anyone who lets a flat to anyone, whether they're stupid enough to pay the rent themselves or not, usually takes the trouble to find out something about their tenants. I mean it's only sensible."

"Ring for the dessert, Vera," Arthur said. "I'm sorry but you just don't understand. I am doing this thing because I know inside me that it's the thing I have to do, because of Willie. I am going to Whitecliffs because my instinct tells me to. I am taking Howard and Basil and the others because I want to. And because I want to I'll have nothing to do with reason or with references or with caution or with all the other things I've put first for the whole of my life. This time Arthur Dexter is doing what he must, not what he should."

Vera waited until the plates were cleared and the soufflé brought in before she opened her mouth to say something. Before she had a chance Arthur said: "Have you taken up references from your Louise person?"

"Don't be ridiculous, Arthur," Vera said. "I've known Louise for years; she's not just somebody I've picked up in a public house."

"You've known her behind the desk at the hairdresser's," Arthur said. "You don't know what she's like at home, do you?

She may be a drug addict or somebody's mistress or something…" His imagination could go no further.

"I've told you she lives with her old mother."

Arthur leered. "Well perhaps they're murderers, the pair of them."

Vera began to serve the soufflé which was rapidly descending into its dish. "Arthur, I really believe…"

"I know," Arthur said, making holes in the tablecloth with the prongs of his fork. "You believe, as you've said before, I've gone mad. I assure you I haven't."

Arthur looked at his wife feeling sorry for her, particularly as he had something else to say.

"Vera."

"Yes, Arthur." She sounded tired, deflated.

"There's something else about Whitecliffs. I didn't say anything before because I had to wait until it was all settled." He decided to run straight on. "I've bought a beach café."

"You'll be telling me in a minute you're going to stand behind the counter serving teas," Vera said.

"That's right." Arthur ate his soufflé.

"Arthur, I was joking."

"I wasn't."

"But, Arthur, you've never made a cup of tea in your life!"

"Then I shall have to learn. There are a great many things I shall have to learn. Seriously, Vera, I saw this place last week when I went to settle things with the agents, and I suddenly thought that it would just complete the picture."

"Complete the picture?" Vera looked dazed.

"Yes," Arthur leaned across the table enthusiastically. "I thought we could run it between us, and then everyone would feel they were earning their board and lodging. We could share the profits, if any, between us."

"But Arthur, I thought the idea was not to work."

"You couldn't call this work. It would be something we'd enjoy doing. Fun."

"Washing up other people's cups and saucers?" Vera said.

"We can get someone to do that. It's right on the beach, this place, opposite the Corporation's café. It's called 'Joe's..."

"We'd have to change that for a start," Vera said, then realised she had betrayed herself.

Arthur smiled inwardly and sensed that he should say no more.

When Vera and Vanessa had left the table, Vanessa to say goodbye to Cliff, and Vera to finish her packing, Arthur and Victor sat in silence in a haze of smoke.

"I suppose you think I'm crazy, too," Arthur said.

"No."

"I hope it will be all right, Vic. Don't tell your mother I said so but..."

Victor stubbed out his cigarette and stood up. "It'll be all right, Pop. *Mihi sic usus est; Tibi, ut opus est facto, face.*"

Arthur raised his eyebrows questioningly.

"Well, the nearest I can get," Victor said, "is that you should do what you have to in this world and that everyone else should damn well mind his own business."

Six

At seven o'clock on an August morning Whitecliffs was at its best. The sun, uncertain still whether to make or mar the day for the holiday-makers who lay asleep in the 'Courts' that were not courts, the 'Sea Views' tucked deep into the town and the 'Ocean Breezes' far removed from the shore, peeped playfully out behind a pale rimmed cloud. In 'Beverley', 'Earlsmead', 'Lynton Villa' and 'The Towers', fathers and mothers slept the last, slowly surfacing sleep in striped pyjamas and nylon nighties, and sunburned toddlers in sandy beds lay vulnerably, angelically quiet, long lashes on cherubic cheeks, breathing softly, heads between rounded, upraised arms.

On the shore, in a grey haze of undisturbed beauty, the sand stretched smoothly out to the curly edges of the foam. The pedaloes, blue, yellow and orange, lay in near rows on the promenade where the boatman had tidied them the night before, and the stacks of corporation deck-chairs waited demurely beneath their green canvas shrouds. Black rocks and green seaweed-slimed rocks bounded the bay on either side, and circling above them the gulls called into the early stillness. The wooden beach huts were curtained and shuttered, and along the wide stretch of concrete from cliff to cliff the litter bins stood empty.

The two beach cafés were locked, bolted and barred; the Corporation one with which we are not much concerned, and, coyly continental, 'Le Casse-Croûte' (formerly 'Joe's') known and referred to locally as 'Cass'', 'Cass' Caff' or simply the 'Caff', which was not at all the original idea.

Superior, on the deserted promenade, 'Le Casse-Croûte' averted its face from its municipal rival and waited patiently, silently for opening time. Only its notices, painted boldly, artistically, red on grey, spoke. 'Candy Floss', they said, '6d'; 'Iced Frutie – 6d'; 'Sandwiches Freshly Made To Order': 'Trays For The Beach'. In the 'garden' – a concrete yard bounded by a low wall – the small tables, pink and green, stood bubbled with sea mist and early morning dew, and their chairs painted to match lurched towards them for support. At the end of the garden the store-room, padlocked, safeguarded in sleep its treasure-trove of tins piled high into the rafters; lemon puffs, iced gems, orange finger wafers, small rich tea, rugby wafers, ice-cream cones. Later and throughout the long day 'Le Casse-Croûte' would welcome all; small barefooted children, whose noses reached only to the counter, men in cloth caps or panama hats, ladies wearing not enough bathing costume. Later the stills would hiss and the cash registers ping, the washing-up tumble in the sink at the back, and the sparrows peck the ground for crumbs in the garden. The day, for 'Le Casse-Croûte' had not yet begun. It waited shutter-eyed for the young lady with the keys. The young lady was still asleep. She was not in her own bed and she was not alone.

It was the coy tactics of the sun that woke her. One moment the room was only palely lit, and the next the sun, winking through the opening in the glazed chintz curtains, drowned it in light. On, off, on, off, like the beacon at a zebra crossing. Its persistence pierced the last light vapour of sleep, and Honey lifted her half-inch soot-black lashes from the pale blue eyes they veiled and examined the ceiling. Although it was extremely early, and at the best of times Honey was not unduly perceptive, she realised that the roof beneath which she had passed the night was unfamiliar. The sun continued its Morse message half a dozen times more, right on Honey's face, before she glanced at the source of warmth beside her. It was Basil, of course. Even in sleep he had the three small frown lines between his eyebrows. He was brown as a fisherman and naked. Sitting up, Honey looked round the room. Three sheets of blank, white paper and a blue carbon flopped out of the typewriter and on to the dressing-table, whose top was a sea of paper; sheets and sheets of paper loose and in packets, scribbled on, typed on and blank. Here and there on the sea, like fishes, blue and red, swam threepenny notebooks ruled 'feint' 'memo' and 'cash'. The mess slopped over on to the floor; the wastepaper basket was full. Honey wondered where she had put her clothes; it was the first time she had slept with an author.

Basil opened his eyes; then shut them again; then opened them and stared at Honey who sat like a silky, golden statue bathed in sunlight.

"My God!" he said.

Honey turned to him and her long black hair swung over her shoulders as she did so.

"What time is it?" she said, "I have to open up this morning."

Basil said nothing but shut his eyes, not against the sun, which streamed now more constantly through the curtains, but to exclude Honey, playing desperately the childish game in which he would open his eyes again in a few moments to find Honey gone and himself to have been dreaming. When he looked again Honey was waiting patiently, and she was not a dream.

"I have to open up," she said equably, "what's the time?"

Basil, shame and reproach chasing each other through his mind, handed her his watch from the bedside table. He thought of his wife and moaned at the irrevocability of what he had done.

"What's the matter?" Honey said, running her fingers through her hair.

"Everything. My wife."

"Your wife's in London."

"That's the trouble. If she'd been here it would never have happened."

Honey shrugged. "You did ask me."

"I what?" Now Basil sat up, too.

"You asked me, last night, to come up here."

Reaching for his dressing-gown from the foot of the bed, Basil put it on and went over to the window. He pulled open one curtain and had his hand on the other when Honey said:

"Well you did. Didn't you?"

He pulled back the other curtain slowly and felt the warm sun on his face before he said: "Yes, I did."

"Well then."

Basil sat on the chair from which he did his typing, and with his arms folded across its back looked at Honey.

"Honey, do you know why I asked you to come up here last night?"

"Of course," she said. She seemed to have remembered hearing somewhere that authors were a little peculiar.

Basil shook his head. "I don't believe you do."

Honey glanced at the bed. "I should have said it was pretty obvious."

"I asked you to come up here so that I could get some material for my novel. I wanted the story of your life. I've never known a striptease dancer."

Honey swung her legs out of bed, and they were long and golden like the rest of her. "Well you should have said."

"I suppose I should. I never thought, though, that you would think I…"

Honey was getting bored. "Look, don't worry about it. There's no damage done."

Basil winced. How simple life was to the simple. Honey went into the bathroom and Basil, thinking hard, tried to reconstruct the previous evening. He remembered clearly their walk along the sea-front in the starlight, with the sea banging rhythmically against the shore and drowning, sometimes, with its roar, his words. He was talking about Henry James and his influence on the novel, and Honey had said she was cold and he had given her his jacket; then he was explaining about existentialism, the theory of which he had studied, and Honey said her feet hurt and they had turned back. He knew that he had asked her into the flat, because he had no notebook on him and he wanted to get the exact details of her career, family background and so on, but what wasn't at all clear was how they had got into the bedroom and into bed. He had vague recollections of a bottle of whisky in which they had made considerable in-roads, the evening having become chilly, and even hazier memories of Honey's long arms twining themselves round his neck. As far as he knew he had not made a single note in his notebook, and was doubtful that he had even got as far as unscrewing the cap of his fountain pen. There were in his mind, playing tag with each other, odd sights and sounds, Honey's low laugh, her hair in his eyes, the warmth and perfume of her skin, but they refused to form a consecutive picture.

Honey, back from the bathroom, looked for her clothes.

"In the sitting-room," Basil said, surprised at his subconscious for remembering.

Honey went to fetch them. Even for mid-August there was very little. A negligible pair of pants, a cotton dress, her shoes. She used his comb and picked up her handbag. She looked fresh as a daisy.

"See you later." No one could deny that standing in the early sunlight she was desirable. Basil hoped she would not come any nearer.

"I shan't be very late," he said. "We were cleaned out of toffee-apples yesterday. I shall have to do some more."

Honey came over to plant a kiss on his forehead and, as though her lips unlocked a door, Basil remembered with shocked clarity the more important details of the night before.

"You'll be late," he said shakily.

"I'll run," she said.

The door closed behind her and the room seemed terribly empty.

If 'Le Casse-Croûte' was peculiar in that one of its assistants was by profession a stripper, and its toffee-apple maker an author, it was equally unconventional in the rest of its staff. There was Howard, serious-faced, with paunch starting to come and hair starting to go, more familiar with torts than tarts, and incapable of addressing even small children in other than his weighty courtroom tones. He filled the cornets, threepence and sixpence, with the same gravity with which he prepared advice on evidence, and had one not known the words he uttered to some grubby urchin to be 'strawberry, vanilla or six-five special?' one might have imagined him to be asking his 'Ludship', with due solemnity, for the custody of the child.

The tea urn mirrored in its fat, silvery belly, for the greater part of the day, Louise, making her shorter and plumper than she really was. Its taps were turned and its handles pulled by the ivory, elegant hands with the perfect, almond-shaped nails always so much admired in the beauty salon where she was more accustomed to enquiring 'Shampoo and set, madame?' than 'Drinking it here or taking it on the beach?'

There was Victor, eighteen, ex-Public School, selling the buckets and spades. His twin sister Vanessa dreamily, romantically twirling the candy floss, equally well endowed with brains and beauty.

And at the cash register, Dr Francis Gurney.

The man responsible for the whole peculiar arrangement was, despite the entreaties of the sun, still asleep.

Had anyone told Arthur Dexter, in the week before Willie Boothroyd died, that he would not only be living at Whitecliffs by the sea before the summer was out but that he would own and run, with sleeves rolled up, a beach café, he would have thought them more than a little mad.

That 'Le Casse-Croûte' (the name was Vera's which was all she would have to do with the project), a beach café, belonged to him, Arthur Dexter, and that he was personally responsible for running it, he had to repeat to himself, aloud and very often. Frequently in the morning, he would search unthinkingly in the wardrobe for his City suit, his sober waistcoat, and hope there would not be too much traffic on the way to town, and that he would be able to find somewhere to park the car. Then he would go to the window, and the great weight in his chest would lighten as he saw the dream was not a dream and that not half a mile away the sea roared comfortingly and that the air carried neither smoke, dirt nor petrol fumes but only spray, refreshing, from the sea. And there was more joy in that he hadn't to go home today or tomorrow or after the weekend or at any time at all until if and when he was ready, and he would let the curtain fall with a sigh of contentment, for Arthur Dexter was happier than he had ever been.

While Arthur slept Honey was busy in 'Le Casse-Croûte'. In the gloom of the self-service bar she had already lit the still beneath the counter, in which the water would boil for the teas, and was now about to prepare the day's first urnful of coffee on the gas-stove in the back kitchen. Into a large saucepan she emptied three quart bottles of milk, three quart bottles of water, filled from the tap, and six measures of powdered coffee. She waited impatiently for the mixture to boil and hoped it would not take too long. There was something she wanted to do before Vanessa arrived to help her with the heavy shutters. It was something to which she looked forward, and the reason why she never minded when it was her turn to open 'Le Casse-Croûte' in the mornings. When the coffee had boiled, properly hot although not very strong, Honey poured it carefully into the urn on the counter, mopped up the drips with the swab, which had been left in bleach from the night before, and left the saucepan, filled with cold water, in the sink. Slipping off her shoes she let herself out of the back door of the café. Opposite, in the Corporation Café whose shutters were already down, Honey saw the skinny Iris putting on her regulation white overall. Honey looked the other way, not wishing to waste her time. The promenade, cleanly swept, was cold beneath her bare feet. A man, newspaper clutched behind his back, stood by the deck-chairs contemplating the morning. There was no one else about. An anticipatory smile of pleasure on her very lovely face, Honey crossed the cool, damp sand, which marked the imprint of her toes behind her, and walked quickly towards the sea. Having reached the water she stopped. On the edge of the ocean which lapped about her ankles she stood quite still and held up her face, eyes closed, to the morning sun. For five long minutes while the breeze lifted her hair and wrapped the tight dress tighter round her body, Honey was a goddess. In her heart, in her blood she knew she was a nude, a stripper, a showgirl, blazed on by bright lights, living by night and sleeping by day, stared at, slobbered over and desired by a changing panorama of hot-eyed men. But for five minutes of every day that it was her turn to open 'Le Casse-Croûte', before the customers arrived and the day began, she was one with the clear, cold water at her feet, the wind and the morning light. She was untouched, virginal, pure. She was Honey DuPont, as she might have been had she not been born Doreen Maloney in a small, damp house where there were already too many little Maloneys.

She walked back across the beach more slowly than she had come, avoiding her own footprints. A small girl in shorts ran down towards the water with a boat. The man with the newspaper had gone.

Vanessa was looking anxiously out of the café door. "I wondered where you were."

Simply, expensively dressed, looking younger than eighteen, Vanessa's eyes were kind. No longer a goddess, Honey said: "I went down to the sea."

There was a year only between them, but looking at her Honey felt, as she always did, that it was a year and a world. Not bothering to rub the sand from her feet she slipped on her shoes, conscious, beneath Vanessa's well-bred gaze, of the corns on her feet.

Seven

"The Lord Chief Justice is late," Honey said, putting sugar lumps from a brown paper carton into small bowls for one, two or three, on the counter.

Vanessa, wrapping currant buns in small squares of cellophane paper, went red in the face, but Honey didn't notice.

There was plenty for the two girls to do. Together they had removed the heavy shutters from the self-service bar, the ice-cream window, the candy floss and the fancy-goods. It was nine o'clock, the water was boiling for the teas and the coffee was made. Officially 'Le Casse-Croûte' was open, but the work had only just begun.

"Sometimes I wonder," Honey, from whom words flowed like a quicksilver stream, went on, "if he goes to bed in his stiff collar." This time she glanced down the length of the counter at Vanessa.

She wished she could remember the time when the mere mention of a man had made her blush.

"Do you think we shall need all the buns?" Vanessa said, her voice a little taut. "The clouds do seem to be clearing."

"I think it'll settle. We don't want to be caught out. I should finish those, then I'll help you start the sandwiches. How old do you think he is?"

"Who?"

"The Lord Chief Justice."

"Howard? I don't know. Getting on for forty, I suppose."

"He'll never see that again, Vanessa. Of course, he's not bad-looking, but he needs some of the stuffing taken out. I know the type."

"Do you mind awfully if we don't discuss it?" Vanessa said politely.

"Not a bit," Honey said easily. "I never knew it was like that."

"It's not like that. I just don't like pulling people to pieces." She wished she didn't sound so prim.

"Oh dear," Honey said, "you want to mother him. That can be awfully dangerous."

She could see that it would be unwise to pursue the conversation. She opened up the record-player which stood near the cash register and started sorting through the pile of records.

" 'Around the World'?" she said, " 'That's my Baby'? 'So Young'? 'Rock me Daddy O'?"

"I don't mind," Vanessa said, dealing with the last of the buns. "What about 'I like your kind of Love'?"

Honey said nothing, but finding the record put it on. Vanessa began to butter bread dreamily and Honey, less inhibited, danced close to an imaginary partner up and down the narrow space behind the counter.

At the time when he was normally driving through the traffic to Southwark, Lambeth, Edmonton, Marylebone, Bloomsbury or Shoreditch, the 'Lord Chief Justice' or Howard Pennington-Dalby was walking smartly along the green sward that ran along the cliff top towards 'Le Casse-Croûte'. To look at him one would believe that he was on his way to a county court or at least to his chambers, for even one hundred yards from where the sea rolled against the beach and beneath a midsummer sky which looked very little like rain he clung to his bowler hat, set correctly on his head, and his rolled umbrella whose ferrule made small holes in the grass as he walked. He had, however, as a concession to the seaside, exchanged his black jacket and striped trousers for a plain, dark grey flannel suit.

How infinitely more pleasant this was, he thought, inhaling the sea air for four paces and letting it slowly out for four, than early morning in the Temple. How absolutely unbelievable that he, on an ordinary, working morning, should be hurrying to serve ice-creams in a beach café instead of unenthusiastically preparing to fight a possession action or an allegation of nuisance by somebody's upstairs tenant. Of course, he had had dreams. That was partly why he had agreed to come to Whitecliffs at all. He was over forty and his dream was not materialising. He had to admit it, and he had to think about it. With his feet up on his desk in his musty room in chambers, a few uninteresting letters on his desk and a pile of old briefs, he had not been able to get the distance from which to face his problem objectively. Now, the length of a bay, beautiful in the morning light, away from his undemanding day's work, he took out his dream and examined it.

That it was the same as every other barrister's dream, he knew. That he had come no nearer to realising it than most other barristers, he also knew. Whether the time had come to abandon it, he had come to Whitecliffs to decide.

At twenty-one, with the stars still in his eyes, he had come down from Cambridge, eaten his dinners at the Temple, and been called to the Bar. He had bought a pupilage in good chambers, which he had been fortunate to get, and had opened his dream at page one. The first few chapters, he was sensible enough to realise, were only the beginning at which everyone must start; by the middle of the book, things, he hoped, should little by little become interesting. In the early days the dream seemed barely remote; the flat in town, the place in the country, the books, the wine, the yacht, the cigars, the food, the women, the silk dressing-gown, the valet, the first nights at the opera, the theatre; the illustrated papers: Mr Justice Pennington-Dalby at home; Mr Justice Pennington-Dalby embarks for the States;

Mr Justice Pennington-Dalby rides to hounds. The knighthood, he had been prepared to admit, would come later, but he was not a greedy young man and did not expect everything to come at once. Neither was he lazy, and he had been prepared to work. And work he certainly had. He had kow-towed to solicitors he couldn't stand the sight of, had worked disproportionately hard preparing advice on evidence for the few briefs he had, studied his successful superiors, and had become meticulous in his knowledge of the law. He had been at the Bar now for twenty years during which time he had changed chambers three times, received many more briefs than he used to, and become pedantic, pompous and stodgy. He was making a sufficient living to supply his own bachelor needs, but he appreciated that, at three-quarters of the way through the book, he was no nearer reaching his dream. The yacht, the country house and the fame had simply not materialised. He had a service flat in Twickenham and augmented his income by sessions at legal advice bureaux, evening class lectures to which nobody listened, and writing unimportant articles for even less important journals. He had enough to eat, a small car, took the occasional holiday abroad and spent most of his money on gramophone records. That was all. He had never married for he was waiting for his dream. He had a first-class brain, they had said at Cambridge, but so, he now had to admit, had many of the hundreds of other barristers who waited hungrily in equally dreary chambers for the daily share-out of briefs which was never enough to go round. At twenty-one Howard had known he could realise the world. At forty-three he had pulled in his vision. After forty, a man can see, if he wishes to look, what he is likely to achieve. Howard was not afraid of looking, and he did not particularly like what he saw. He had welcomed the invitation to Whitecliffs as a respite, during which he would try to discover how the dream had escaped and whether he would continue to pursue it.

A few fathers in shorts and open-necked shirts walked by him on the green carrying the bread and newspapers they had been sent to fetch. They looked at Howard curiously. The children, skipping at their heels, did not give him a second glance.

In the back kitchen of 'Le Casse-Croûte', Howard hung his hat and his umbrella behind the door. Taking off his jacket, he placed it carefully on the hanger he had provided for himself during the opening week, removed his cuff-links, which he tucked into his waistcoat pocket, tied his white apron neatly round his middle and went into the café.

"Good morning, good morning," he said, making for his ice-cream counter.

"Good morning, Your Worship," Honey said, cutting tomatoes and waggling her hips in time to a rhumba.

Howard was not amused. "Good morning, Vanessa," he said to Vanessa who was replenishing the stock of cigarettes on the shelves behind his counter.

"Good morning, Howard."

Howard lifted the heavy black lid of the ice-box, and put his head into the steamy interior. "I have twenty-four sandwiches cut from yesterday," he said seriously. "I shall have to replace the biscuits." He put the ice-creams, whose wafers had gone soggy overnight, on his counter and took down a fresh packet of wafers.

"Shall I help you?" Vanessa said. "I've filled you up with cigarettes."

"How kind," Howard said. "How very, very kind."

By the time Arthur Dexter arrived at 'Le Casse-Croûte' the seaside day, upon which the sun had finally decided to shine brilliantly, was well under way. On the beach, brown-legged men in shorts and woolly caps with pom-poms on were pushing the pedaloes down to the water; fathers and mothers with sundry small infants had wandered back and forth a few times over the sand and stones and finally put down their deck-chairs and staked their claim to a few yards of the shore. The children, stripped to the first pair of dry trunks of the day, flew their kites, dug their castles, took their buckets and searched for shrimps in the water, filled the dog-bowl from the Corporation tap, nagged for an ice-cream, put up convincing arguments that it was time for a bathe. The fathers refused to dig castles or make boats, removed their shirts, tested with a handkerchief which way the wind was blowing and settled down behind the newspaper. The mothers, distributing their numerous bags and hold-alls which were packed tightly with dry swimming clothes, towels, beach robes, bottles of milk, chocolate biscuits, Elasto-plast and their knitting, rubbed anti-sunburn cream into sandy shoulders and said no, it was too early for a bathe and be careful of the rocks and put your shoes on if you're going on the promenade.

Already 'Le Casse-Croûte' had served a few early teas and coffees, and Howard, leaning earnestly from his serving window, was deep in argument with some small child as to the respective merits of strawberry and vanilla.

Arthur Dexter, happy because he was caring for his new baby, was in a good mood.

"Morning everyone!" he called, rolling up his sleeves as he walked quickly hither and thither. "Let's get cracking, eh! The sun's going to shine all day and the tide'll be up this afternoon; we'll get them all on the promenade. Ring up the dairy, Vanessa, we're a bit short of milk; Basil, carry the candy-floss machine out to the front for her before you start on the toffee-apples; don't forget the rain-covers, just in case, see that they're well out of sight, Van. Morning, Doctor Gurney, get the floats handed out, there's a good chap; Victor, hurry with the ladder and get those picture postcards outside; they're coming down to the beach like flies; where's Charlie? — We need some cigarettes from the store and we'd better have the umbrella out today and we're getting short on grease-proof. Honey, darling, get the ham from the deep-freeze and hold it for me while I cut it; watch your fridges, Howard, old man, I can hear the ice-cream van."

Basil, starting to melt the sugar for his toffee-apples in the back kitchen, found himself within an inch of Honey, who was holding the piece of frozen ham steady while Arthur sliced it in the old-fashioned machine. Having buttered the round marble slab on which he would put the coated apples to set, he opened a new crate of apples and started to insert the sticks.

"What did you do last night, Basil?" Arthur said, and then to Honey, "Leave that one for the salads; it's too thick for sandwiches."

Basil stirred the melted sugar and added a small amount of vinegar. "Nothing very much," he said casually, "I went for a walk."

"Gets chilly here at night," Arthur said, "even though it's August. I suppose you went dancing, Honey-child?"

Honey looked at him across the ham slicer. "Oh, no!" she said innocently, "as a matter of fact I went for a walk, too!" She felt Basil pinch her behind in warning. "And then I went to bed," she said, "it does get chilly in the evenings."

"Basil!" Arthur said. "Are you sure that sugar isn't burning?"

At his fancy-goods window, from which he had a panoramic view of the entire beach, Victor laid out his stock: tins of bubbles for the children, fishing nets, kites, boats, flags, windmills, sunglasses, water-pistols, hairnets in small cellophane packets, brooches, toys, small books, games, and perhaps most important of all, buckets and spades. Every few moments he would stop and survey the changing pattern of the beach. When he was in the middle of preparing his tray of coloured brooches, pinning them securely to their cushion as a precaution against light-fingered customers, he suddenly stopped what he was doing. "Hey, Howard, come here a minute."

Howard stuck the chocolate flake into a 'six-five special' and handed it to a fat lady in sunglasses. When he had put the money in his till he moved over to Victor at the next window.

"What is it?"

Victor pointed to the beach. "Look! There. Between the two huts. Near the man in braces with the newspaper over his face."

Howard followed his pointing finger. "I can't see anything."

"My God," Victor said, "can't you really? You'd better go back to your cornets."

"What is it anyway?" Howard moved back to his own counter.

"It's a girl! With the prettiest little bottom you've ever seen. I wish we sold binoculars."

He leaned as far as he could out of his window. She was fair-skinned and wearing a black bikini. Her hair was blonde and tied in a knot, as far as he could make out, on top of her head. She was standing up, her legs planted apart, and appeared to be searching the beach as though looking for somebody. Her profile, against the sky, was classic.

"Hey Dad!" Victor called into the back, "can somebody look after my window for a moment?"

"Why? You've only just arrived."

"Urgent business. I shan't be long."

"Ask Howard if he minds," Arthur said.

Howard said he really didn't see how he could give his proper attention both to ice-creams and fancy-goods, but before he had finished grumbling Victor had gone.

Vanessa looked up in sympathy from her candy-floss stand beneath Howard's side window. He could see the smooth line of her throat and the evenness of her teeth as she smiled. He noticed quite suddenly, and with a small shock, that she really was a very pretty girl.

Eight

"Excuse me," Victor said. "Were you looking for someone?"

The girl turned towards him, put one hand on her hip, tilted her stomach towards him, the navel well in evidence above her brief pants, pouted and stared at him.

"I might be," she said, her baby face assuming an expression she believed to be sultry.

"Well…er…could I be of any help?"

"On holiday?" she said.

"Not exactly. My father owns that café," he pointed towards 'Le Casse-Croûte'. "I help him."

"What happened to Joe?"

"Joe?"

"Had the place last year."

"My father bought it from him."

"Smartened it up a bit."

"Oh, yes, we've done a lot of work on it. You see when Joe had it…"

She wasn't listening. She had forgotten to pout and was looking up and down the beach again.

"You'd better go. I'm expecting someone."

"Look," Victor said. "Can I see you sometime?"

She gave him her attention again, looking him up and down from where the hair flopped over his eyes, to the open-necked shirt, his grey trousers and his sandals.

"Please," Victor said. The top of her bikini scarcely covered her breasts. He could see where the suntan stopped in a clearly defined line like Neapolitan ice-cream.

She intercepted his glance. "Praps you'd better ask your Dad," she said, to punish him.

"I'm twenty-one," Victor lied, hurt. "I know I don't look very old but..."

"I was joking. I'm on the darts at Merrydown Park. The first darts as you come in." She was searching the beach again. "You'd better go," she added suddenly, forgetting to undulate or pout. She turned her back on him.

"I don't know your name."

"Petal," she said without turning round. She began to comb her hair. "Now beat it."

Victor, stepping over beflagged sand-castles, made his way towards the promenade. Halfway up the steps he found his way blocked by somebody coming down. He stood to one side. "Sorry," he said, and looked up. Astride, across the steps was one of the largest, meanest looking Teddy boys he had ever seen. He was about six feet tall, had oily, black hair which swept thickly back from his low forehead and trickled down a black suit which narrowed rapidly from ridiculously broad shoulders to ludicrously narrow trousers, luminous green socks and black shoes with no laces but elastic sides. His mouth drooped downwards, in a pallid, puddingy face beneath a prominent nose; his eyes leered dully from beneath heavy lids and his tie appeared to be nothing but a piece of black string. He made no effort to progress down the steps in the space Victor had created. Having been taught, the hard way, during ten years of Prep. and Public School, that one of the primary requisites of any male is to act at all times like a gentleman, Victor retreated to the soft sand at the bottom of the steps. Only then did the apparition, hunching his enormous shoulders and fixing Victor with a blood-curdling glare, descend to the beach.

"I say! Don't say thank you, will you," Victor said to the draped, receding back. Fortunately for him the wind was blowing in from the sea, and his remark was heard only by some small girl clutching a pair of water wings who was waiting to come down the steps.

When the long August day finally ended the sun, a great fiery sphere, having extinguished itself in the sea,. Arthur Dexter, alone, still sat in the back kitchen of 'Le Casse-Croûte' doing the books. The tide had come up, bringing up with it the crowds from the beach, clamouring for refreshment, and was now lapping slowly out again into the evening sky. 'Le Casse-Croûte' had filled and refilled. Sticky hands had helped themselves to buns and sandwiches, sun-dried voices asked for orangeade and tea, purses spilled half-crowns and shillings.

Arthur Dexter, busy, a sandwich by his side, was in his element. He was working, it was true, but not so hard that he had no time to think. He was wondering, as he often did, how he had actually made the stupendous effort of tearing himself away and coming to Whitecliffs at all. Vera had opposed him, there had been tears, rows, threats and pleadings; Vanessa had argued with him; it had not been easy for him to arrange for his business to jog along without him (only to keep going; he knew that in his absence it would make no profit and might indeed fail altogether); but there had been, in those strange weeks immediately after Willie's death, something driving him on. It was something which Vera did not recognise, and Doctor Gurney could not cure; it was something which he had been unaware dwelt within him, and which he had allowed to have its head; it was perhaps the last flicker of what remained of the world-compassing hopes of adolescence, the strength of young manhood to accomplish anything at all, the fight that still remained with the coming of maturity, the upsurge of second wind as the race was nearly run. Whatever it was, it had got him to Whitecliffs and had been sufficiently strong to sweep with him, his wife and children, Basil, Howard, Honey and Louise and her old mother. Whatever it was, it had cajoled, persuaded, removed obstacles, attacked and conquered. But whatever it was that had moved all these mountains, Arthur admitted to himself four months later, had now gone. He had still the results of his tremendous endeavour to live with, had yet to see that what he had done was good and right, but for the moment he was glad that strength had been given him to do it, and that he was, for the time being at any rate, Arthur Dexter of 'Le Casse-Croûte', rather than Arthur Dexter of Dexter Toys, daily buried afresh in the smoky coffin of the City.

Arthur wrote down 'buns, rolls, small Rich Tea, ice-cream cones and two gross of boats with sails' and thought about the little family he had brought to Whitecliffs. The slowest worker was undoubtedly Howard, the most scatter-brained surely Honey, the most industrious, the capable Louise, and the quietest, Doctor Gurney, who stood all day at the cash register and appeared to be thinking of something else.

The early days had been fun for all of them. There had been the exhilarating freedom of unbounded access to the sea and to the sun, the task of settling in their new flats in Shore Court, and the greater one of creating order and a smart little beach café from the tumbledown shack that had been 'Joe's'. They had made mistakes, many of them, but after three weeks of really hard work, 'Le Casse-Croûte' had stood, spanking fresh, opposite its Corporation rival, as though it had always been.

Arthur and Louise, the most business-minded of them all, had dwelt with the equipping, general ordering and stock. Basil and Vanessa had redeemed the back yard and created a 'garden', painting the tables pink and blue and yellow. Doctor Gurney and Howard had composed all the notices and price lists, and Victor, doing research along the coast, and provided the idea of selling candy-floss, fancy-goods and toffee-apples. Honey had kept them laughing and provided them all with cups of tea at appropriate moments. None of them knew anything about catering. How could they know how many scoops of tea to a half gallon tea-pot? That toffee only adhered to certain types of apple? That it was an uneconomical (although charming) gesture to provide paper serviettes? That their wish to provide good quality teaspoons would be frustrated by the fact that they nearly all disappeared during the opening week? That to make sandwiches with too much ham, too much egg or too much tomato, would eat a big hole in the profits? Between them they produced several good and workable ideas. The first, one upon which they agreed unanimously, was that all food should be wrapped. It was also to be promptly served in order to avoid the formation of a queue such as there invariably was at the Corporation Café opposite. They agreed to provide music, to attract the young people, from a record-player, pictures on the walls and aspirins for headaches. The cups were to be examined carefully for stains and cracks before they were allowed on to the trays, and the customers, in accordance with policy, were to be always right. They found a small, wrinkled man, as old as the sea and as grey, to keep the garden swept, the crocks cleared and the tables wiped, a Mrs Boil, whose name nobody believed, to do the washing-up, and a firm to paint the outside of the café for them and supply them with their particular brand of ice-cream.

After days of preparation, excitement and speculation, 'Le Casse-Croûte', painted, stocked and christened, was opened to the public. On the opening day, Doctor Gurney, whose task was to operate the cash register, stood too near to the unfamiliar machine as he took the money offered by the first customer, tapped out 2/2 ½d smartly, and was winded for several moments as he was struck in the solar-plexus by the drawer. Apart from this and one or two other minor mishaps, all went smoothly. They had ordered too many biscuits and not enough rolls; they had trouble with the tea-leaves in the pots for the beach, until somebody thought of tea-bags; they forgot the ham in the ham sandwiches and sometimes gave the wrong change; they persevered, all glad to be occupied, until things began to run smoothly, and divorce petitions (Howard), midnight oil over chapters that wouldn't come (Basil), shampoos and sets (Louise) and the glare of the spotlight (Honey) were forgotten temporarily in a whirl of teas and buns and ices and milk shakes and trays for the beach and the garden.

Whitecliffs was unused to Arthur's arbitrary business methods.

"I want a dozen cases of butter puffs," Arthur said on the telephone during the opening week to one wholesaler.

"Certainly, sir, our van will be calling Tuesday or Wednesday of next week."

"Useless," Arthur Dexter said. "I want them first thing in the morning or I shall take my order elsewhere..."

At Whitecliffs, sleepy on the seashore, they were unaccustomed to such haste. One or two wholesalers, however, had recognised a businessman and what was likely to be a good account when they saw one, and had agreed to supply 'Le Casse-Croûte' on Arthur Dexter's own terms. Now, Arthur had only to lift the phone and announce his name before the ice-cream wafers, the chocolate tea-cakes or the fifty pounds of tea (catering quality) were on the road.

At ten o'clock, Arthur, satisfied that all was in order at the café, walked beneath the stars and within sight of the black, mysterious sea towards the flats. As he went up the little path towards the entrance of Shore Court he saw, through the glass, a shadow come out of Honey's flat which was on the ground floor, and a flash of white. Inside he heard light footsteps running up the stairs and, as he stood outside his own flat searching for his key, he heard the door of Basil's flat above click softly shut.

Vera was already in bed. He looked at her, not yet sleeping, thinking, here's the rub.

"I'm going to town tomorrow," Vera said.

"All right."

"I think I shall need a sleeping tablet. They're in the drawer, Arthur."

"If only you'd relax, Vera…"

"In this place?"

"Try to be happy…" He passed the box of small pink tablets.

"Do you know what the time is, Arthur?"

"After ten."

"You're working harder than you did at home. What are you trying to prove?"

"This isn't work. This is something to keep me occupied. I'm free, Vera, free; sometimes I just stand in the kitchen, or behind the counter or on the beach…"

"You look so foolish with your hanky on your head; why don't you buy a panama?…"

"…and simply think about anything that comes into my head. Or watch the children…"

"…you were never all that interested in your own…"

"I hadn't time…and smile when I think that no one's coming to dinner, and that we don't have to go out, don't have to change, make polite, repetitive conversation…"

"There's not a soul to talk to. Will you want a tablet?"

"I sleep like a log and wake a young man…if I forget to look in the mirror…but when I do I think of Willie. Vera…?"

"Yes, Arthur?"

He had wanted to say, "Please try! Please try to be happy." He had no language with which to communicate.

He said: "Try to remember we're out of fishing-nets."

"I shall be in town."

"Of course. Goodnight."

"Good night, Arthur." Vera turned over and waited for the sleeping pill to work.

Upstairs, Basil and Honey sat grimly, one each side of the dressing-table.

Basil, his dressing-gown over his shirt and trousers, had been writing to his wife before going to bed when his front door bell had rung. Wondering whom it could be so late, he opened the door.

Outside in the dim light of the landing, smiling, stood Honey. Basil groaned, and half shut the door.

"Oh, Honey, no!" he said. "Go away. Last night was a mistake, and I'm sorry about it. Go away, there's a good girl, before somebody sees you."

Honey, in tight, white trousers and a black, sleeveless shirt, opened her eyes wide.

"I thought you'd be pleased," she said. "I hurried with my ironing and I came to tell you about me. You know, for your book; like you said."

Basil hesitated, wishing she wouldn't wear her clothes so tight.

"Are you sure that's why you came?"

"Why else? There's never any time during the day."

"All right," Basil said ungraciously, and held the door wide so that Honey did not have to walk too near him as she passed.

He took Honey into the bedroom, which was his workroom, before he realised that perhaps it was a mistake. He pulled a chair up opposite his own on the other side of the dressing-table from which he had removed the mirror.

"You sit over there," he said firmly and, finding a notebook and his pen, told her to begin.

"I don't quite know where," Honey said nervously, lowering her eyelashes until they sent long shadows down her cheeks. "Perhaps it might be easier if we had a little drink."

Basil sighed and going into the sitting-room poured her a whisky.

"Aren't you joining me?" Honey said, raising her glass.

"No, I am not. And when you're ready I think you'd better begin at the beginning," he said sternly.

Honey DuPont had been born Doreen Maloney in a 'single-end' in the back streets of Liverpool. Her grandmother, who was still alive, and still prided herself on her looks, had been a Gaiety girl. Her mother, once a palely pretty blonde, had been a soubrette until the seemingly endless stream of little Maloneys started to arrive, and although she still continued to read *The Stage* weekly from cover to cover and still spoke of herself as being in show business, she had never managed to make her often threatened come-back. Honey's father, whom she had never seen but from whom she inherited her black hair and laughing blue eyes, had been a seaman who returned to Liverpool sufficiently often to father another small Maloney, then disappeared to far-off lands leaving his wife to cope as best she could, which wasn't very well. Having fathered Honey, William Obadiah Maloney had grown tired of Liverpool and still more tired of his wife Annie, who grew fatter and less comely with every flying visit and, disappearing as usual into the muddy waters of Liverpool, forgot on this occasion to come back. Annie Maloney waited only so long for his return, then took up with one George Hackett who was something, what exactly she was never sure, to do with greyhounds. Whatever it was he did brought him a large amount of cash money, which he was willing to spend as fast as he got it on Annie and her little brood. The family prospered, changed its name 'en masse' to that of its benefactor, and moved from its dockland slum where Honey spent her school days. She was brought up in a free and easy, if at times ribald, atmosphere, in which her own good nature blossomed, and found life singularly uncomplicated. She listened goggle-eyed to stories of the theatre from her mother and grandmother, and at school sat yawning through her lessons, waiting for the gym or games sessions in which she could practise her backbends, cartwheels and high-kicks before a circle of friends who marvelled at her agility. At fifteen she was neglecting her homework to sing, after school, with the band at the local dance-hall, and at sixteen, calling herself

Honey DuPont, she got a job as soubrette with a seaside Follies company. It was here that she met and married her husband, Jimmy, who was the comic in the show. After this she followed the customary round of the bottom rung of show business; pantomime at Walham Green and Hackney; fit-up concert parties at Strutton in Devon, Rock in Cornwall; number three, tatty dates, the Hume Theatre, Manchester, Collins' Music Hall, more Follies in the summer, an endless succession of dreary digs, spangled dresses, often grubby, and tights, as often as not with holes in. Then came the break. Jimmy landed the job of comic at the Ambassador Luncheon Club and managed to persuade them to take his wife as a show-girl. Honey's was the more enviable task; poor Jimmy had to crack the same gags three shows a day, often to the same set of business-men who were unwilling to be amused, and had come only to see the girls. In any case, they were not very good gags to begin with, but the pay was good and the comic act was necessary to give the club a vaguely respectable front as a 'show' rather than merely 'showgirls'! From the luncheon club Honey progressed to the Revue in which Arthur Dexter had found her, and where she firmly believed that it was the few lines she sang in a not unpleasant contralto that brought the applause, rather than the fact that she was wearing only a feather when she sang them. Her ambition still was to be a pop singer, preferably on the TV or radio, and she believed that with her West End date she was now well on the way to achieving it. As far as her marriage was concerned she and Jimmy had long ago come to an amicable arrangement in which they helped each other up the ladder of show business (Honey had got Jimmy the comic's spot in the Revue) and shared the same flat and the rent. Whether they happened to share the same bed depended upon whether either of them was otherwise engaged at the time. They welcomed each other's friends to the flat and several times a week gave jolly parties at which everyone sat on the floor and talked about themselves, most people got drunk, and which only the dawn disrupted. Since neither of them started work until after lunch, unless there happened to be a rehearsal, this did not matter at all, and they usually woke at noon to a welter of empty bottles, full ashtrays and ejected olive stones.

Honey's mother, having watched her family depart, one by one, to various quarters of the globe, lived now in brassy-haired respectability in Surbiton with the faithful George Hackett who had stuck by her, and to whom, as far as Surbiton was concerned, she was married. Of her youngest daughter she was exceedingly proud, show business being to her the epitome of achievement, and she bored the neighbours frequently with stories of 'my daughter on the West End stage'.

Honey leaned back in her chair and sipped her drink. Basil, pen poised over his blank notebook, looked at her expectantly.

"We'd better," he said, "start with your childhood."

"All right," Honey said, and, holding her glass to her, closed her eyes.

"I was born in India," she said. "My father was a Maharajah..."

Basil's pen sped smoothly over the paper.

Nine

Vera, conspicuous as the 'fat, white lady' of the poem who walked through the fields in gloves, stalked up the village High Street towards the station in her elegant navy blue and white ensemble. Along the street, holiday-makers in shirts and shorts, sun-dresses and brightly flowered skirts, jostled her with their shopping baskets and bumped occasionally into her firmly corseted figure. That she had to walk to the station at all annoyed her, but Arthur had been too busy at the café to drive her there, and the local taxi was spending the morning in dock for some repairs to its chassis. There seemed no other means of transport. The High Street was uninteresting and the shops even more so. Vera glanced at them as she passed. 'Footwear Repairs,' with its dusty window of dusty old shoe trees, shoe brushes and cards of 'segs'; the needlework and wool shop with its droopy matinee jackets, knitting patterns and traycloths to embroider; the baker's window full of bath buns, congress tarts, battenburgs, jam tarts (red and yellow), macaroons, currant scones, flies and dead wasps lying on their backs; Barclay's Bank; a firm of solicitors with quaint names; the showrooms of the South Eastern Gas Board with wash-boilers and tempting hire purchase terms; the hairdressers' window with Alice-bands in assorted colours and faded showcards advertising old-fashioned hairstyles; the fishmongers (Local Plaice, 2/6); the 'Bandbox', with dowdy hats and dowdy dresses dowdily presented, royal blue and salmon pink, bottle green jumper suits; gift shops, toy shops, sweet shops, food shops. Vera's heels click-clacked impatiently towards the station, and already her feet had begun to puff over the fronts of her navy and white shoes.

The train was dirty and empty, the business men having already gone, and it was a relief on arriving in London to take a taxi, of which there were rows and rows, to her own little world which was bounded by Curzon Street on the north, Piccadilly in the south, Bond Street in the east and Park Lane in the west. In this right little, tight little corner of London from which she made only rare excursions to Harrods and the Brompton Road, or sometimes as far north as Berners Street (by taxi) when she needed to choose fabrics, paint or wallpapers, Vera fed herself, shod herself, clothed, corseted and coiffed herself. It was Mayfair, her spiritual home, and indeed almost the only part of London she was familiar with, apart from the small area of Hampstead in which she lived. In New York, she had walked dutifully round the Metropolitan Museum of Art; in Spain she had skimmed through the Prado, and in Italy trotted wearily behind a guide round the galleries of the Uffizi and the Pitti Palace; she had never, however, been into the National Gallery, the Wallace Collection the Tate Gallery and it was doubtful if she knew where they were. She was interested in little beyond her body, her appearance, her wardrobe and her family but in these things she was happy. She did, of course, as was fashionable, go to the theatre, cinema premières and the Summer Exhibition at the Royal Academy; her opinions, however, together with those of her friends, came practically verbatim from the columns of criticism in the Sunday newspapers from which the 'Veras' may be said to obtain their higher education. None of them uttered before Kenneth Tynan or Dilys Powell; when they did, it was the one who had remembered the most of what she had read who delivered the weightiest opinion. They thought their discussions extremely intelligent, often bordering on the intellectual.

They did read, Vera and her friends, again, books prescribed by the Sunday papers; safe books by lady novelists who knew their customers and dutifully provided words to be cosily curled up with, heroines with whom the reader could identify herself, journeys into strange lands in which, because only the mind travelled, there was no discomfort, the odd, titillating foray into worlds of sex and vice, read with guilty, page-turning excitement, the comfortable ending, concluding sometimes with sadness, never with violence. They spoke, too, Vera and her friends, occasionally of Renoir, Modigliani Matisse, but only after their names had been exhumed for brief moments of sudden glory by the newspapers because their works had been bought or sold for some fantastic sum or were about to be exhibited in some gallery in Bond Street it was considered smart to visit. They were as familiar with the words Impressionist and Post-Impressionist as they were with the names of the salads in Fortnum's, but if you asked them what they meant they faltered only for a moment then told you about last night at the Caprice, or the cruise they had booked for next spring, or their son's examination successes. For they were not entirely stupid. They were quick-witted enough to charm each other and their husbands' business friends with layers of sophistication passing for culture, with warm-hearted hospitality passing for friendship and with money, which was the mercury in the thermometer of their success, and which was life. These women, of whom Vera was one, who hunted, usually in pairs, in the purlieus of Mayfair, were not entirely to blame for their ignorance, their blinkered eyes, their painful, pitiful insularity. They were merely acting out their birthright. They had been nurtured in the lull of years between the two wars, richly and comfortably, to an early, satisfactory marriage. Their minds were tuned to wavebands of material comfort, to pleasantness, to success. Having crossed the first and most important hurdle, they bore their children quickly, reared them in the confines of 'the best' and expended their energies and resources on clothing themselves and their children, running their homes luxuriously and efficiently, and occasionally putting in a minimum of work on some charity committee, whose aims were quickly forgotten, over numerous luncheons, teas and coffee mornings. By the time they looked round from all this activity, if ever they did, their minds had inevitably closed against all that was fresh, intellectually stimulating or original. They would never thrill to the consummate performance of a virtuoso, feel weak before the brush-strokes of a master, shed tears over the wonders of the world. They were to be pitied, these matrons, but not too much. For they were happy and they did not know.

If the 'Veras' were to be pitied, what of the 'Arthurs', the half-worn husbands they trailed in their wake? The 'Arthurs', too, had only half completed their education through no fault of their own. They had passed straight from school to family business, often by way of commercial course, and scattered their dreams like rose-petals along the path to middle age. They lived in a world of money and of commerce, and relaxed in a world of money and of family. Money was the dominant factor, and in the pursuit of this they lost their figures, the carefreeness of youth and their hair. At the office they were bosses, snarling lions to be respected, at home they were subordinate, baring, only occasionally, their fangs when the demands made upon them grew too incessant. Unlike their wives, they made no effort to acquire a pseudo-culture, and contented themselves with the *Financial Times* and the occasional detective story. On the whole, they were more honest. They were good in business, and they knew and talked about it. With that they were satisfied. They pampered their wives and indulged their children, until the rare occasions when the bounds of reasonableness were passed and the parental foot was put irretrievably down. If the 'Arthurs' were content, for the most part, to walk behind the 'Veras' it was in docility rather than in submission, and there still existed the masterfulness, dormant but by no means dead, which had attracted their wives in the first place, which was brought out on appropriate occasions and which had enabled Arthur Dexter to get Vera and his family to Whitecliffs. If the wives were to be pitied, the husbands were possibly to be praised. Through years of following, agreeing and paying, they had emerged, fattening and balding and occasionally irascible, but for the most part equable, sensible and still paying. They grumbled about changing into evening dress and going out when, after a day's work, they preferred to sit comfortably by the fire, but they did it; they protested at having the Greens or the Smythes to dinner yet again, yet they played the host jovially and expansively; they complained about having the furniture re-upholstered so soon, but they provided the wherewithal. They gave in, agreed, smiled, submitted and acquiesced, for just so long until, like Arthur Dexter, they turned in their tracks and snarled. When they did this they could not be opposed. They were kings of the jungle; masters.

Vera, feeling weary after her journey, but happy to be among her own familiar shops, stepped out of the taxi on to the bright, hot pavement. She gave the driver a small tip above the fare and, looking down her nose, ignored his glare. She knew what was what and did not, despite her husband's wealth, like to be 'done'. She prided herself, together with the other 'Veras', on her knowledge of the value of things, her ability to find a bargain (albeit a costly one) and the fact that it was difficult to get the 'better' of her. She was, though, as were they all, the easiest person in the world to dupe. The model milliners, the tailors, the dressmakers had only to knock the odd guinea, with a semblance of grudgingness, off their already extortionate prices, to send Vera happily home to boast of her 'bargain'. The furrier, as soon as she trod the plush carpet of his showroom, added ten guineas immediately to whatever he had to show in order to have the pleasure of removing it later in order to clinch the sale. He said it was because she was an 'old customer', a 'special, favoured client'. He had a sick wife and a son at University. He had to live. Vera, he knew, would be back next year. He was one of her retinue: one of those from whom for Mrs Dexter there was always a 'special price'. She was favoured, flattered, fussed, pampered, by those she imagined she cheated. To them it was a small price to pay. Vera Dexter and her friends fed their families, financed their holidays, bought their cars and paid for their daughter's weddings. For this they could well afford to make her feel constantly, continuously, that she was the most important person in the world. In a way she was; she was their bread and butter, predictable, fashionable and with a well stocked, if not bottomless, purse.

"Darling, you're not the teeniest bit brown," Eve Gardner said making room at the tiny table in the restaurant where she had been waiting for Vera.

Vera hitched her skirt, took off her gloves and settled herself and her large, baby-calf handbag.

"It's not exactly Cannes, dear." Vera shuddered as she thought of Whitecliffs. "It's so windy it's impossible to sit on the beach."

"You poor thing," Eve said, but there was no sympathy in her voice as she studied the menu she knew by heart. "Is Arthur still peculiar?"

"Absolutely wrapped up in this café thing. I'll have my usual."

"What about the children? Two 'health salads', waitress, please; and coffee."

"Rolls and butter?" the waitress asked, writing on her small pad.

Vera and Eve looked shocked and shook their heads.

"The children are happy," Vera said, "although I think Vanessa misses Clifford. She sits up half the night writing to him, and can't wait for the postman in the morning. I shan't be sorry if she forgets about him at Whitecliffs. Not that she'll find anyone else down there. Nobody goes there."

Eve knew that she meant anyone who was anyone.

"I thought Clifford's people were rather nice," Eve, who only had sons, said.

"Charming," Vera said; "I've known Bessie Stafford for years. But it'll be years and years before the boy qualifies; he's hardly begun. And even when he is qualified he won't be earning enough to get married on; he's going to specialise in something or other, Vanessa was telling me."

"Does she want to marry him?"

"She hasn't said so. But one has to think ahead. I haven't encouraged it, but it's obvious that Clifford thinks Van is wonderful and she he."

The two middle-aged women smiled at each other with the thrill of a vicarious romance.

"They just rush into these things," Vera said, "without thinking."

"Didn't we?"

Vera sat back to allow the waitress to put the salads on the table.

"No," she said. "No, I don't think somehow we did."

There had been nothing 'rushed into' about her marriage to Arthur Dexter. Vera's parents had known the Dexters for many years, and when Vera was nineteen she and Arthur had been deliberately placed next to each other at a dinner party carefully connived at by the two families. After the dinner, during which the two young people, acutely aware of the parts they were playing, scarcely spoke, Arthur had taken Vera into the garden and kissed her chastely. He found her proximity not unpleasant and Vera, whose very first kiss it was, nearly fainted from excitement. Two years later, after a suitable and sensible courtship, the young couple were suitably and sensibly married. After a rather miserable honeymoon in Torquay for which both of them, owing to their previously sheltered lives were unprepared, they returned home to set up a house and routine which was an exact replica of that of their parents. Then followed, quite unexpectedly, what were probably six of the happiest months of their lives. And they came, quite by accident, because of a book. Arthur had bought it in the Charing Cross Road, and they kept it, covered in brown paper at the bottom of the linen chest to which Vera had the keys. It explained to them, quite simply, many of the things that had puzzled them about marriage. They read it separately, each a little ashamed and hot-cheeked, but together in the darkness, they practised what they had read. To Vera, at twenty-two, with dark eyes in a pale face, very pretty, it was a miracle. As well as loving Arthur for his gentleness, his good sense and his fondness for her, she discovered that she adored him. From her usual rather quiet self, she became joyful, carefree, relaxed, happy and very much in love. Her day hinged on the moment when she heard his key in the door, and the nights were never long enough. To Arthur, his wife of a few months was wonderful, remarkable and eminently desirable. He congratulated himself on his choice of such a jewel among women. In his father's business he worked happily and hard, and the two families who had fostered the union had every reason to congratulate themselves.

Their delight in each other seemed as though it could never end, only grow from strength to strength. It lasted for six months until Vera became pregnant with the twins. Even then it died a slow and lingering death. Arthur was patient, gentle. Until well after Victor and Vanessa were born he waited to recapture the old rapture he had known with his wife. The twins, however, despite the nurse they had engaged, seemed to absorb all Vera's thoughts and energy. The attention she gave her husband was grudging, diffident. Her mind was in the nursery. When the twins were a year old Arthur, unhappy, had consulted a doctor about his wife's changed attitude. A holiday was advised. From Arthur's point of view the holiday was not a success. Although once or twice, beneath the Attic sky and partly assisted by the wine Vera had drunk at luncheon or at dinner, the old magic had been for a brief moment resurrected, it was soon forgotten. He had wooed her, pleaded with her, explained to her and finally got angry with her. Unable to relive in memory past delights, she looked blankly at him. She no longer understood.

At home things were no better. At night Vera had to cream her face, pin her hair, preserve her night's rest for an early appointment, sleep off fatigue. What had once been a trembling joy to her, on the occasions she permitted it, became the final chore at the end of a long day, the inconsiderateness of a husband, the penalty to pay for a marriage that had given her her two beautiful children in whom the sun rose and set.

For many years, at varying intervals, Arthur continued in his attempt to storm the bastion, to fan the dying spark. He still loved Vera who had borne the twins of whom he was justly proud, and wished more than anything to prove it to her, tenderly, passionately. Finally, he gave up. He found his desires waning from unfulfilment, and bothered Vera only on the rare occasions when he felt he must and when she satisfied him in martyred fashion. As the years progressed, the hurt, the humiliation and the anger died. Arthur thought less and less often of how it might have been. Vera never thought of it at all.

"When we got married," Vera said to Eve who had started her salad, "we were introduced to suitable people. Things have changed since the war. Standards, I mean. Victor and Vanessa meet all kinds of odd people and one can't really stop them. They don't seem able to discriminate."

"I don't think they want to. I'm sure Vanessa will be all right. Clifford is probably a passing phase and you're worrying for nothing," Eve said comfortably. Neither of them liked talking about anything other than themselves or their own families for long. Vanessa was Vera's worry. As long as she was invited to the wedding she wasn't going to give the matter too much thought. Besides, just now she had some news to impart.

"You know that man I went to see," she said, leaning confidentially over the table towards Vera; "the Second Opinion?"

"Yes."

"Well, he says there's no question about it, I've got to have it out."

Vera tut-tutted sympathetically, feeling no pain.

"The lot! It's one of the worst cases he's seen. A major operation!"

"You poor dear. When?" Vera said, wondering whether she should bother to complain about the greenfly she had found in her salad.

"Well, he's going away for two months, so when he comes back…"

"Couldn't someone else do it?"

"My dear, there's not another man in London. He does the Royal Family."

"How long will you be in?" There was another greenfly.

"Weeks. And after that I shall have to take it very easy for a long while." Eve, who never took it anything but easy, looked sorry for herself. "Of course, I shall go away afterwards," she said, but Vera wasn't listening.

"Waitress," she said, holding her plate, "will you kindly take this back to the kitchen…"

The London afternoon was smouldering, but although her feet bulged more and more over her shoes Vera did not care. From the sun-sparkled windows she chose a hat, a lampshade for the flat, an Alice-band in mother-of-pearl for Vanessa. Her last hour and a half she spent relaxed in the muffled, scented luxury of the hairdressers. Closing her eyes beneath the dryer, she let the glossy magazine they had given her slip to the floor and dreamed about the party she would give when Arthur gave up his foolish idea and they returned to town. She arrived back at Whitecliffs on the fast train with all the business men. As they walked towards the sleepy-eyed ticket collector in their dull black hats, evening papers beneath their arms, they breathed the fresh air which seeped up the High Street from the sea and smiled. Vera adjusted her parcels and looked for Arthur. He was outside in the cobbled yard with the car. The seat was almost too hot to sit on.

"Had a nice day, dear?" he said affably.

"Wonderful. What about you?" Both enquiries were polite, mechanical.

"Not too bad. We ran out of strawberry and the last lot of buckets had faulty handles. The kids have been bringing them back all day."

Vera closed her eyes, only partly in weariness, she thought. Buckets with Mickey Mouses on and strawberry ice-cream!

"Arthur, dear," she said.

"Mm?"

She wanted to ask him if he hadn't had enough of foolishness, of Whitecliffs, of playing at cafés. If he didn't think he should be getting back to his business. It had been a long, tiring day. She did not want to start an argument.

"Nothing, it doesn't matter."

He took his eyes from the road for a moment and smiled at her. She was surprised to see how brown he had got, his eyes were clear and his face seemed less lined, to bear an imprint of another Arthur Dexter; a young man, half remembered.

Vera felt a sudden surge of affection. "I bought you some cheese from Fortnum's," she said. " 'Tombe de Savoie'."

"Good," Arthur said; "that's one thing I miss down here."

Ten

When Vera, changed into more comfortable shoes and an expensive silk dress, came into Vanessa's room to give her the Alice-band she found her daughter, in her underwear, of which there was not very much, standing on her head, her feet supported by the wall, her eyes closed. The odd, off-beat sounds of some unintelligible song moaned from the radio by the bed. From the walls some two hundred and fifty young men, glossy, showing their teeth, most of them pop singers, looked down. Some of them had signed their names across their chins. On the chair, on the dressing-table, on the bed and on the floor were items of Vanessa's clothing. Vera sighed.

"Vanessa!"

Vanessa's eyes opened. "You spoiled my concentration."

Vera lowered the radio from which a young man was threatening to 'getta noo baa-aa-beee'. "How can you concentrate with this row going on?"

"I was diverting my senses from the external world and breathing through my fingertips. Yoga," Vanessa said. "You'd be surprised how difficult it is."

"I can quite believe it," Vera said and, picking up one or two of the garments scattered about, tried to straighten the bed-cover. "Are you tired? You mustn't let Daddy keep you standing there all day with that wretched candy-floss, you aren't used to it."

"I'm not a bit tired. I love it. It's such a change from school. I love to watch the children's faces as I twirl it on to the stick. I can almost hear them begging me not to stop. I try to be fair, but sometimes it's difficult." Vanessa closed her eyes. And I love the feel, she said to herself, of knowing that Howard is there behind me. That I have only to look round to see his solemn face, wise, yet sad somehow, the hair greying above the ears, the hands, beautiful, serving ice-cream cornets. Perhaps one day he will know that I exist.

"I bought you something in town," Vera said.

Vanessa opened her eyes again. "Thank you, Mummy. What is it?"

"If you could stand the right way up for a moment, I'd show you."

Vanessa sighed and let her legs drop to the carpet. "Phew!" She looked at the clock by the bed and turned the radio up again. "Seventeen and a half minutes! Not bad."

She took the Alice-band, kissed her mother dutifully, and tried it on.

Vera, looking at her, wished she was eighteen again with a tiny, firm bottom and a bust that wore a brassière only as a token rather than a necessity. She ran her hands over her firmly corseted figure, and wondered when the insidious spread had begun, and the loose skin beneath her chin and the lines round the eyes. I, too, once looked like you, she wanted to confide, but she knew that Vanessa, uninterested, would say, Yes, politely, unable to imagine it, probably not even believing. At eighteen one did not believe one could grow old.

Vanessa was prattling about the Alice-band, and saying that she would wear her new pink cotton tonight, and that being in the café hadn't really given her a chance to get tanned.

Vera pointed to a letter on the dressing-table. "From Clifford?" she said.

Vanessa, her hands adjusting the Alice-band, became completely still. Her face, which a moment before had been open, laughing, closed down, blank, guarded.

"Yes. It's from Cliff." She reached for her cotton robe from the chair and tied it firmly round her. She turned the radio off, her mood no longer rocking and rolling, and, choosing one from her dozen bottles of nail-varnish, sat on the dressing-stool.

"How's he getting on with his exams?"

"All right."

"Of course, it will be years before he qualifies, won't it?"

"Years and years."

"So it's silly to think about marrying Cliff."

Vanessa looked up from the nail she was varnishing. "Who said anything about marrying Cliff? You are funny, Mummy, just because a boy happens to write to me. Lots of boys write to me. It would be jolly funny if every time a boy wrote to me you thought..."

But Vanessa, Clifford writes twice a day, Vera wanted to say, sometimes Express post. He telephones, too. You wait for his letters, a look comes into your eyes. I am a woman, your mother, why can't we talk? I would understand. I understood your cries as a baby, your first words, your tears when you went to school, your bewilderment at womanhood, your pride when you passed your exams. Why have I suddenly become acceptable only for small, meaningless talk, for buying your clothes and entertaining your friends?

"I only wanted to tell you – warn you," Vera said, "before you get too keen on him. I mean one has to have something to get married on, however little, and you're used to every comfort..."

"But nobody's mentioned marriage. Cliff's a friend..."

"I know, I know. I'm only trying to say... You know quite well what I'm trying to say... Why do you pretend? I was young once." Now she had said it and she hadn't meant to. It sounded stupid, pathetic, a plea for sympathy; it widened the gap she was trying to close.

There was an uncomfortable silence.

"I ordered the material for your chair," Vera said, "a kind of wallflower pink to tone with the bed-head. The man's coming next week. Would you like it box-pleated or tailored?"

"Whatever you like," Vanessa said, but she was smiling again having stepped on to safe, familiar ground, the only place where they could meet each other.

"I think perhaps box-pleats, it's daintier for a young girl's room."

After dinner Vanessa walked out into the evening which was still warm and light. With a white stole over her pink dress she strolled over the green above the beach towards the lighthouse. She knew where she was going, although she hadn't admitted it to herself. Each night, from her bedroom window, she had watched Howard, book in hand, walk purposefully along the green in the direction she was now going. After about an hour she would see him stride back, smoking his pipe, through the dusk. The grass soft beneath her sandalled feet, Vanessa tried to analyse her feelings for Cliff, and reconcile them with how she felt about Howard. For two months since she had met him at a dance, she had seen Cliff practically every day. With growing wonder they had discovered they liked the same things, thought the same thoughts, were happy only when they were together. Then she had come away, firmly believing that without seeing Cliff every day, without kissing him, touching him, walking beside the tall, thin figure in the old favourite sports jacket and with the unruly blond hair that was almost white, she would be unable to live. Each time she closed her eyes she could see his clear face, his smiling mouth and the eyes that looked so deeply into her own. Then she had met Howard. He had arrived in Whitecliffs after most of the others, and had rung the Dexter's doorbell late one night in order to get the keys to his flat. Vanessa had opened the door. He was tall and heavily built, wore his City black jacket and striped trousers and looked tired, blinking like a child; his face was stubbled with the end-of-the-day's darkness but his shirt was still impeccable. He had introduced himself, and Vanessa had fetched the keys from her father who was already in bed. He had thanked her solemnly and gone. A moment or two later he was back.

"I suppose you haven't any milk?" he said. "I'm frightfully sorry to trouble you but I hadn't expected to be down until the morning. My case finished sooner than I anticipated."

"If you'd like to come in, I'll make you something," Vanessa said, "a sandwich and some coffee."

"I dined before I left town," Howard said. "If you just have some milk. I generally take a glass before I retire."

She'd watched him, the milk bottle incongruous with his black jacket, go back to his flat. When she shut the door she knew she was in love with him. But what of Cliff? Cliff who thought the same, talked the same, knew her almost better than she knew herself? He hadn't changed. His letters were wonderful and full of love. She hadn't changed either, she wrote back that she loved him, too. She did. But, as the weeks progressed, she had forgotten what it felt like in his arms, how he looked when he smiled, the near delight of him. She was writing to nothing, and when she shut her eyes she saw Howard with his sad, kind face, the chin growing heavy, the deep forehead, the greying hair. Particularly, she liked the back of his neck which was all she usually saw of him when she turned round from her candy-floss. She could not understand her own emotions, or whether it was possible to love two people at the same time. She walked faster along the green searching for Howard who would be shattered if he could look into her heart.

She found him sitting in a shelter, facing the sea. He was smoking a pipe and reading his book, and was wearing a cloth cap against the evening breeze. She thought it made him more good-looking than ever. Like a country squire in a way.

She sat down next to him. "What are you reading?"

"Good evening, Vanessa. I didn't see you coming."

"You were too busy with your book. What is it?"

"Joad's Guide to the Philosophy of Morals and Politics."

"Oh!" There seemed nothing else to say.

"It's getting too dark to read. I generally stay here for about an hour. I like the soothing sound of the sea. Do you believe that the universe is ethically neutral?"

"I don't know what you mean."

"That the universe itself contains no principles to guide our conduct, no Being to watch over our endeavours, no goals to reward our efforts. That it's all the hurrying of material, endlessly, meaninglessly."

"I believe in God, if that's what you mean."

"How old are you, Vanessa?"

"Eighteen."

"I'm forty-three. I wish it were so simple."

"Why do you worry so?"

"Because I must. I believe we are here for a purpose, but I have to convince myself. Socrates, Plato, Kant, the more one reads the worse it becomes." He looked out into the deepening sea as if the answer he sought would come floating to the surface.

"Don't you ever relax?" Vanessa said, watching his well kept hand round the bowl of his pipe. "Go to the pictures or dance, or anything like that?"

"I told you. I'm forty-three."

"Well, you aren't married or anything. It doesn't do to get too stuffy."

He turned sharply to look at her.

"I'm sorry," she said. "I didn't mean exactly that, only...well ...you don't seem to enjoy life. You make it all so serious."

"It is, Vanessa. What are we here for? What do we mean? What happens when we're dead? What have we learned from civilization? Why must we all learn afresh?"

"I don't know. I really don't. Why have you never married? Did you have an unhappy love-affair? Or is it because all the divorces you do put you off?"

"Neither of those things. I just haven't." He did not say that he had been waiting for his dream to materialise.

"I went to a divorce court once. It was horrible. I didn't know that you could just walk in like going to the pictures, only this was free; then someone told me that you could, and I went. It was a couple, not very old, and they had one child they were squabbling over. It was a year old, they said, and I could imagine it, all golden curls and dimples, and at ten-thirty one winter's morning it became 'legal custody', the 'child of this association', the pawn moved to and fro. And the parents, how happily they must have started, all dressed up, and the wedding dress, and the church, and the orange blossom and confetti; and then suddenly their hopes and cares and dreams dragged out on to the muddy carpet one cold morning by some soulless barrister who, in the middle of messing up a life or possibly two, loses his papers, his glasses, his gown from his shoulders and his train of thought. And the Judge, wanting his lunch, and the private enquiry agent with his frayed suit and beady eyes, and his pocket full of pens and pencils in case he missed something. And the woman having to speak up and everyone laughing and sniggering at what should be private and sacred..."

"In all probability," Howard said, sucking calmly at his pipe, "there was no white wedding, no orange blossom and no confetti. A hurried and necessary marriage in a registry office; a room with the in-laws, a shared kitchen, an indolent, alcoholic husband, a nagging, shrewish wife and the baby a snivelling bundle of wet nappies. But then I'm not, as I told you, eighteen. And hanging round the divorce courts, if you've no objection to my saying so, is no pastime for you."

"I wasn't hanging. I just went out of interest. And I wondered if it was that which had put you off getting married."

It was almost dark. "No, it was not that," Howard said. He could not explain that he had been waiting for something that could never happen.

"How do you like serving ice-cream? It must seem strange after acting about in your wig and gown."

"We don't act about, as you put it. And I like doing the ice-creams. It gives me time to think."

"What do you think about?" She took the book from his lap and flicked over the pages. "I'll tell you. Objective intuitionism, objective utilitarianism, society, its nature and origin, the theory of democracy."

"And other things," Howard said. He did not know she was laughing at him.

"What other things?"

"I don't know. Legal Aid, the Rent Act, my chambers, I need a new carpet…"

"And those things are actually going through your mind as you hand out strawberry and vanillas?"

"Why not?"

Vanessa handed him his book. "I believe you are beyond redemption," she said, standing up. "I'm going to walk back; it's getting cold."

He stood up, as she had hoped he would, and fell into step beside her along the grass which was now almost black. He put his hands in his pockets and stooped forward slightly, his stride long and regular.

"What do you do on your afternoon off?" Vanessa asked when they had walked almost half a mile in silence. Arthur allowed them all one free afternoon a week.

"Anything. I went to Richborough Castle last week. Of course, there's very little now remaining, but it was quite fascinating. Occupied about the third century BC. Some outstanding excavations in the Museum there; Samian pottery, Kimmeridge shale from Dorset, jet from Whitby, Anglo-Saxon sceattas of the late seventh century – of course, there's a break of more than two centuries in the archaeological record at Richborough…"

Vanessa watched the stars popping one by one through the velvet curtain that was now drawn across the sky, and sighed.

"What are you doing next Wednesday?"

"I'd rather like to go over to Walmer."

"What's at Walmer?"

"Walmer Castle, of course."

"Of course."

In the cool breeze of the soft summer night within sight and sound of a gentle sea that whispered to the shore, the man and the girl walked in silence again to the small white block of flats that stood upon the cliff top.

At the door Vanessa said: "Will you take me to Walmer with you on Wednesday?"

"Delighted. I didn't know you were interested."

In the light from the door Vanessa looked at his serious face, his eyes blinked solemnly, his broad shoulders bent a little as though beneath the weight of his thoughts.

Suddenly he smiled. Vanessa, now completely sunk, closed her eyes.

"I'm very interested," she softly.

"Good. We must leave early and do the moat as well. Good night, Vanessa."

"Good night."

In the flat, Vanessa found her parents playing gin-rummy.

"My trick," Arthur said.

"Daddy, can I be off on Wednesday afternoon this week?"

"No, dear. That's Barrington-Dalby's day. You'll have to lend a hand with the ice-creams as well as the candy-floss. Your deal, Vera."

"Oh, Daddy, just this week."

"Out of the question. Come on, Vera."

"Why on earth can't she have the afternoon off?" Vera said. "You're getting as carried away with that café as if it were your bread and butter."

"She agreed to help. She can't just go gallivanting off whenever it suits her. A job's a job. She has to realise it sooner or later. She's free on Thursday so I don't know what all the fuss is about."

Vera patted Vanessa's hand. "You look very pretty tonight, dear, and it'll be all right for Wednesday. I'll come and take your place."

Arthur looked at his daughter. "Thoroughly spoiled," he said, but there was pride in his eyes. He added up the figures on the scorer by his side.

"That's half-a-crown you owe me," he said to Vera.

Eleven

Arthur and Louise had got on together from the very beginning. Expecting to meet some 'refeened' type, coming as she did from Vera's hairdressing salon, Arthur had been agreeably surprised to meet the quiet, genuine warmth that was Louise. Had it not been for her good sense and efficiency he would have found it difficult to get 'Le Casse-Croûte' going at all. Helpful and willing as were Honey, Basil, Howard, Vanessa and Victor, they had not a business head between them, and it was many weeks before they were able to give the correct change or add up the items on people's trays without the help of their fingers. Louise, accustomed to dealing both with people and with money, took them all beneath her wing. When Vanessa stood with temporarily paralysed brain before her till, trying to subtract five and sevenpence-halfpenny from a pound, she would look round to find Louise, ready to help, behind her; when Howard pondered while the delivery man, whistling through his teeth with impatience, waited, how many blocks of strawberry, or nut-crunch or coffee ice-cream he was going to need, Louise would appear from nowhere, sweep an eye over his neatly stacked fridges and say, "What about two dozen of each and three of the strawberry to be getting on with, Howard?" and, of course, those were the very words Howard had been struggling to find.

In the first days Louise had thanked Arthur for giving her, through his wife, the opportunity to come to Whitecliffs.

"I'm extremely glad that she had the good sense to ask you," Arthur said, as together they sorted through great stacks of cracked crockery, grimy legacy from 'Joe'. "You're the only one with any sense."

"The others are children," Louise said. "Let them be children," and although Howard was as old as she, and Basil not so very much younger, Arthur understood what she meant. For many years now Louise had had to be the breadwinner for her small family; she knew what it was to have others dependent upon her, to be responsible. He understood that at times, for a woman alone, the burden must seem very great. In the first days at Whitecliffs, Louise's face, with its London mask, had been drawn, hard and pale, the lines deep from nose to chin. Now her face had a warm glow, the skin a tang of the wind and the sea, the lines were less harsh, the features softer.

On her free afternoon she sat at the dressing-table in her mother's room combing her hair.

"Where are you off to now?" the old lady asked.

"I'm taking the Gurney children to the concert party. I'll be back by the time you've had your rest," Louise said.

"I don't know why you have to go out on your afternoon off. It's bad enough that you work all the week and leave me with nothing to do."

"You know you like to go to bed all the afternoon, Mother. I'll be back by the time you wake up. Anyway you look much better for the sea air, and I do think you're rather enjoying it here if you'd only admit it. Miss Price was telling me about those two ladies you meet every morning for coffee."

"Miss Price talks too much. She never stops," she said of her companion.

"She's good company. It was clever of Mr Dexter to find her."

Her mother sniffed. She liked Miss Price.

"When are we going home?"

"I don't know. I like it here. I like the café and everyone in bathing suits and bare feet, and no smell of perfume all day, and not having to wear a dark suit all the time, and the air."

The old lady said nothing.

"I'm glad I came, anyway," Louise went on. "I feel younger, healthier. You can go on doing the same thing too long, you know."

"You only think about yourself. Nobody ever considers me."

Louise, looking at herself in the mirror, at the hair no longer chic, from the sea air, in which the grey was steadily encroaching upon the blonde, thought that she had probably not thought of herself enough, and wondered whether things would have been different if she had. It was difficult now to believe, it seemed so long ago, that there had been another Louise, a Louise who laughed and was gay and did not spend all her free time making Ovaltine and filling hot-water bottles and steaming fish and fetching shawls and listening to grumbling so incessant that most of it she didn't hear, but was only aware of like a tap that dripped and dripped and dripped. She had been big and blonde and shy when she left school and, so everyone said, beautiful, with the classic grace of a Greek statue. She had worn her hair back from her face and in a knot at the back of her head, and this she supposed and helped achieve the effect, although in those days it had been an unconscious effect, and one she had in no way striven for. Her father had been a stockbroker, and they had lived in Bournemouth where she had been born, and where in their lovely house among the pine trees her mother, younger then, of course, had nagged not only about her Ovaltine and the television picture, but how untidy were Louise and her father; and why Louise didn't put the music away when she had finished with the piano, and why Louise and her father didn't fold the newspapers and plump the cushions when they got up, and empty the ashtrays, and hang their coats up more tidily, and wipe their feet and not leave the doors open because of the draughts. Only then there had been two of them, Louise and her father, and together they laughed it off, and teased her mother that she'd really like them to walk around with no shoes on her highly polished floors, and come in and out through the keyhole. And occasionally her mother had laughed, too, at her own obsessions, but not too often and not with very much conviction. When Louise had left school there had been no need for her to earn her living, and she had occupied herself with work on charitable committees and two afternoons a week at a local crèche among babies which she loved and before whom she was able to lose her intolerable shyness. She went to dances, one or two, with nice, selected young men, but mistaking her shyness for haughtiness they didn't call again. Louise didn't care; she was a happy girl and, because of her strict upbringing, young for her age, and wasn't yet worried about getting married. She was twenty-two when the war came and the Air Force descended upon Bournemouth and slept six in a room in the luxury bedrooms of the big hotels, and often in the bathrooms and ballrooms as well. And there was barbed wire along the front, and concrete blocks, and they blew big holes in the two piers, and the charity committees and the crèches became suddenly unimportant. Louise had joined the WAAF, and told her parents afterwards. She scarcely heard her mother's grumbling about being left alone all day in the big house among the lonely pines, while her father was in town all day, or what she was to do if there was an air raid or the Germans came, bayonets pointed, scrambling over the barbed wire on the beach. In the Air Force, she moved for the first time since she had left school amongst people of her own age. They were not people her mother would have selected, and at first they shocked Louise herself a little. She learned to speak a new language, to live among a coarseness and immorality to which she was not accustomed, and to lose her shyness. She found a new Louise, not prim, but laughing and gay, she had not dreamed existed, and a young pilot, taller even than herself, with whom she fell madly, and for the first and only time, in love. He worshipped her, pulled the pins from her hair until it fell in a golden cascade round her shoulders, and called her Lulu.

One wintry November day which she would always remember, when the sea was rising in great waves that swamped the promenade, the sky grey and the wind howling through the pines, she had brought him down to Bournemouth to meet her parents. They had stood kissing on the doorstep, and when her mother opened the door their faces were pink with the cold and love, and they were laughing.

"Your father's had a stroke, Louise," her mother said. "We tried to get you."

And Louise had stopped smiling and, forgetting Johnny who had removed his peaked cap and was standing politely on the doorstep, had gone slowly up the stairs. And when she came down again she had wound her hair up into its knot and said, "Johnny, you'd better go," and shutting the door behind him, knew with a sudden understanding how it would be. She had, the next moment, opened the door and called 'Johnny' into the wind but only the pines leaned towards her and the jeep had gone back towards the town. At first it had been just compassionate leave. But the only nurses available were old and not very efficient, and smoked in their bedrooms and left dirty dishes and their stockings in the kitchen, and her mother would not tolerate them. So she had had to leave the Air Force, and had written to Johnny because she could see no future for them. He had called once to see if she wouldn't change her mind, but it had been uncomfortable because things were not the same any more, and though she thought her heart would break as she watched him sitting there like a blond god in his uniform, the wings across his chest, she knew that she no longer belonged to his world, and couldn't laugh and drink and do crazy things because of the mixed-up world and death lurking in the skies he rode nightly. Her mother, for once, had shown a spark of understanding, and for comfort said: "Your father needs you,

Louise, you know that. The boy will most probably be killed, anyway. They all are." But Johnny had not been killed. He had survived the war and been decorated and had become something of a hero and married a beautiful girl from South Africa where he had gone to live. And looking at their wedding picture in the evening paper, which she still kept in her stocking drawer, Louise had cried unashamed tears for what might have been, and her own foolishness. Yet she knew that because of her upbringing, had she the same decision to make again she would have made the same choice. Her father had been five years dying. While Holland was occupied and France fell and even Bournemouth received its solitary bomb she ran up and down stairs with drinks and bottles and appetising food, prepared from meagre rations, and clean linen and newspapers from which she read that this was their 'finest hour' during which she was carrying bedpans. Her father lay helpless, undemanding. He spoke often of his appreciation for what she did, and from his words she drew her strength to carry on. Her mother fussed and moaned and nagged, and left most of the work to Louise. Her chief concern was that the sickroom should be tidy and the sheets straight for the visitors who rarely came. Her father slipped eventually, almost imperceptibly, from half-life to death. Had he lived another week he would have known the war had ended. Because he had been so long ill there was no money left and they sold the house in the pines, and because Louise's mother wouldn't consider a flat, 'a hole in a box, Louise', they had taken the small, semi-detached house in the suburbs so that Louise could commute, night and morning in the rush hour, uncomfortably to the job she had found. It had not been easy either, with no training or qualifications, and all the men and women coming out of the Services. The Mayfair hairdressing salon liked her though, for her statuesque appearance and obvious good breeding, and had put her behind the desk in the reception, where she remained. They did not regret their decision, and Louise was satisfied that each week she took home a wage packet sufficiently large to support her mother and herself. She had even, unknown to her mother, who would, she had no doubt, have found some other use for the money, managed to save a small amount each week which had now grown into a comfortable little security for her own old age which she had no reason to suppose would be otherwise than lonely. Because of her mother, whose demands for her company were incessant, Louise had no friends of her own, and had long ago given up any thoughts of marriage.

Tying her hair into the knot she made without thinking day after day, year after year, she wondered if her mother ever considered, ever thought, that she might once have wanted a life of her own. She knew that she never did. She was too selfish, and she realised that probably by her own acquiescence she had encouraged her in her egotism. With the offer to come to Whitecliffs Louise had recognised the opportunity she would never have consciously striven for, to get away from the daily grind a little; away from the shop and the dreary semi-detached and the pictures on Fridays and the television she watched and hated; to consider, as she should have done long ago, if there was anything else she would be happier doing. Already she was feeling the benefit of the change of air, she felt lighter, happier, younger even, and free from the City dirt.

Her make-up didn't take long. Her blonde skin was still good, and here at Whitecliffs she didn't trouble with the eye-shadow, the mascara and the pencil she had to apply so laboriously for the necessary degree of sophistication in the salon. Her lipstick was pale and she did not bother with the lip brush.

"What about my tea?"

"I'll be back for that, Mother. The show only lasts about an hour."

"I could've gone with you."

"You wouldn't enjoy it. It's very noisy and for children."

By the time her mother was in bed and properly supplied with her tablets, her glasses, her water, her book and her clean handkerchief on the bedside table, Louise was almost late. The Gurney children were at the open doorway of their flat in a dither of excitement. They wore blue jeans and striped T-shirts, and the one with the missing teeth said:

"We'll mith the beginning, Louithe. We've been thtanding here for hourth and hourth and hourth."

"About ten minutes," the elder one said. "Come on, we can run."

"Louithe ith too old," Jennifer said.

Amanda, going down the steps, looked back at Louise, apologising for her younger sister.

"How old do you think I am, Jenny?" Louise said.

Jennifer pushed open the glass doors. "About a hundred," she said.

"Don't be silly, Jenny," Amanda looked prim. "She's not much older than Mummy."

"And how old is Mummy?" Louise asked.

"Twenty-one. How old are you?"

"Somewhere between the two," Louise said, but she felt years younger already.

They took the bus along the front, and got off at the stop where the people were streaming over the green to the pavilion. On the bus Amanda told Louise that she had an inkspot on her pale blue skirt. Fastidious, as her mother had taught her to be, Louise was about to get angry and upset, when Amanda removed the metal 'ink blot' she had put on her lap. The two children produced in rapid succession from their pockets, a 'bleeding finger', a realistic looking, bent piece of metal which looked as if Jenny had a nail through her finger, 'pretend soot' and what Amanda called a 'stinking bomb' which Louise could only just prevent her throwing in the gangway of the bus. Laughing at their exuberance, Louise realised that it was too long, much too long, since she had laughed.

They took their seats in the open-air pavilion, just as the band, in red jackets and white trousers, with red bow-ties, were happily and noisily playing the opening number. A skittish chorus of not-so-young ladies kicked up their legs and tap-danced with many coy shakes of their permed heads to the next number, and sang a soprano song of welcome whose last line only was intelligible '...and we hope you have a jolly good tiiiime'. They danced themselves out, their smiles fading before they left the stage.

'Uncle Harry', well-built and good-looking with very white teeth, trailed the microphone wires behind him and introduced himself to the children. Every time he said "'Hallo" they had to call out "Hallo, Uncle Harry". He said "Hallo". The response was deafening. "I can't hear you," Uncle Harry said. "I asked you to shout, not whisper!" The children roared. "We'll try again," Uncle Harry said, showing all his teeth. "Hallo, children!" "Hallo, Uncle Harry!" The noise was incredible. "A little better that time," Uncle Harry said. The children rocked in their seats, enslaved, spellbound. They sang, refrained from singing, uttered gibberish at his command. When he went off, trailing his wires behind him, having introduced Sophie who was going to sing 'Only a Rose', they sighed and clapped till their hands were sore. They suffered Sophie who had forgotten to remove the plum from her mouth and shied a little at the high notes, and applauded her politely. Encouraged, she remained to sing 'Because'. There followed some slapstick comedy between uncle Harry and the dwarf of the company dressed in baggy sponge-bag trousers which he kept losing, then another piece by the orchestra during which the children sucked sweets or looked round for ice-cream. The next item was a children's talent contest, and when Louise turned to ask Jennifer and Amanda if they wanted to take part she found the seats empty and children already on the stage with a cluster of others, mobbing Uncle Harry who chided them gently with jokes. With the aid of Sophie, a hard-looking cookie when she wasn't singing, he created some sort of order, the stage microphone was lowered to the height of a four-year-old who sang 'Baa-baa Black

Sheep' with her thumb in her mouth, and the competition was on. Jennifer began to recite 'Albert and the Lion' but had to be restrained at the twelfth verse, and Amanda, Tennyson's 'I come from haunts of coot and hern' with such solemnity the audience was unable to refrain from giggling. The competition was eventually won, as the loudness of the applause indicated, by a sophisticated miss in a satin dress who confessed to seven but sang 'Mad, Passionate Love' with such feeling there could be no doubt as to the outcome. All the competitors received a stick of rock as a consolation prize, and justice having been done and seats resumed, the show went on. There was a sketch, in which Uncle Harry with knobbly knees and suspenders, was a fairy and the dwarf a policeman, then a jolly number from the band during which they stood up, sat down, juggled, joked among themselves and threw paper streamers at each other; then there was Sophie again, this time in a different frock, then the finale by the chorus who looked as if they wanted their tea. Finally Uncle Harry came on the stage and told the children, who were reluctant to go home, that he hoped they would come again, and there was a special concert for the Mummies and Daddies every night at eight o'clock, including a talent competition and lucky programme, and that was that.

Looking at her watch, Louise knew her mother would be annoyed but she could not take the children home without at least giving them an ice-cream. She took them to a little tea place on the green. They queued up for cups of tea and cheese and biscuits in small bags (Amanda and Jennifer – it was Louise who had the ice-cream) and Louise carried the rusting metal tray out onto the green where there were tables and slatted chairs. Jennifer was only halfway through her first biscuit which she ate plain in order to enjoy the cheese later, when she stood up and shrieked: "Look, there'th Uncle Harry!" and Uncle Harry it was, striding across the lawn in his white trousers and red jacket, still with his make-up on.

"Hullo, kiddies," he said, "did you enjoy the show?"

They said they did and offered him cheese and biscuits, but Uncle Harry said he was gasping for a cup of tea and went off to join the queue, promising to come back. And when he did, balancing his cup of tea, they asked him to sit down, and Uncle Harry looked questioningly at Louise but there was nothing she could very well say, so he pulled up a chair and sat astride it and made noises like a duck and then a dog, and sent Amanda and Jennifer into hysterics. And while they were laughing, the tears rolling down their faces, he asked Louise if she had enjoyed the show, and she saw that under his make-up he was not as young as he had looked and that his teeth, though nice and shiny, didn't fit very well. He seemed kind though and they had a jolly time and Uncle Harry gave the girls sixpence each to buy chocolate bars. And when they'd gone across the green to the kiosk that sold chocolate Uncle Harry asked Louise what she was doing that night, and Louise, not understanding, said nothing, and then she did and she blushed and grew confused and didn't know what to say and finally said: "I have my mother to look after." Then Uncle Harry said: "Well, if you can get out come and have a drink at the pavilion bar," and Louise said she was sure she couldn't but thanked him very much, and Uncle Harry said, "Well, try," and wouldn't take no for an answer. Then the children came back and they said goodbye to Uncle Harry who said "Don't forget," but not to them, and Louise took their hands in self-protection and they walked towards the bus.

At home her mother was still sleeping noisily, her mouth open and her expression disgruntled even in sleep. In the half-light of the bedroom where the curtains were still drawn, Louise peered into the mirror and examined her face to see what Uncle Harry had seen. Of course she had no intention of seeing him at the pavilion that night or any other, but it was nice, in a way, to know that she had not grown too old, too plain, too past it; that she still had a little way to go before the shapeless black dress and the lavender shawl and the two pairs of glasses and the Ovaltine.

It had been an enjoyable afternoon, and she smiled to herself as she remembered the feel of Jennifer and Amanda's arms round her neck as they thanked her, and the chocolate they pressed into her hand, which was better than words. She tied an apron round her pale blue skirt, and going into the kitchen began, humming quite happily, to prepare her mother's tea.

Twelve

'On the red, twenty-four
On the green, twenty-one
On the yellow, thirty-three...'

The chant of the Bingo men was audible as soon as he passed under the archway brightly lit with neon lights proclaiming 'Merrydown Park', and underneath in smaller letters, not lit, 'The World's Gayest Funfair'. 'On the blue, twenty-two, on the green...' Victor walked slowly, almost carried along by the tide of people, down the slope towards the funfair itself. Past the fish and chip shop, past the winkle stall, past the tavern, past the 'Ladies', past 'Two eggs and chips 1/6d' chalked on a blackboard, into the level of the amusement park itself which spread out wide before him as far as he could see. "On the yellow..." Now the chant was louder, and coming from various directions. And there were other noises. "Three for six, lady, three for six...come along, sir, try yer luck...win a 'andbag for the missus or a walking-doll for the kiddy...orl yer do is roll 'em dahn the slide...can't miss...prize every time...come along, sir..." and from the firework display on Victor's left there were long 'ooooooh's' as the bumper rockets were released into the air and drawn-out 'aaaaaah's' as the rain of stars, golden and red and blue streamed down through the inky sky. The men and women in cowboy hats shuffled endlessly past the stalls, dragging behind them sleepy children rubbing surreptitiously at their eyes; and there were anxious calls of "Maureen" and "Jimmy where've you got to? Stick wiv' Dad or e'll clock yer one!" and "Mum" and "Dad" and "Nana" and "Why can't we see the bearded lady Mum?" and screams from the big dipper which swooped down high above them all, and the smell of hot dogs and onions and the flop-flop of darts. Victor walked past the weight-guessing (a ruby ring if I'm aht more that free pahnds), the flea circus, the ghost-train, the ghost-house, the water tubs, his ears gradually becoming accustomed to the cries of the stall-holders and the shrill shrieks, and his nose to the smell of fish and of vinegar. He was looking for Petal.

She had told him to look for the first darts stall on the right. As he entered the amusement park, though, he had deliberately turned to the left and followed the people, borne along in their midst as they shuffled, their faces varying red and green from the overhead lights, round the funfair. He wanted to think. Not that he hadn't been thinking about the same thing ever since he'd met her on the beach, before that even, since he had noticed her from the window of his fancy-goods. He was interested in Petal for one reason, and it was that which was making him nervous. He wanted to sleep with her. At eighteen, his mother called him girl-mad. It was only partly true, although it was how he liked to appear. In actual fact he was only curious and confused about the opposite sex, and it was a problem which, though he did not wish it, occupied his waking and sleeping moments. At school the talk, amidst the final battles with English, History and Latin, had turned always, ultimately and inevitably, to sex. At eighteen, tall, tousled and with small affectations of dress or manner, sprawled on chairs in studies or in common-room, he and his friends were men who were not yet men. They boasted to each other of the girls they had met in the holidays, the girls they wrote to and to whom they had sworn undying love, the girls they had conquered when in fact there had been no conquests. One of the ringleaders of these discussions, a short youth, bespectacled, who in thirty years' time coming respectably home from the office, would linger at the bookstalls in Charing Cross Road, had hitch-hiked to Paris in the holidays and brought back, wrapped in his pyjamas, a book which was passed from hand to hand in the common-room and which brought, to Victor at any rate, only more confusion. He wished there was someone he could discuss it with. The other boys, despite their boasting and their bravado, were, he knew, as disturbed as himself. Twice he had considered approaching his father, once when they were alone, man to man, drinking sherry before one of his mother's charity dances, and once when they slept, just the two of them, at the Whitecliffs flat together before the women of the family arrived. He thought of that night. Victor, less fussy, had been first in bed in the starlit room in which there were as yet no curtains. His father was busy, in and out of the bathroom, washing, brushing his teeth, preparing his clothes for the morning. Each time he came back into the bedroom Victor moistened his lips for what he was about to say. Each time he found the words his father had disappeared again before he could speak them. He waited until they were both in bed. Arthur, having hung up his dressing-gown as Vera had taught him to, and placed his slippers neatly underneath the bed, lay heavily onto the mattress, the springs creaking as he turned to find comfort.

"Dad?" Victor said.

"Mm?"

"Do you mind if I ask you something?"

"What is it, Vic?"

He had thought that in the darkness it would be easier, but now that it had come to it there seemed nothing to say. The words floated away from him. What do I do about women, he wanted to say. I know how things are. I've known since I was thirteen, more or less, that's how it is at school. But now; what do I do now? I know that one should not be promiscuous, that one should wait until one gets married, it's the middle-class code we live by. But I am eighteen, Father. I shall be at least three years at Cambridge, then I shall have to get some sort of job, and it'll be years and years before I get married. I know what you'll say. Wait, my boy, wait. That is, if you say anything at all. But you're fifty, you've forgotten how it is at eighteen. The thoughts and the fears, and most of the time the desire that can drive you crazy and about which you must say nothing, for it is your own. There have been dances and pretty girls, nice, too nice, and the ride home in the car and "No, Victor!" or "Victor, you mustn't!" when his hands have wandered. "It's not that I don't like you, honestly it isn't, but..." He recognised the 'but', and knew that it was home and Mummy and upbringing and starry-eyed innocence, and he hated himself for upsetting them. Father, he wanted to say, what do I do? What did you and other men do at eighteen? Tell me what I should do. He cleared his throat.

"What's troubling you, Vic? If it's about Cambridge, it's all right, old son. I'll hang on to the business for you in case you change your mind. I know how it is. You don't want to settle yet. I suppose if I'd had the choice I wouldn't have either."

"It isn't that, Dad."

"What is it then? Short of money again?"

Victor closed his eyes. With the talk of business and of money the moment had somehow passed.

"It's nothing, Dad. I thought...there was something but...it doesn't matter... How long are we going to be at Whitecliffs?" he ended feebly.

"I don't know, Vic."

"Good night, Dad."

"Night, Vic. And if anything does trouble you you know you can rely on me."

"Yes, Dad." He was glad he hadn't said what was on his mind. Looking out into the stars he realised that it was something he had to work out for himself.

In Petal he had seen a means to solve his problem. She was extremely desirable, the very sight of her in her swimsuit had brought his problems rushing back, she was not what he thought of as a 'nice girl', and she belonged to the world of Whitecliffs and Merrydown Park where he was not known. Such were his predatory thoughts as he shuffled, flanked by the slowly moving crowds, round the perimeter of Merrydown Park.

He watched her first from a distance. Hidden by a stall which sold bottles of pop and ice-cream, he saw her calling the customers, enticing them, in particular the men, to her stand. With the light shining down on her hair she was as pretty as he had remembered. Tonight she was wearing a green shirt blouse open at the throat, and when she smiled he saw her even, pointed teeth like those of a little fox. She was working hard; calling her wares, handing darts, taking money, selecting prizes, flirting with the customers. He wondered whether the burly man who worked on the stall with her was her father. He came out from his hiding place and pushed his way across the stream of drifting people.

"Five for six, mister," Petal said, holding out the darts towards him.

"I was wondering whether you could come out for a drink," Victor said.

Petal looked at him, not remembering.

"On the beach," he reminded her. "You said I could come. Don't you remember?"

"Oh! It's you," she said. "For the moment, with a jacket and tie, I didn't recognise..."

"Can you come out?"

She left him to pick some darts someone had thrown out of the board at the back.

"You playing, mister?" The burly man was ugly, his muscles bulged.

"It's all right, Dad. He's a friend."

Petal's father passed a calculating pair of eyes slowly over him then moved away.

"I'll meet you in ten minutes," Petal said, "by the winkles." She moved to serve two drunken sailors with darts.

Victor walked away. Leaning against the side of Petal's darts stall was a group of Teddy boys. Among them he thought he recognised the beefy character Petal had been waiting for on the beach. One was picking his teeth, one filing his nails, one tossing something up and down in the palm of his hand. One stepped out of the group as he passed them, lithe and black in his drainpipe trousers; he was pulled back by the restraining hand of one who was taller than the rest. The tall one muttered something, and the one who had been tossing whatever it was up into the air stopped. The little group became immobile, watching. They were watching him and it made him nervous. He held his head high and walked on. He found it difficult not to look back.

Petal had put a faded mac over her blouse and skirt. As they walked away from 'Merrydown' and across the road which was full of cars and people and lights in the darkness, she winked up at him. He took her arm, crossing the road and kept it beneath his own, she did not object.

"What about the pavilion bar?" he said, having spied out the land before going to Merrydown Park.

"Suits me."

They walked along the promenade in silence, Petal's hair illuminated now and then by the light from the lamp-posts.

The bar was crowded. Victor ordered whisky for himself and port for Petal. They found a small table.

"Do you work every night?" Victor asked.

"Most." Her eyes were green like a cat's. She raised her little finger as she held her glass.

Victor pressed his knee against hers under the table. She drank her port as if she hadn't noticed.

"I say!" Victor said suddenly.

"What on earth...?" Petal said.

"Well, don't look but over there, at that table near the door, there's Louise, with a man. She works at our café; we brought her down, but she's frightfully old-maidish, I never thought..."

"You mean with Uncle Harry?" Petal said.

"With whom?"

"Uncle Harry. Bloke with the red bow-tie. He's the compère with the 'Jollies'. Hope your Louise knows how to look after herself."

"How do you mean?"

She looked sideways from the port. "How do you think I mean?"

"Good Lord!" Victor said. "Do you think I ought to tell her? I mean I don't think... I'm absolutely sure...she lives with her mother, you see."

"I should mind your own business if I were you," Petal said wisely.

Across the heads and through the smoke Victor's eyes met Louise's for a fraction of a second, then Louise looked away.

"Let's get out of here," Victor said to Petal, and, pushing back his chair, stood up.

They walked again along the promenade and this time Victor put his arm round Petal. She seemed co-operative and he tried to lead her away from the pier to where the people were thinning out and it was dark.

"Let's go and dance," Petal said, looking up at him.

"All right," Victor said, wishing to tread lightly.

The 'Merrydown' ballroom was full, the music, at its high-pitched loudest, hot. She was a practised dancer and led him, stiff-legged with unfamiliarity with the steps, round the floor.

"Twist," she called, laughing, "now step back and turn."

He did not wish to twist. He wanted to hold her in his arms again, but he did as he was told. In the slow numbers she did not seem to mind how tightly he held her; once she deliberately arched her back and pressed her body closer to his. They didn't talk much. The music was too loud, and there was nothing to say. Looking over her shoulder as they weaved round the floor, Victor saw a cluster of black round the ballroom doors. He was sure it was the same group of Teddy boys. They were looking over the heads of the dancing couples, searching for someone.

"Look," he said to Petal, sensing an urgency. "We've some wonderful records at our café. How about us going there one night? I'll get the keys and we can dance."

Petal looked up at him, the green eyes considering.

"OK," she said. "Wednesday."

"Wednesday," he said. "I'll call for you at eight o'clock?"

She nodded.

Victor felt a hand on his shoulder. It was heavy.

"That'll do, sonny boy." The face he looked into was pasty, the lips heavy, the shoe-string tie did not hide a grubby shirt.

"You'd better go, Vic," Petal said, letting go of him. "This is my friend."

"How do you do?" Victor said above the noise of the band.

"...Meetcher," the Teddy boy said. He pushed Victor aside and, pulling Petal firmly to his large chest, glided off. At the door Victor had to pass the small group of his pals. They wore heavy boots and their eyes followed him out unblinking.

He walked back along the sea front, the lights and the people changing gradually to dark emptiness, and the green sward punctuated only by shelters in which pairs of lovers cuddled close.

At the door of the flats he met Louise. He could smell the gin on her breath. She looked as if she had been crying. Disinterested, because she was neither young nor beautiful, he hadn't really noticed her much before, except to exchange the odd words in the café. He realised suddenly that other people, older people, might, too, have their problems. She seemed sad, not bright and polished as she usually did. He looked at the moon, three-quarters full.

"It's a lovely night," he said, not mentioning the pavilion bar. "I walked along the cliffs."

"You can smell the sea," Louise said, "even at night."

Victor held the door open for her. "Good night, Louise."

"Good night, Victor," she searched in the dim vestibule light for her keys.

"See you in the morning," Victor said, and went up the stairs to his flat.

Thirteen

The rain, which had fallen incessantly from a colourless sky since Friday night, showed no signs of stopping by Sunday morning.

The beaches were empty, sodden, puddled by water from the sea and the sky. There were pools of water in the green canvas shrouds of the deck-chairs on the promenade; the pedaloes were awash; it dripped sadly from the roof of 'Le Casse-Croûte' and from the tables in the garden. In the boarding-houses, despondent parents watched their year's savings dissolve in rain and slapped or played with fractious children who wanted to know why they couldn't go on the beach. In the village the cafés were full, steaming with humanity who came in gratefully from the wet with shiny mackintoshes and dripping umbrellas.

Arthur Dexter had decided, influenced by the weather, that it was time they all had a day off. Although the holiday-makers would certainly be in search of tea and coffee today, it was unlikely that they would come down to the beach to find it. If they did they would find 'Le Casse-Croûte' closed, as was the Corporation Café, and would have to go elsewhere.

The staff of 'Le Casse-Croûte' were taking a well-earned rest in their own or each other's flats, sorry only that on this day of nothing to do, they were not lying indolently sunning on the beach.

In number Four, Arthur and Vera lay against their satin bed-heads, breakfast trays by their sides, reading the Sunday newspapers; Vanessa and Victor, in the manner of youth, were still asleep, waking now and then to hear the steady fall of the rain, then turning over to a new dream, a fresh sleep which, if undisturbed, would last till lunchtime.

In the bathroom of Number One, Louise, up to her elbows in soapsuds, her hair to the shoulders of her paisley dressing-gown, was washing under-garments and stockings for herself and her mother, and thinking of Uncle Harry. Occasionally she smiled at herself in the mirror above the basin in an attempt to see herself through his eyes.

Amanda and Jennifer Gurney in Number Three, having spent nearly an hour drawing on the steamy window with their fingers and grumbling at the rain, had now settled on the floor to a game of Monopoly at which both cheated unashamedly. They were supposed to be looking after the baby who, crooning to itself an unintelligible lullaby, was happily tearing up the latest copy of the *British Medical Journal*. Doctor and Mrs Gurney, taking advantage of the peace and the rain which obviated the necessity to get up and do anything, had remained in bed and locked the door of their bedroom.

Howard, in Number Five, having prepared himself a painstakingly cooked breakfast of bacon and eggs, with his own special brand of coffee despatched each week from the coffee man in South Molton Street, had gone back to bed with the *Sunday Observer* and Rousseau on inequality. He was indifferent to the fact that it was raining, and could think of no better way to pass the morning.

Number Six was empty. The bed had been slept in, but the bedroom looked as if a bomb had hit it, as did the rest of the flat. Its tenant was standing gloomily by the window downstairs in Number Two.

"You know something, Basil," said Honey, who was in bed watching him. "You know all about me, but I really don't know anything at all about you."

Basil dug his fists into the pockets of his yellow wool cardigan until they were stretched almost to his knees.

"All I know is that I'm fed up," he said, looking at the rain as it fell monotonously on to a sea-front empty except for a small, hooded child who sought every puddle with its Wellingtons.

"Why are you fed up?" Honey sat up and, drawing her knees up beneath the bedclothes, rested her head on the hump they made.

"I don't know. This place gives me the creeps; the sea and the wind and the stupidity of the people in the shops and the slowness of the bus-conductors and the customers in the café not being able to make up their minds what they want, and parochialness of it all – once you've walked down the village street everyone knows who you are – and I've all day to think and all night to write, and you know how much I've written of the chapters and chapters I was going to? Nothing! Not a single, solitary word. I put the paper in the typewriter, then I read the newspapers or write a letter, or make a phone call, or change my socks, anything at all, to put off the moment. And when the moment comes, when there's nothing else that I can possibly pretend to do, something happens to my brain. It freezes, atrophies, becomes utterly blank. All my plots, my brilliant, sensational ideas I came here to put on paper, just disappear. I sit there so long until there seems nothing left to do but weep, then I go out and get drunk. No, that's not quite true, sometimes I stay home and get drunk. It doesn't help anyway." Basil turned round from the window. The bed was empty.

"Honey! Where are you, damn you? Have I been talking to myself?"

Honey came in, in her nightdress, with two tumblers of whisky. She gave one to Basil and got back into bed with hers.

"If it wasn't for you, I'd go stark, staring mad," Basil said.

"Tell me about Elisabeth."

"Why?"

"I'd like to hear. You love her, don't you?"

Basil drained his whisky. "Yes, I love her. Why don't you bring the bottle in?"

"I'll get it."

"Stay where you are. I'll get it myself."

Back in the bedroom, Basil slumped into the armchair which was strewn with Honey's clothes, filled his glass and put the bottle down on the floor beside him.

"The story of a failure," he said, "Chapter One." He closed his eyes. "The beginning was good," he said. "The beginning has to be good or the whole bloody book's no good. But this beginning was particularly good, real 'happy ever after' stuff. It just shows how you can't tell, about anything, the plot runs away with you. I met Elisabeth while I was working in a bookseller's in Knightsbridge. I'd always wanted to write, you see, so I never bothered to train for anything in particular, although I did a year of sheer purgatory on a local paper. Then after that I just took whatever job happened to be going so that I could keep myself, in order to be able to write. It had to be a job which didn't entail very much thinking, so that I was able to keep myself fresh for my writing in the evenings. The bookshop job was particularly good from that point of view. Anyway, one day after I'd been there only a few weeks I was checking our stock of French dictionaries (I remember clearly it was French dictionaries) when I looked up and I saw this girl come in. Being in Knightsbridge there were lots of pretty girls about, but usually they just walked by outside on the pavement and more often than not didn't bother to glance in the window. Anyway this girl came in. She was quite tall and beautifully dressed and she had some sort of fur round her neck and a silly little dog under her arm as they do in Knightsbridge, and I supposed she had come for a book, 'something light' to 'give to a friend in hospital'. You get used to summing them up as soon as they come into the shop. I said, 'Can I help you, madam?' and she said, 'Have you got Victor Hugo's *Feuilles d'Automne*', in a very soft, sweet voice. And I said, 'You mean in the translation?' and she said, 'No, the original', and then she smiled and I just stood there gaping like an idiot. But she was so pretty, so quiet, yet so obviously full of hundreds of undiscovered things that for the moment I was completely paralysed. I did manage to move eventually, and went to find what she'd asked for. It took me longer than it should have. For one thing my hands were shaking and for another I kept peeping at her standing there behind the books. I didn't want her to go, you see. I took as long as I could wrapping the book and taking the money and giving her her change, but then she had to go, and she did. After she'd gone I thought what an idiot I'd been. I should have said we were out of stock, that I'd let her know when it was in, or send it to her. I should at least have known then where she lived. I spent days after that at the window watching all the fashionable women go by, in the hope that among them would be one quite tall and very beautiful with a little brown dog under her arm. I spent so long at the window, in fact, that I lost my job. It didn't worry me too much, as I had lost jobs before. I just decided to have a real lunch for once, with my last week's wages. I was shown to a table at the smart Italian restaurant opposite Harrod's, and the manageress asked me if I'd mind sharing and I said not at all and there, sitting at the table which I was to share, was Elisabeth. She smiled when she saw me, that wonderful smile, and took her dog off the chair so that I could sit down. I said 'I don't suppose you remember me?' and she said, 'What makes you think that? I enjoyed *Feuilles d'Automne* and I was coming in for something else. I think French lyric poetry so beautiful, don't you?' She smiled again and her eyes were a sort of deep violet, and I knew it couldn't end with a copy of Victor Hugo and a shared table at lunch. There were difficulties, although not emotional ones. Elisabeth, in her quiet way, cared as much for me as I for her. She had, she admitted, been attracted to me that first morning in the bookshop, but hadn't had the courage to come back. No, the difficulties were social. Elisabeth's father turned out to be Sir Godfrey

Bainbridge, MP, OBE, and lord knows what else. He took a pretty dim view of me, and I can't say I blame him – no job, no prospects and no money. My only claims to fame were a story in *Argosy*, an article in *John Bull* and two paragraphs in *Tit-Bits*. Elisabeth was his only child though, and together, she and her mother, a charming woman, managed to get round him, and he gave us his blessing. He did more. He offered to give Elisabeth an allowance which was more than enough to keep us both for a year, in which time I should have completed my masterpiece."

"Didn't you mind your wife keeping you?" Honey said, wide-eyed, from the bed.

Basil sat up and refilled his glass. "No. You see, by the end of the year, with no worries and no living to earn, I was convinced that I could produce something so good that I would be able to keep her as she was accustomed to living, for many years. I was only, as it were, borrowing the money from Sir Godfrey."

"And did you write your masterpiece?"

Basil finished his drink and lay back again in the chair. "By the end of the year I had forty-seven rejection slips from short stories I had submitted and five hundred pages of the most putrid drivel on God's earth. I also had the unpleasant fact to face that my wife was no longer able to keep me. Elisabeth was good. She loved me, you see, and although her faith seemed to have been rather misplaced, she only said, gently, that I had better see about getting a job. I got several jobs and, just as before I was married, as fast as I got them I lost them. I was thinking all the time about writing, you see. Sir Godfrey, seeing how it was with me, didn't want to have anything to do with me any more. Elisabeth was loyal, she said she wouldn't see him either. We saw her mother and she tried to help us, although by the way she looked at me I could tell that she was thinking her daughter might have married anyone, and had landed herself with a failure like me. We moved from our flat in South Kensington to a very tiny one in Hampstead, and Elisabeth got a job selling baby clothes in a shop near the Heath. It was inevitable that we had rows. Elisabeth came home tired, she had never been used to working, and she wasn't as patient as she used to be. I used to go out in order to avoid the rows. Usually I came home drunk – on Elisabeth's money!"

"You're a real rat, aren't you?" Honey said. "I never believed you were like that."

"That's what Elisabeth said every time we had a slanging match. She believed better of me. Knew I was capable of holding a job, staying long enough to be promoted. She didn't understand, and you won't either, but if I take a job to which I must put my whole mind, I am sunk. As a writer, that is. I know, as well as you do and Elisabeth did, that there are daubers who delude themselves that one day they will be hung in the Royal Academy, strummers with dreams of Salzburg and the Festival Hall, rhymesters with absolute convictions of immortality. I don't class myself among those. They have only hopes. I have certainty. I know that one day you will be able to read my soul in books, as surely as you can see Rembrandt's soul on canvas, and hear Beethoven's every day, if a little distorted, on the radio. This knowledge is the strongest thing I have, my only good, the one thing I must hang on to, and because I was unwilling to let it go, unable to let it go, I sacrificed Elisabeth."

"What happened?" Honey said.

"She was tired. Fed up with working. She got me a job with her uncle in Industrial Chemicals, a good job."

"Well?"

"He threw me out. He said I was brainless, shiftless and incapable of earning a living, in addition to one or two less complimentary things I wouldn't care to repeat."

"Hard on Elisabeth."

"Of course it was hard on Elisabeth. She was a saint to have stood it as long as she did. But don't you see it was Elisabeth or my own integrity? Once you throw away your integrity, what you know you are destined to do, to be, you have nothing. You are nothing."

"What happened to Elisabeth?"

"She went back home. Her father didn't mind that as long as I wasn't around."

"And you?"

"I came down here. You know the rest. You know how much I have written. Nothing, nothing at all. And you know why? Laugh, if you like. It's because I can't do a thing without Elisabeth. I'm lost, half alive. I've all the leisure in the world to do exactly what I've always wanted to, and I can do precisely nothing. It's a bloody paradox, but that's how it is."

"You had a whole year before, when Elisabeth's father was keeping you. You had no worries then, and you had Elisabeth. Why didn't you write?"

"I'll tell you. Every time I sat at the typewriter I could feel Elisabeth's father hanging over me with a whip, watching, waiting for the end of the year. And the days slipped away and the weeks, until it grew nearer and nearer the time when he could say to Elisabeth, 'I told you so'. It's impossible to work at the end of a pistol, for an artist with any sensibility."

"It looks as though you find it impossible to work at all," Honey said. "I feel really sorry for Elisabeth."

"Oh God!" Basil said, putting his head in his hands. "Women!"

Like a shot Honey, who did not like to see anyone miserable, was out of bed. She knelt beside Basil and stroked his hair.

"You know what the trouble with you is?" she said, but didn't wait for an answer. "You're stale. In show business, when we get stale we're useless; we're out if we don't do something about it. So we rest. But not just a rest while we look for another job. We really rest. We don't live the theatre, eat, sleep and dream the theatre. We forget it; kick over the traces. Pretend it doesn't exist. Then suddenly you wake up one morning and you're better. The lights and the make-up and music have crept back into your veins, but fresh and throbbing and full of life, and you're capable of anything again. How long have you been writing your famous book?"

"Ten years."

"You're crazy." Honey pulled his hands from his face. "Burn all that rotten paper in your room, lock up the typewriter, concentrate on your toffee-apples and the café, and write to Elisabeth."

"I keep writing to Elisabeth."

"Write to her again." Honey crossed the room and turned on the radio. The fast blare of a rock and roll rhythm filled the room. Honey, laughing, her limbs gleaming through the transparent nightdress, contorted her lips and jerked her long, black hair back and forth over her shoulders in time to the music. She didn't stop until Basil was laughing at her exaggerated gyrations.

"...'A star danced and under that I was born.' You should have been called Beatrice. Does nothing ever get you down, Honey?"

Honey stopped dancing, and for the first time Basil saw her face serious. "When you have to look out for yourself," she said, "you don't let it. You mustn't."

Basil, standing up, took her in his arms. "For a Maharajah's daughter you're a lovely girl."

Honey blushed. "I didn't think you'd swallow that. Would you like to know the truth?"

"Very much," Basil said, crushing her to him, "but not just now."

"You don't have to, you know," Honey said, removing her mouth from his. "I understand – about Elisabeth."

"Damn Elisabeth!" Basil shouted. "And damn the whisky and the rain and most of all damn, damn, damn myself." He picked Honey up in his arms and strode with her to the bed, turning off the radio on the way.

"And a damned good job, too." Arthur Dexter, sitting up in bed in the upstairs flat, said. He was referring to the sudden quiet. "Making a row like that on a Sunday morning!"

Fourteen

Basil, lying in bed beside Honey, thought, I haven't told her half. I have told her about Elisabeth working in the baby-shop and me trying to write and then my job with her uncle and how he chucked me out, but I haven't told her how it really was with me and Elisabeth. I haven't told her why it was that Elisabeth, darling Elisabeth who was willing to stick anything, finally left. He glanced at Honey who had fallen asleep, her customary happy smile still on her lips, her face almost buried by the cloud of dark hair which smothered the pillow and flowed onto his shoulder. Elisabeth had been right, of course, but that same devil that egged him on to try to write at the expense of earning a living had made him, time after time, after time, hurt and humiliate her. He thought of the last months in the flat. Each night as it grew dark Elisabeth had let herself in with her key, laden usually with the shopping she had collected on the way home. At one time, in the early days, she had crept up behind him as he sat at the typewriter and putting her arms round his neck and her cheek against his, whispered words of love. That had stopped a long time ago though, together with the laughing and the joking and the hundred and one silly things they had shared together. Recently she had only come in, moving quietly as she always did, but with the quietness of defeat, and tired and laden she would go straight into the kitchen to dump her parcels, then into the bedroom and the bathroom to wash off the dirt of the day's work and only then into the little study where he worked, to glance over his shoulder at the blank paper in the typewriter or the crumpled pages hurled in desperation to the floor. And in self-defence he'd say, "Well, why don't you say it straight out? I'm no bloody good and you should never have married me." And, hurt, she'd disappear into the kitchen to get the supper. Except sometimes when she'd answer back that they had loved each other once and why couldn't he face up to his responsibilities like other men? Then he'd say how misunderstood he was and she, goaded, would say she was fed up with keeping him, and he would say then why didn't she get out, and the words would fly back and forth more vituperative and more hurtful as the argument progressed, until finally it was he who got out, slamming the door behind him and leaving his wife to sob while he found solace in as many double whiskies as he could afford which usually wasn't very many. And when he came back he'd sit at the typewriter again, and at midnight or often later Elisabeth, bearing the olive branch, would come to the door in her dressing-gown and say very softly, "Basil, come to bed now", in such a way there could be no doubt she still loved him and wanted him and he, not looking at her would say, "Later", and without looking round know she had gone, and he would be left to sublimate himself in the work that never materialised. When he finally did go to bed Elisabeth would be asleep, only sometimes sobbing occasionally as she slept. And by the morning, refreshed, he would feel remorse and overwhelming love for what he was slowly killing and stretch out his arms for her but she with red-rimmed eyes would say, "Not now, Basil, I have to go to work", and so she had, and the whole dreary day would start again. And all the time there was the demon that was holding him back for the greatness he felt he must achieve so that he was unable to give himself to any job of work, unable to give himself even to his wife except on rare occasions, as if they had been married thirty years instead of three. Perhaps had he not known what he was doing it would not have been so bad. But with every fibre of his being he knew that he was, day by day and night by night, destroying that which he loved most. And he could not stop himself. He stood and watched the murder, so that his hands would remain clean for a task that in ten years he had not been able to begin. Whitecliffs had seemed a chance. He believed that by taking it he would at last give birth to what had been growing inside him for so long. That the period of gestation would be over; that by his achievement he would win Elisabeth back. All he had done was to prove faithless to a marriage he had himself wrecked, and achieve precisely nothing. Looking at Honey beside him, he knew that he had only ravelled more tightly the tangle into which he had got himself. He had sought from her the solace Elisabeth had longed to give him. He wished he knew what had made him so cussed, and why he loved what he did not love and turned his back on that which he would die for.

It was still raining. He could hear it hissing through the trees. He got up and dressed and, smiling at Honey who still slept as though she had not a care in the world, went back to his own flat.

He started on his notebooks. He ripped the pages, some covered with his writing, out of the covers, and tore them into small pieces. It was satisfying. When he had finished he turned his attention to his papers: flimsy quarto sheets, some with notes, some with doodles, some with chapter headings and nothing more, received the same ruthless treatment. When he had finished, the bin in the kitchen was full and his dressing-table clear. He put the lid on the typewriter, snapped the hasps and, lifting it down from the dressing-table, took it into the hall where he stowed it in the cupboard beside the electricity meter. When there was no trace any more that he was a writer, or rather a would-be one, he sat down on the bed. He felt lost, desolate, worse even than when Elisabeth had left. There was an emptiness in himself, as well as in the flat, that seemed unbearable. In an hour he had thrown away the burden he had carried for ten years. The hollow it left was intolerable. I have something to say, he thought, and I cannot say it. Soon something must break. Not bothering to put on his coat, he left the flat in its unaccustomed tidiness and walked out into the rain.

On the promenade, now soaking wet, he watched the sea, angry, collect up in grey, foamy waves and hurl itself against the concrete, swirling the top with water which slowly ran back into the ocean. It had been his own fault as everything had been his own fault. On that last night he had been at his typewriter as usual when Elisabeth, going to bed, had come into the room and faced him.

"I can't go on like this, Basil," she'd said. "I don't think you love me any more." Her face was white and the violet eyes looked large. She waited for him to speak. When he said nothing she said: "Well, do you? I think it's time we had the truth." Inside himself he had been weeping with love for her. He had said nothing, aware of his own failure; had not been man enough to say anything. She had gone to bed. Next day, towards evening he had sat as usual waiting for the sound of her key in the door. It hadn't come. By the time it was dark he knew it would not, and that he had only himself to blame. He stepped nearer the edge of the promenade and looked down into the gloomy depths of the sea whose surface was dimpled by the rain. If I took one step more, he thought, all my damned worries would be ended, but I'm not even man enough for that.

"Not contemplating suicide by any chance?" a voice said.

Basil turned round, his shoes squelching in the water. Doctor Gurney, well wrapped up in raincoat and cap, was watching him, his hands deep in his pockets, his head bowed against the rain and the spray.

"Why should I be?" he said.

"Well, for one thing you're absolutely soaked through; you've no coat and you must have known it was raining. And for another thing I know you sensitive plants."

They stepped back as a large wave sloshed towards them.

"How do you mean?" Basil asked against the wind, and aware now of the wet blowing into his face.

"The frustrations and indecisions and the sense of inadequacy and the moodiness and the fits of depression…it's a common syndrome. Do you mind if we walk along?"

Basil fell into step beside him. "You mean other people feel the same?"

"We're none of us unique," Doctor Gurney said. "We all fit roughly into one category or another. I've watched you since we've been down here. I didn't think you were very happy."

"Have you a cure?"

Doctor Gurney put his arm round Basil's shoulders. "Listen, old boy, I'm not down here in my professional capacity. Why don't you pull yourself together, change into some dry clothes and come and have a drink before lunch? There's a nice little road-house up towards Canterbury."

"What a splendid idea!" Basil said, and they walked towards the flats.

The 'Landscape', a picturesque old house with a pleasant, timbered bar, stood amongst trees set back from the main London Road. The car park was full, and inside the coat racks laden with raincoats and hats. In the bar one could forget that it was raining; forget that it was August and should not have been raining; forget everything in the warmth and the peace of a Sunday morning drink. There was not very much noise, only a gentle hum of conversation and a slowness and unhurriedness one did not find in London bars, and the smell of beer, and sometimes one caught the drift of roast beef cooking as a door was opened, and what might have been Yorkshire pudding and probably was. The landlord, tall and with a handlebar moustache, said, "What will it be, gentlemen?" as Basil and Doctor Gurney pushed their way to the bar, and he stood as though he had all the time in the world.

They ordered, and with their drinks turned to find somewhere to sit. At a table in the corner, next to the window with its leaded lights looking onto the dripping garden, they found Arthur Dexter and Howard.

"Bloody weather for August," Basil said to Howard. "How did you get here?"

"It is a little inclement," Howard said. "Mr Dexter found his Sunday morning mood disturbed by Honey's radio, and he asked if I wanted to come for a drive. I'd heard about this place. It's owned by a man I once defended. He hasn't recognised me yet. I was interested to see what it was like."

Basil, grinning as he thought of Honey's radio, found his mood lighten suddenly. He pulled his chair in. "Well," he said, "we're almost back where we were when we first met in Fleet Street. Only Doctor Gurney wasn't with us, and now we're all off our treadmills."

Arthur said: "It's peaceful. On Sunday morning at home I'd be drinking, too, but not like this. Not with people I want to drink with. I'd be at home all dressed up as carefully in my casual clothes as I would be in my City ones during the week, and the house would be tidy and I'd be making polite conversation to people Vera thought I ought to make polite conversation to, either at my home or theirs. Do you know," he leaned towards Doctor Gurney, "for the first time in years I've been sleeping without my tablets, and I've been dreaming, too: I suppose you'll laugh, but not about mortgages and properties and toys and imports and exports, and a hundred and one other things I'd been worrying about during the day, but about children! Children playing on the beach and paddling in the water. And when I wake up in the morning I feel as if I've slept and not as if I'd been pacing up and down all night. What about you?" he said to Basil. "After all it was more or less your idea."

Basil said, "Perhaps it wasn't such a clever idea after all. I'm beginning to think that there is no treadmill except in our imagination. That it's ourselves we're trying to run away from, and there is, when you come to try it, no escape, however hard, however fast you run."

"Talking of treadmills," Howard said, putting his glass down on the polished oak table, "there's a story of a Judge, in the days when in prisons there actually were treadmills, who was being taken round a prison on a tour of inspection by the Governor. The Judge, when he saw the prisoners turning the wheel step after step after step, asked if he might be allowed to get on. He wanted to know how the punishment felt to which he committed those who came up before him. The Governor asked the prisoners to stop their weary task and the Judge, an elderly man, took his place. After one or two turns of the mill, with the learned Judge doing his share of the work, the Governor was called away. The Judge, having had enough, asked the prisoners to stop the wheel so that he might get off. To the prisoners it was a chance to retaliate for the sentences that had been meted out to them. They had no intention of stopping, and the poor old Judge had no choice but to tread step after step after the others. By the time the Governor remembered the old boy he was in a state of collapse. They say it actually happened. And then there was the story about the Judge who, or so the story goes..."

Doctor Gurney wasn't listening. Arthur Dexter would ask him next, he was sure. Ask him if he was pleased he had come to Whitecliffs, happy to be away from his practice. They had come, of course, in the first place for Jonathan, whose health had been much improved by the sea air. Had it not been that he was worried about him he would never have left his practice. It had been strange at first for Mary and himself. Used to listening in a state of constant tension for the first ringing of the telephone, they had been unable to believe in its uncanny silence. At night they had for the first few weeks still slept in a state of semi-tension, sure of being disturbed. Only in the last few weeks had they allowed themselves to sleep deeply, and marvelled in the morning that no one had rung, to be prescribed two aspirins, to be visited or to be advised. No one had rung at all, and neither had they during the day. It had been difficult to get used to. No coughs, no colds, no throats, no abdomens, no backs; no injuries, no illnesses, no surgical interventions, no going out at night, suit hurriedly over pyjamas; no histories, no diagnoses; no palliatives, no treatment; no sedatives, no tranquillisers, no antibiotics, no steroids. Only his wife and his family and the sea and the beach, and at the café his not very arduous task of looking after the till. At mealtimes he still bolted with a sense of urgency whatever was put in front of him, but although he still ate quickly his mind was no longer on the gall bladder or the middle ear infection he had to see, and he noticed what he ate. Occasionally he would worry if the locum he had left in charge would recognise Mrs Beechley's attacks of pancreatitis, manage to talk young Toby Burns round when he started to get depressed, watch the small babies carefully for ears and appendices, deal firmly with Mrs Barbary whose frequent illnesses existed only in her mind. He had told Arthur Dexter that there was nothing of a vocation about his practice of medicine, that he did it, as he might do any job, because by it he earned his living. He was watching himself carefully to see if this was in fact true. If it was there was no reason why he should not get some other job, give up medicine and follow some less nerve-racking occupation where he could be sure of a night's sleep and not wear himself out before he was fifty. He had not yet convinced himself. At the till in the café he watched the people pass, his eyes wandering over their trays; two teas, one ham sandwich, three chocolate wafers...two-and-seven...unilateral exophthalmos, looks a little as if she has a goitre...two lemon squash a shilling, old thymectomy there...one Bovril fourpence...she ought to get rid of that pigmented mole. Perhaps it was just habit. One couldn't lose the training of years in a few weeks. Besides, such observations passed the time away: the time which seemed too slow in passing because there were no surgeries to do, no homes to visit, no sick to treat and well to comfort.

Howard was saying: "…I must say I find it extremely pleasant down here, quite amusing even. If only one hadn't to scratch a living somehow…"

"A living, yes," Arthur said. "I've been scratching for too much. Far too much."

"Some people scratch and scratch just as hard as any of us and get nothing for it," Doctor Gurney said, thinking of some of the patients who came to him sick with despair and overwork, but still unable to make ends meet.

"We're back to the old treadmill again," Basil said. "How about another drink?"

"You've been very quiet about all this, Doctor," Arthur said. "A bit of a dark horse. Are you happy at your cash register, or would you rather be incising boils or doing some of the other horrid things you usually do all day?"

"I reserve my judgement," Doctor Gurney said. "I'm not sure that I hadn't become fonder than I'd imagined of my own particular treadmill. Not that I'm not grateful," he said to Arthur, "of the opportunity you gave me to get off. It's nice in a way to stand back and watch the wheel going round and round as it did before without any effort from yourself. I don't know if we can get away with it, though. If we've been given a part in this play, perhaps we have to play it."

"Or is it an endless hurrying…" Howard said.

"Shut up, there's a good chap," Basil said, standing up. "Let's just drink and be merry for once without analysing every bloody thing we do. There's no reason to suppose that we're not here for our own good. Same again all round?"

Fifteen

By Wednesday the weather, which had cheated many of their summer holiday since Sunday, seemed to have taken pity on those on whom it had rained, blown and chilled for three days. An innocent sun, as though it had never been away, shone from a clear sky, drying the beach, the soaked huts and the promenade and like a magnet drew parents and frustrated children from hotel and boarding-house in their hundreds.

In 'Le Casse-Croûte' they were all busy. Arthur, anxious to compensate for the meagre takings of the past few days, was behind them all. "More sandwiches," he said, the sun was going to shine all day. "You'll need all those apples today, Basil. Honey, help him put the sticks in, there's a good girl." The customers were already arriving for the first cups of tea and coffee. "Good morning, madam, Good morning, sir," Arthur said from behind the counter. "Take a tray, if you please. What a splendid day! Two teas? With pleasure, with or without?" And at the fancy-goods: "You've broken your bucket? Victor, there's a small girl here who says the handle's come off her bucket. See what you can do for her, will you? One Bovril, madam, and have we some dry bread? We can do better than that, dear. Honey, bring out one of those scones from yesterday from the kitchen, will you, dear? Not at all, madam, it's a pleasure. Louise, this gentleman would like a tray for six for the beach. Yes, sir, ten shillings deposit which you get back when you return your tray to this window. You've only half-a-crown in your shorts pocket? All right, sir, you've an honest face. Doctor Gurney, the gentleman will leave two-and-six deposit; give him a disc, will you."

Outside, her machine humming as she twirled candy-floss for two small boys who watched open-mouthed, Vanessa smiled. She was hardly able to believe that it was her father. Her father who, in town, came home irritable and tired from the office with hardly a word for anybody. Who was immersed either in his newspaper or in the papers he kept in a large box-file and which seemed to give him an enormous amount of worry. With his City suit he seemed to have shed whatever it was that in London kept his brow permanently creased, his mouth firm and straight, his eyes tired. Had anyone told her, six months ago, that he was capable of rolling up his sleeves, of calling an old lady 'dear', of slicing ham, she would only have laughed. She had always thought of him as buttoned permanently into a dark suit, or on Sundays fawn with a Prince of Wales check, and set irrevocably into his rut of City and armchair, card games and cruises in which there seemed very little joy. With each birthday, on which she and Victor spent hours trying to think of something original and usually ended up with socks and ties which he invariably exchanged, he had seemed to grow a little greyer, a little more as she remembered her grandfather had looked. It had not seemed possible that he could bare his forearms, test the temperature of toffee, supervise the making of tea. In the months they had been at Whitecliffs, his face, which ever since she could remember had been pale, had become not tanned but glowing with the look of skin that was alive, the lines that seemed always to have been between his eyebrows were less obvious, and his eyes, at home always slightly blurred with weariness, were clear as stones.

This morning there had been a letter from Cliff. 'Van, darling, you don't write very much. I am sweating blood over this Anatomy but every time I close my eyes and try to commit something about the flexor retinaculum or the internal iliac lymph glands to memory I can only think of you. Why did you go away, and when will you be coming back?'... She hadn't wanted to go away. Hadn't believed that without Cliff... She handed the two fluffy, cotton-wool sticks of candy-floss to the children, and took the warm shilling they gave her. Turning off the machine that stopped with a slow whine, she looked up behind her towards Howard. He was in profile, serving his customers with ice-cream. Solid, such beautiful hands, beautifully kept. How could he not know? She felt as if her thoughts must be electric. He did not turn round. This afternoon they were going to Walmer Castle. Only a few more hours. Suddenly he turned towards her and trapped the naked look of adoration in her eyes before she had a chance to hide it. He looked uncomprehending, then surprised. He served his customer then looked again towards Vanessa. She had her machine whirring again and her back was towards him.

In the kitchen, Basil, stirring the toffee, said to Honey: "It's the oddest feeling. A very miserable sort of emptiness. Yet with it there's a kind of peace. It's like playing truant from school; one feels almost too guilty to enjoy one's freedom. I can hardly believe that I've cut the chain between me and that wretched typewriter. Stay near me, Honey." He watched the line of her throat as she stuck sticks into the apples she removed one by one from the case.

"I know how it feels," she said. "Each night, as it gets dark and I'm free to watch the evening through the window, I begin to miss the lights and the music and the make-up and the fights in the dressing-room, and the gossip..."

"What did you gossip about?"

"Sex." Honey thought for a moment. "I can't remember anything else."

"It must be quite a sight in the dressing-room," Basil said, "all you girls running around in your birthday suits."

"Don't be silly," Honey said. "We put something on as soon as we come off stage."

"I suppose half the audience queues up for you at the stage door."

"There's no stage door. We have to come out through the bar. And they don't queue up. They usually send round notes. It's surprising," she said, "the amount of men who imagine that just because you take your clothes off on the stage you are no better than if you walked the streets."

Basil looked up from his toffee.

"I mean we're only working-girls no different from shorthand-typists or anything…" Basil took the apple she held out to him and kissed her nose.

"You really are rather sweet. Do you get diamonds and furs sent to the dressing-room?"

"Chocolates and sherry," Honey said.

"What do you do with them?"

"Keep them." Honey looked surprised. "We do quite well at this place. I once got a pair of diamanté earrings. Of course, occasionally you meet somebody really nice who's been to see the show, like Mr Dexter, for instance…"

"Mr Dexter's seen you dancing around in your…?"

"Of course," Honey said. "He said he enjoyed it."

"I'll bet he did. Would you believe it?"

"Of course, I like men you can *talk* to," Honey said, "somebody interesting, like you. And there was an archey…archy…oh you know, somebody who digs up old stones and things, once; he was awfully sweet, and then a doctor who cut up dead people all day and…"

"Let me keep my illusions, darling," Basil said. "I seem to have nothing else left at the moment."

"Has Elisabeth answered your letter?"

"She hasn't answered any of my letters."

"Perhaps you should stop writing. Perhaps she'll get worried about you."

"What makes you think that?"

"That's what a woman would do. We're funny like that."

Basil shrugged. "I could try it. This toffee's hardening. Can you hand me the others quickly, Honey-child, or I'll never get them all coated."

Victor, selling postcards and buckets and spades as fast as he could go, had little time to think about Petal. When he did he counted the hours until nightfall, and imagined how it would be when he called for her at her darts stand at Merrydown Park. They would walk, he thought, along the sea-front, leaving the crowds behind, until they came to 'Le Casse-Croûte.' He would have his arm round Petal and he would feel her warmth as they walked together in the darkness. He wondered whether there would be a moon. Perhaps there would, and it would shine through the windows of 'Le Casse-Croûte' as they danced cheek-to-cheek in the space before the counter where today people in bathing suits, pink from the sun, were lining up for tea and coffee, cakes and sandwiches, little imagining… And then when their dancing had grown slower, they would stop to kiss, and Petal's lips would be soft and her hair pale in the wash of light and the piles of silent plates and saucers, ghostly, and then gently, very gently, he hoped he would not tremble and that she would not realise it was his first time…

"I think you've given me the wrong change." He looked down at the fat lady in the navy blue dress who held a pile of silver and copper in her pudgy hand for his inspection. "I had two cards and a fishin' net and one of them rubber balls." Victor, relinquishing Petal with a sigh, said, "I'm frightfully sorry," and tried to add up.

Louise, in a moment of respite between filling the large, steaming teapot from the hissing tap, pouring endless cups of good, strong tea, filling pots with one, two or three tea-bags, milking cups expertly, just so much, serving cups of coffee, fingered the knot of hair at the nape of her neck and wondered if she dared. Harry said it would make her look years younger. She had a nice face, he'd said, why did she spoil it with that dreadful, old-fashioned hair style? He had been even more surprised when she'd told him that her work, her proper work, had been in a hairdressing salon. She'd tried to explain that the fancy, fashionable styles, the urchin fringes, the casual curls, the bouffant, were for the customers; the women to whom the hairdresser, no matter where they were, was a necessary adjunct to living. The week was not complete, the party could not be attended, the dinner not eaten, without the washing, the conditioning, the setting in rollers and clips, the net, the cotton-wool for the ears, the drying, the combing out, the lacquer; not to mention the perming, the straightening, the bleaching, the tinting, the rinsing, the oil treatments, the scalp treatments... All that was for women whose night was a theatre, a dinner, a party, not a bus home in the rush hour, a hastily prepared supper – a kipper perhaps or scrambled egg on toast – and an evening listening to the television and her mother grumbling. She took advantage of the facilities the salon offered its staff for free shampoos and sets. One of the girls, Miss Irene usually, did her hair for her, and years ago they had stopped asking her wouldn't she like to wear it short for a change or brightened a little or the ends permed. Now they just washed it, dried it loose under the drier and left her to wind it into the knot with which she was so familiar. The only thing she did accept was her weekly manicure. She was proud of her hands, which were very much in evidence as she took money, gave change, entered appointments in the large book in front of her. It was on her hands that she lavished varnish, creams and lotions, her hair she had given up long ago. Her mother would have something to say, of course, but that didn't worry her. What worried her was if she really wanted herself to experiment, if she dared. What worried her even more was her own willingness to do this for a man she had only just met, and so casually, a man who, she had to admit, but only in the deep recesses of her own heart, wasn't really her type at all.

That she had accepted his invitation at all was difficult to believe. Drinking in a seaside pavilion bar was hardly something to which she was accustomed, and if it wasn't for her mother she would never have gone.

On the day that she had taken the Gurney children to the concert party her feeling of contentment and good humour had persisted, in spite of her mother's moaning that she had been left for the whole afternoon, until after their supper for which Louise, because of her good mood, had prepared a tasty dish consisting of fillets of sole, a fish which was plentiful and beautiful in Whitecliffs, and sauce in which were sweet, white grapes. With the cookery book in front of her, she had hummed the tunes which the band had played as she peeled the grapes, melted butter and carefully stirred her sauce. During the meal her mother had said nothing, only carefully scraped every bit of sauce from her fish to the side of her plate, and left her half-dozen grapes untouched. When she had put down her knife and fork Louise, still in her good humour and only half annoyed because she had expected nothing else, said: "I don't know why I bother," and gone into the kitchen, carrying the plates, to fetch the crème caramel she had made. When she came back her mother was sitting very still and upright, her hands clasped on her lap, her lips in a thin line. She should have recognised the signs. "I don't know why you do, either," her mother said.

"Why I do what?" Louise put the dish down.

"Bother. That's what you said, wasn't it? Can I help it if I'm an old woman and my legs aren't very good?..."

Louise was still cheerful. "Come on now, mother, don't start. Eat your caramel and we'll listen to Variety Playhouse, or I'll take you for a little walk along the front while it's still light, if you like."

But her mother was not to be diverted. "When I think," she said, not even picking up her spoon, "of the years I spent looking after you, you never were an easy child, Louise, and then your father day and night in the sick-room, and when it comes to my turn for a little attention..."

Louise had put down her spoon. "Just a minute, Mother," she said, her mood having completely evaporated and been replaced by an unfamiliar, tight feeling which seemed to be constricting her chest. "You know quite well who it was that looked after father, day and night, and meals and beds and everything else..."

"And why not? Your own father..."

Because you were his wife and because of you I lost my only chance of happiness, Johnny. "No reason why not, but don't pretend you did it all, Mother, because you didn't; you didn't."

"Don't think your father wasn't aware, Louise, that when you nursed him it was grudgingly, your mind all the time on that Air Force fellow..."

Louise stood up. "I loved my father," she said distinctly, "he was the sweetest, kindest...how can you say a thing like that...when Father's not here to defend me? When you know it isn't true?"

Her mother, now she had succeeded in riling Louise and had the upper hand, began calmly to eat her crème caramel. "Well, you did want to go off with that fellow, didn't you?" She made her voice sound reasonable as she slung her darts with sure aim.

"I did, yes, and you made sure that I threw away my chance. My only chance, as it happened."

Her mother looked up. It was not like Louise to answer back.

"That's just what I said. You bore a grudge and your father sensed it..."

Louise said, "Whose name was it he called into the night, every night? And when he was dying, and he must have known it because you were careful that he should, whose name did he call?"

Her mother opened her mouth to answer but before she had a chance Louise said: "You're a wicked, wicked old woman, and if I said I don't know why I bother, I meant what I said; I meant it because it's never occurred to you that I, too, might have feelings, need someone to care..."

"Louise, where are you going?" The voice followed her into the bedroom where she had run before she said too much of what was in her heart.

She hadn't been going anywhere except to dam the stream she had been bottling up over the years and which threatened to overflow.

"I'm going out," she said.

"I'll be alone again… You said we were going for a walk…" the voice, unsure, was whining again.

Louise had her coat on. She was pale when she came into the lounge which was also their dining-room. "I have to get out for a bit. It's your own fault, Mother. I shan't be long."

Outside she had run, a middle-aged woman, tears streaming down her face, towards the bus which would take her to the pavilion.

Only when she pushed open the door of the bar, and the smell of the drinks and the smoke had hit her in the face, had she wanted to turn and go back, but he had already seen her. She accepted the chair at the small, glass-topped table, and the cigarette and the gin he put before her. Only when he said: "I'm ever so glad you came," did she really look at him. He had changed from the red jacket uniform of the concert party, and now wore a pale grey suit on which the chalk stripes were at least an inch and a half apart, and the shoulders well padded. His shoes were brown and white. After her third gin she stopped noticing that his teeth clicked when he talked, and when he covered her hand with his she did not protest. It was warm and friendly in the bar, and it was not until she had told him practically all there was to know about herself that she thought suddenly, I don't know what has come over me sitting here in a bar drinking with some frightful man – and she knew he was frightful – and telling him my life story like some eighteen-year-old. Looking again at his face, which was not unkind, only a little sad from too many dreary digs and third-class shows in fourth-class seaside towns, and too much knocking around for too long, she thought he will probably take out his wallet soon and be surprised to find it empty, and say, "I'm most terribly sorry, I thought..." and she would pay for the three gins she had had and for his whiskies... Suddenly she knew she didn't care. Whatever his motives, and she had seen too many films, read too many books from the library to believe them anything but suspicious, he had made her feel, for an hour at least, that she was a woman, still not too old for beauty, not too staid for fun. She had left him to walk back alone along the sea-front, having declined his offer of company which he did not press too hard, but had agreed to meet him again in the pavilion bar. When he said, "Good night, Louise, try to make it Wednesday," and clasped her hand in both of his she'd said, "Good night, Harry," and hadn't cared that she was making a fool of herself, and knew that she could come again because she had enjoyed the evening and she felt relaxed, wanted, if only by Harry who she knew was probably up to no good, for herself.

Now in the café, at her place behind the urn, Louise, too, had something to think of besides whether she had done the right thing for herself and her mother in coming to Whitecliffs, and as she poured teas and filled pots she decided yes, she would have her hair cut and perhaps try to take a little weight off, she was, after all, not much over forty but until now she hadn't cared...

"You're all half asleep this morning," Arthur said, coming through to the café from the stock room. "Come along Victor, Louise, Basil, we'll have them all going over to the Corporation if we don't pull our socks up. Let's get this queue cleared quickly if we can; we'll have the trippers down at any minute on a lovely day like this."

And indeed, pouring out from the little station and flowing down in a colourful stream towards the beach, for which they had risen at six and packed sandwiches and filled thermos, was a steady line of Mums in floral dresses and Dads with scrawny Adam's apples in open-necked art silk shirts in blue or green, carrying floppy bags, and Grandads with caps, and Nannas with varicose veins, and children of all ages with black plimsolls and tired London faces but smiling with anticipation. And as they neared the front and 'Le Casse-Croûte' they decided that having been up so long they could do with a cup of tea and an ice for the kiddies, and they were served by Vanessa who thought of Howard, and Louise who thought of Harry, and Victor who was waiting for the night.

Sixteen

If Howard had correctly interpreted Vanessa's glance as she looked towards him from her candy-floss stand in 'Le Casse-Croûte' he had shown no sign, no sign at all. In a dither of excitement Vanessa had rushed back to the flat at lunchtime, and hurried to change in order not to keep him waiting. When she had opened her wardrobe she had been overcome by indecision about what to wear. The pink cotton was nice but he had seen her in it; the pale yellow with the stiff petticoat was pretty but she knew it made her look younger; what she was looking for was something that would make her look older, more sophisticated, more likely to catch the attention of Howard, who was so much older than she. In the end she kept him waiting nearly twenty minutes while she decided on a straight navy blue cotton skirt with a white shirt which, although she was unaware of it, because of its simplicity made her look younger than ever. She took trouble with her hair which obstinately refused to do what she wanted and put black mascara on her blonde lashes. Howard appeared to notice neither what she was wearing nor that she was late. He was sitting outside the flats in his car, a small grey Hillman, and was reading. When she opened the door and slid into the seat beside him he said: "Did you know that William Pitt the Younger resided there between 1792 and 1806?"

"Where?" Vanessa said, smoothing her skirt beneath her so that it should not get creased.

"Walmer Castle. There have been some most illustrious Lords Warden of the Cinque Ports. The Duke of Wellington, Viscount Palmerston, King George the Fifth, when he was Prince of Wales, the Marquess of Reading, the Marquis of Willingdon; I suppose you know who the present Lord Warden is?" Howard put down his book and started up the engine.

In her mind Vanessa went back to school. Lord Warden of the Cinque Ports? It sounded awfully familiar. She didn't want to appear dim. Of course!

"Winston Churchill," she said.

Howard appeared not to have heard. He was about to turn into the main road, and was looking carefully both ways to see if anything was coming.

He drove soberly, carefully, taking no risks, through the country roads between flat fields of stooked corn, maize growing high, and cabbages, through the narrow old streets of Sandwich, past the lifeboat on the shore at Deal and on into Walmer. All the time Howard talked, and Vanessa, lulled by the sound of his voice and busy with her own thoughts because she was actually sitting beside him if only by her own invitation, heard only half of what he said. "Fortifications constructed by Henry VIIIth to counter any attempted landings...work of coastal defence begun in 1583...most extensive work of its kind undertaken in England until the last or even the present century...perfection in the style of its period... Spanish Armada ...encroachment of the sea... Civil War in 1642...besieged by the Royalists... Walmer Castle no longer used as a fortress... fabric altered in order to fit it for residence by the Lords Warden."

They joined a party which was being guided round the Castle by the Curator. Together with a group of serious-faced Brownies, two French girls who commented continuously and volubly in their own language to each other, an American with a camera and two old dears in brown felt hats, they shuffled past cordoned-off rooms, including Queen Victoria's bedroom, with its high, canopied bed from which she could see the passing ships, and saw in glass cases the Duke of Wellington's boots and his silk handkerchief, also his camp bed whose simplicity, according to the Curator, he preferred, and his reading chair, unusual in that the book rest was on the back and could be used only by one sitting astride. The Curator assured them that the ascetically minded Duke had preferred this arrangement but the Brownies looked doubtful. When they had finished the tour of the Castle, including the bathrooms, recently added and built into the immense thickness of the walls, and the parapet with its cannons, where the Brownies were warned not to remove any of the cannon balls (they discovered, amidst giggles, that they were unable, even by combined effort, to lift one an inch from the ground), they were released to explore on their own the gardens and the moat. Howard stayed behind the crowd and entered into earnest discussion with the Curator about the removal of the stairs from the central column of the keep. He stood solemnly on the flagged floor in the damp dimness of the entrance hall and muttered, arms folded, about the panelling, which had been added comparatively recently to most rooms, and the work carried out by Earl Granville in the last century. Vanessa, telling him that she would wait for him in the gardens, but not sure whether he had heard, escaped into the sunshine and sat on a wooden seat beneath the yew trees to admire the laid-out lawns. When Howard finally came he did not apologise for keeping her but led her enthusiastically down the steps to the moat, where now dahlias, larkspurs and grape vines grew in their sheltered position among lush grass. When there was nothing more than even Howard could think of to see, Vanessa suggested they should go down to the beach while the sun was still shining, and Howard said: "Interesting. Most interesting," thinking still of the Castle.

On the beach, which was nothing but a narrowish strip of small stones washed clean by the tide, they sat and watched the sea which lapped invitingly towards them, sparkling in the sun.

Vanessa looked at Howard who, in his stiff collar and dark tie, looked as if he was just passing through.

"Why don't you take your jacket off?" she said, lying back on the warm stones.

"I'm quite comfortable," Howard said, although he looked anything but.

"Don't you ever relax? Think about simple things, the sea and the sun? You are at the seaside."

"Nothing is simple. The sea has been rolling like this for thousands of years, and the sun shining. And long after we're dead and forgotten, and our children and our children's children are dead and forgotten, the sea will still be rolling in exactly the same way, only perhaps a little higher – it has been encroaching upon the Castle for some years now – and the sun will still be shining on a world we shall know nothing of."

"Why don't you think of today?" Vanessa said, admiring, as she always did, the back of his neck. "I don't know why you worry about thousands of years from now when we shan't even be here to see it."

"That's the whole point. It's so important to find out why we're here at all like so many grains of sand or pebbles on this beach. Are we any more important?"

"It's a pity we can't swim," Vanessa said, changing the subject. "It looks lovely here."

"You carry on," Howard said. "Don't worry about me."

"I haven't brought my swimming things." How could he be so obtuse? She wanted to shake him, shock him out of his apathy into some awareness of her. "Of course, I could go without. There's nobody around except us."

Howard turned round to face her as she lay defiantly on the stones.

She held his gaze, saying to herself, please notice me, Howard; look into my eyes and see how much I love you.

It was a few minutes before he turned away from her. When he did he ignored her remark and said: "What about having dinner tonight at the 'Landscape'?" He sounded quite different from when he had been talking about Walmer Castle. His voice was softer, less pompous. He spoke like a man to a woman. Vanessa sat up, her back aching from the stones.

"I'd like that very much," she said.

The car-park of the 'Landscape' was full. They found a small space for the Hillman between a bronze Bentley and a racy red sports, and Vanessa, her high-heeled sandals crunching on the gravel, got out and shook out the skirt of her pale blue organza dress into which she had changed. Faint sounds of dance music seeped out of the road-house and floated over the still, dusking air towards the car-park.

"It sounds quite gay," Vanessa said. "I didn't know there was dancing."

"Neither did I." Howard put a hand beneath her elbow to guide her over the stones.

The head waiter shook his head.

"I'm terribly sorry," he said to Howard. "You see, on Wednesdays and Saturdays we have dancing, and being August we're packed out tonight. Every table is booked."

Howard said: "Can I speak to Mr Westropp? He is the owner, is he not?"

"That's right, sir. I think he's busy in the bar just now though."

Howard took out his wallet and from it removed a small visiting-card. "Will you give him this, please? I'll wait."

Mr Westropp of the ginger, handlebar moustache was out of the bar and coming towards them, hands extended, within three minutes.

"My dear chap," he said to Howard, "I'm honoured, deeply honoured. How did you know this was my place?"

"I was in the bar the other day. I didn't get a chance to talk to you."

Howard introduced Vanessa and Mr Westropp, his moustache twitching, said: "Charmed, dear young lady. If it hadn't been for your...your...er... Pennington-Dalby here I would have been in an extremely nasty spot to er...say the least of it."

"What made you come down here?" Howard said. "This isn't exactly your line, is it?"

Westropp glanced round furtively with his pale-blue bloodshot eyes.

"I thought I ought to have a change of scenery," he said. "A complete break until the hooha died down, see what I mean? 'Smatter of fact this is my last season here. I've put the place on the market and I'm going back to town. Strictly on the level, of course. I've enjoyed it here, mind you, made lots of friends. Of course, in the winter I only have the bars going. The dinners and dancing are only summer stuff for the visitors, extra bunce, what? Can't say it hasn't been peaceful here though. Quiet in the day all winter, and a spot of the old conviviality in the evening with the old log fire in the bar and my regulars. Getting itchy fingers again now though...on the level of course; yearning for the old metropolis. When you're London bred and born... Mustn't bore you though; you want to dine and dance, do you?"

"That was the idea," Howard said.

Mr Westropp beckoned the head waiter from the door of the dining-room. "Anything these good people want, Mr Oliver...a bottle of champagne...and on the house if you please, Mr Oliver."

Howard started forward to protest but Mr Westropp, advancing until the moustache nearly tickled Howard's face, said: "If it hadn't been for you I might only have been able to offer cocoa from a tin mug, what? Never forget, never."

The table was on the floor near the band, which compensated for its musical ineptitude by the enthusiasm of its members.

"I can hardly wait to hear what Mr Westropp has been up to," Vanessa said, against the noise of the music, when they had ordered from what seemed to be a very good menu.

"I can't really divulge that," Howard said. "It was nothing very interesting anyway."

"Oh, Howard!" Vanessa said. "Don't be so stuffy."

Howard looked surprised. "Am I being stuffy?" he said. "I hadn't meant to be tonight. That's what you get from going out with someone more than twice your age. I'm sorry."

Vanessa was touched. "I didn't mean it. I just wanted to know about Mr Westropp."

Howard looked at the eager young face and the clear eyes and the brown, smooth shoulders covered only by a thin, pale blue strap. He smiled and Vanessa, bursting with happiness at his softened face, smiled back.

"I don't even remember all the details," Howard said. "He was mixed up on the fringe of some bank robbery. He was a rear gunner in the Air Force during the war, and when he got out he was looking round for a bit more excitement. An ordinary job of work seemed so dull to him, as it did to a lot of these chaps who'd been heroes for so many years. He couldn't settle to a regular job, five and a half days a week year in year out, so he got involved with a rather unpleasant crowd."

"Was he guilty?" Vanessa's eyes were large.

"I believe so. Fortunately for him, the jury didn't."

"But you got him off?"

"That's right."

"Do you often have to defend people you know are guilty?"

"People I *believe* to be guilty – yes."

"It isn't very honest, is it? I mean Mr Westropp really should be in prison, shouldn't he?"

"So should a lot of people."

"That doesn't make it any better. Don't you ever think about that when you're thinking about the sea and the sun and us being like grains of sand and all those things you think so much about?"

"I do. But you see, Vanessa, I have a living to earn. If somebody comes to me, as young Westropp did, and says 'I'm supposed to have been involved in this bank robbery but in actual fact on the night it took place I was...er...ah...having dinner with some woman in Shepherd's Bush' all I can do is to agree to take his case, if I'm not completely stupid, that is, and present the facts, as he has told them to me, to the jury. It is for them to decide if he is telling the truth, not me."

"But you knew he wasn't telling the truth."

"It's not my job to dispute what he has told me - only to present his case to the court. Had he come to me and said, 'Look here, I was mixed up in this bank robbery all right, but I want you to say I was having dinner at the time with some woman in Shepherd's Bush; I can fix it with her,' then I'd have to tell him that I couldn't appear for him and he'd have to find somebody else. My job is only to present the facts as he tells them to me, not to conspire with him in putting forward some tale he has told me is cooked up, and not deliberately to divert the course of justice."

Vanessa sighed. "I can't see the difference," she said. "If you *know* in your own mind that he's not telling you the truth about this woman in Shepherd's Bush."

Howard said gently, "But it isn't for me to decide that. It simply isn't my job. It's the jury's."

"Well, I think it's dishonest," Vanessa said, and sat back so that the waiter could serve the soup.

During dinner they spoke of 'Le Casse-Croûte' and life at Whitecliffs, and discussed the dancers who sped in time to the music, smoothly passing their table. The girl in the mauve dress, Vanessa said, looked like a model; Howard thought she probably sold shelf paper in Woolworth's. The good-looking man in the smart hacking jacket looked to Vanessa like an actor or a film star; Howard thought he spent his life knocking at doors with insurance policies. There was a middle-aged woman Vanessa admired, dancing so nicely with what must be her son; Howard said most probably she was keeping the young man who was far too attentive to be her son.

"We don't seem able to agree on anything," Vanessa said.

" 'Two men looked out through prison bars'," Howard said.

"Some people can't even see as far as the mud." Vanessa looked at him. "You seem to get awfully disillusioned at the Bar. I don't think it's good for you."

"It's not the Bar," Howard said. "It's old age. Would you like to dance?"

To Vanessa's surprise, he danced well. She imagined him in London spending his evenings in night-clubs dancing with pretty girls, but she didn't like to ask him if he did. He was comfortably taller than she and, a little whoozy from the champagne, she was wondering whether she dared lay her head on his shoulder, which looked broad and inviting, when he said: "Shall we go? It's awfully hot and smoky."

They went through to the bar to say goodbye to Mr Westropp. At the table by the window where Howard had sat with Basil, Doctor Gurney and Arthur Dexter on Sunday morning, Louise was sitting with Harry.

Howard and Vanessa stopped and Louise introduced Harry who said:

"How de do?" without standing up and kept his eyes for a long while on Vanessa. Louise who had flushed, said: "We were just having a drink," as though it wasn't obvious, and Howard, taking Vanessa's arm, said, "Nice to have seen you, Louise; we're just going."

In the car Vanessa said: "What a dreadful type she was with. Do you think he picked her up?"

"I've no idea." Howard backed the car.

"Perhaps she needed rescuing." Vanessa's eyes were wide with romance.

Howard smiled at her. "I'm sure she's old enough to look after herself. I'm afraid we embarrassed her."

"I thought she sat in with her mother every evening."

"It isn't really our business, Vanessa."

"I thought she was too old for that sort of thing."

"The trouble with you," Howard said, "is that you think everyone over twenty-five ought to be in a museum."

"Only women," Vanessa said, looking sideways at him.

The roads back to Whitecliffs were dark and they drove through with their headlights on. In the village everything slept; the shops were shuttered, the High Street deserted.

Howard said: "I feel like some fresh air, don't you?"

Vanessa nodded and he drove on down to the beach.

They parked the car near 'Le Casse-Croûte' and Vanessa took off her high-heeled sandals to walk barefoot on the sand. They stood facing the moon at the water's edge, not talking, just watching the sea which was dark and mirror smooth, slap gently on the beach. Vanessa was surprised to feel Howard's arm around her shoulders; his hand was warm where it touched her skin. She turned to face him and thought I can't believe it. He likes me. His lips were very near and she knew that he was going to kiss her. A sound on the quiet beach distracted her attention. Looking over Howard's shoulder, she saw the lights go on for a moment in 'Le Casse-Croûte', then go off again.

"Howard," Vanessa said. "There's someone in the café."

Howard turned round. "There was, you mean. Look!" She glanced towards where he was pointing. Three youths, the moonlight glinting the jet of their hair, had appeared from behind the café and were running up the small slope towards the road. The last one was pulling a blonde girl behind him.

"Hey!" Howard shouted. "Hey you! Stop!" They looked round for a second, then, running faster, disappeared into the bushes. There was the sound of an engine starting up, then driving away fast.

"I bet they've damn well taken my car," Howard said. "Teddy boys! You wait there and I'll go and see if they've done any damage in the café."

"I'll come with you," Vanessa said. "Don't leave me." She sounded frightened, her evening shattered. Howard took her hand.

They went in through the back door which was open. The kitchen was empty. In the moonlight everything appeared to be in order; the stacks of plates, of saucers, covered with tea-towels, ready for the morning.

"They were probably after the food," Vanessa whispered, "underneath the counter."

She trod softly behind Howard as he went through to the self-service counter, and felt him jerk her hand as he tripped over something in the gloom.

"What was that?" she said.

"Put the light on, Vanessa." His voice was authoritative, harsh. She fumbled for the switch and turned on the light which was on the wall behind the counter. On the floor, face down in a pool of blood, lay a young man. Howard, kneeling down, turned him over gently, but even before he had done so they both recognised him.

"My God!" Vanessa said, supporting herself against the counter. "It's Victor!"

Seventeen

For a moment the walls of the café and the notices, 'Trays For The Beach' and 'Sandwiches To Order' seemed to swim away, then Howard said:

"Give me some tea-towels, Van, lots; then dial nine, nine, nine and ask for the ambulance and police."

She could not control her hands which were shaking as she pulled a stack of clean tea-towels from where they were kept beneath the counter, and handed them to Howard. The nines on the telephone seemed to take an age on their return journey round the dial, and although it was only a minute it seemed like ten before the operator answered her call.

When she had finished Howard said: "You wait at the back for the ambulance. There's nothing much we can do," but trying to master her trembling she said: "It's my brother, Howard, my twin," and kneeling in the blood on the other side of Victor she picked up his hand which lay limp and bleeding on the stone floor and bound it in a towel. She tried not to look at his face. His lips and one eye were bruised and swollen purple. From the other eye and from the hair that had been tow-coloured blood was streaming thickly down.

"There were three of them," Vanessa sobbed.

"By the look of his hands he must have put up a pretty good fight," Howard said.

"Vic would. He never was afraid of anything."

The ambulance and two policemen from the local constabulary arrived together. Howard remained behind to talk to the police, and Vanessa rode with Victor in the ambulance to which a man and a woman in navy blue suits and peaked caps had transferred him gently, carefully, on a stretcher covered by red blankets.

In the ambulance, as they swayed to and fro, the bell ringing, Vanessa said several times: "Vic, Vic," but the swollen lips didn't move.

The woman attendant who was doing what she could with dressings and the already blood-soaked tea-towels, said: "He's lost too much blood, dear," and felt beneath the blankets for his wrist.

Vanessa watched her face which was unmade-up and unmoved, as though it was her nightly habit to minister to boys of eighteen whose flesh was scored with razor slashes, and skin pulped by vicious fists.

"Is he…all right?"

"They'll transfuse him as soon as we get in." She rapped twice on the window where the driver was and Vanessa felt the speed increase, and couldn't stop herself shivering. The woman unfolded another red blanket and put it round her shoulders. Vanessa smiled her thanks.

At the hospital they wheeled Vic away on a trolley down a dark corridor, and showed Vanessa, the red blanket still round her shoulders, into a waiting-room. There were two cane chairs and a slippery leather couch. On a table the morning's *Daily Telegraph* and the *Isle of Thanet Gazette* were tidily folded. There was a plant in a pot that needed water.

Vanessa, wondering what she was supposed to do, sat on the edge of the slippery couch. A young nurse, whose cap was crooked, put her head round the door and said: "Are you the young lady…?" then glanced at Vanessa's blood-stained skirt and said: "Oh, yes" and disappeared again. A few minutes later a bosomy Sister with a navy blue dress, frilled cuffs and a bonnet tied with strings, came in with a cup of tea.

"Are you all right, dear?" she said, her voice belying her fierce appearance. She switched on one bar of the electric fire which was set into the wall, and gave Vanessa the tea.

"They've taken your brother up to the theatre. Doctor Potts is up there now."

They never say anything, Vanessa thought. One always has to ask.

"Will he be all right?"

"I'm only from Casualty," the Sister said. "I just came to see if you were all right. You must have had rather a shock. Doctor Potts will send a message down as soon as he's had a look at your brother. Are you warm enough, dear?" She moved the *Daily Telegraph* an inch, then crackled out, her apron standing away from her skirt.

When the door opened next it was Howard. Without thinking she ran towards him and, leaning against him, let the tears she had been holding back flow freely.

His arms were round her holding her tightly, and she noticed that his usually immaculate stiff collar was spattered with Vic's blood.

"Don't cry, my love," Howard said. "Vanessa, please don't cry. He'll be all right. We have to be thankful we were around at the right moment."

Vanessa raised her head from his shoulder. "I never thought of that, of course. We might not have found him till the morning...and by then...for sure...oh Howard!"

Howard dried her tears clumsily on his large breast pocket handkerchief, then led her to the couch.

"What about Mummy and Daddy?" Vanessa said.

"I rang Doctor Gurney from the café and explained. He said he'd go across and tell them. I thought it would be less of a shock like that. He said he'd bring them down here."

"What was Vic doing in the café?" Vanessa said, "at this time of night?"

"That's what we shall have to find out," Howard said.

"Have the police gone after those…those…thugs?"

"They're looking for my car. It might give them a clue."

"Poor Vic." Vanessa, recalling the sight of his face, began to cry again. "We were having such a lovely evening."

Arthur and Vera arrived with Doctor Gurney; Vera was sobbing into a lace handkerchief. Arthur said: "See that they get the best surgeons, Gurney. We can get someone from London if there's time. Tell them not to worry about the expense…"

From the door of the waiting-room a young man in a white coat, with carroty hair, said quietly: "I'm Doctor Potts. I've just operated on your son. He had multiple lacerations on the face and body and had lost a considerable amount of blood, which we've replaced. It was lucky he wasn't brought in any later."

"Will he be all right?" Vera said, her face swollen and plain from crying.

Doctor Potts looked at his nails, then plunged his hands into his deep pockets and rocked back on his heels. He looked at Arthur and Vera.

"I doubt if we shall be able to save his eye," he said. "Mr Wells, our consultant ophthalmologist is coming to have a look at him in the morning. There's nothing more we can do for him tonight."

"Can we see him?" Vera asked.

Doctor Potts said: "I don't advise it, Mrs Dexter. Perhaps your husband…"

Vanessa said: "Don't see him tonight, Mummy," and looking at Doctor Potts in his white coat was reminded suddenly of Cliff. He did not look all that much older. In a few years Cliff would be doing the same job…

Arthur was saying, "If you think we should move him to London, Doctor Potts, the Royal Masonic, if you like, I am a Freemason…"

Doctor Potts said: "Your son has been nearly an hour in the theatre, Mr Dexter. He is lucky to be alive."

"There's no point in moving him," Doctor Gurney said.

"I don't like the idea of these local hospitals," Arthur said. Doctor Potts walked out of the room.

"Where's he gone?" Arthur said.

Doctor Gurney said, "I expect he's done a big job on Victor if he was up there for an hour. I don't expect he was very impressed by the fact that all you could think of was moving him. He's probably saved Victor's life."

Arthur seemed to sag, and sat down on one of the cane chairs.

"I only wanted to do the best for the boy," he said, "I didn't mean anything."

"I'll go and square it with him," Doctor Gurney said. "He'll understand."

Arthur, his head in his hands, said wearily: "Tell me what happened, Howard."

They waited until Victor had come round from the anaesthetic, and Doctor Potts and Doctor Gurney were satisfied with his blood pressure before they left the hospital. It was two o'clock. At midnight a policemen had arrived to tell Howard they had found his car abandoned in a sidestreet in Merrydown. No incriminating evidence had been left behind except the smell of cheap perfume. They were holding the car for the fingerprint men in the morning.

"Have you started looking for them yet?" Arthur asked the policeman, a smooth-faced youth who looked very new to his job.

"Well, sir, we haven't anything to go on just yet."

"Pennington-Dalby here has told you it was Teddy boys, hasn't he? Round them up and question them. What are you waiting for? They can be in Timbuctoo by the morning."

"Round up all the Teddy boys, sir?" The policeman's face was pink.

"Of course."

"Have you ever been to Merrydown at night, sir?"

"No."

"There are hundreds of them, sir. All got up the same. We've got to have something to go on, sir."

"You're so slow," Arthur said, standing up. "My son has been nearly sliced to pieces and is in danger of losing his sight, and you just stand there! Those boys are going to be found if I have to question every one of them myself."

"There's nothing more we can do tonight," Howard said. "Perhaps by the morning Victor will be well enough to tell us something."

"I've instructions to wait for the young man's statement," the policeman said.

"Yes, sir."

Arthur said, looking at him, "I must be getting very old."

In Arthur's flat, to which they all went back in Doctor Gurney's car, they found the lights on and Mary Gurney waiting for them. "I've got the kettle on," she said. "I thought you'd like some tea. How's Victor?"

Her husband kissed her. "He's round from the anaesthetic but they've given him morphia for the pain. They had to do a lot of sewing-up. He doesn't yet know what's going on."

Vera was crying again, and when Mrs Gurney brought in the tea in the breakfast cups she didn't even notice. She didn't notice either that she had put on odd shoes in her hurry to get out.

"What I don't understand," Arthur said, "is what Victor was doing in the café at all. Why did he have the keys? It was Louise's turn to open up."

"Perhaps he changed with her," Vanessa said. "Although I don't see why he should. Vic hates to get up early."

"We'd better ask Louise," Arthur said.

Howard said, "You can't disturb her now. I'll go down first thing in the morning. We shan't be able to open up tomorrow anyway. The police want to investigate the café and want us all to stay here for questioning."

"What happens next?" Arthur said.

"Well, the first thing they have to do is to find out who did it. Once they've done that the police can prosecute."

"I suppose you'll appear for Victor?" Arthur said.

Howard shook his head. "I couldn't do that, I'm afraid, because I found him and saw the boys running off. I should certainly be called as a witness. I advise you to inform your solicitor in the morning, and when it's necessary he'll instruct counsel for you. Of course, you have to face the possibility that they won't find out who did it. There are so many of these coshings and beatings-up these days, so many irresponsible hooligans, that it's not very easy. Most of these boys carry flick knives and razors."

"It's fantastic," Arthur said. "Can't anything be done?"

"A lot of them are backward, come from broken, unsettled homes..."

"But what did they have against Victor? He's only a schoolboy."

"I don't know," Howard said, "unless it was something to do with the girl."

Vera said, "What girl?"

"They had a girl with them. I told the police. A blonde girl. I wonder...?"

"What?" Arthur said. "Have you thought of something?"

"Only that a week or so ago, in the café, Victor asked me to look after his window for him while he went to...er...talk to some girl he'd seen on the beach. She was a blonde; I remember Victor saying so."

"Someone he knew?" Vera asked.

"I don't think so."

"You mean he just went up and spoke to some strange girl?"

"I wouldn't be certain," Howard said.

"Did you know anything about this, Vanessa?" her mother asked.

"Vic never told me anything about his girl friends until he was fed up with them. I didn't know he had anyone down here."

"Of course, I may be wrong," Howard said.

Vera said, "I think you must be, Howard. I hardly think Victor would go and speak to some strange girl on the beach he didn't even know. He went out with such nice girls in London. You remember that Anderson girl, Arthur, cousin of Sir William Anderson...?"

"Do you realize what a mess he'll look," Arthur said, "and he may be blind in one eye! God knows what he went through, too, tonight, poor boy, and you sit there talking about some girl he went out with, which isn't the slightest bit important."

Vera began to cry again. "There's no need to shout at me, Arthur. How do you think I feel? It's the sort of thing you read about in the newspapers. I can't believe that it's happened to us, to Victor."

"It's my fault," Arthur said. "We should never have come here. I must have been mad. What are we doing here anyway?"

Doctor Gurney stood up. "I think you should go to bed," he said to Arthur and Vera.

"I couldn't sleep," Vera said.

"I'll go upstairs and get you something to take," Doctor Gurney said, "something stronger than your pink tablets. I expect you'll both need it."

"Could I have something, too?" Vanessa said. "I keep thinking of Vic lying on the floor...it was horrible!"

"I think she needs it more than anyone," Howard said. "It wasn't very nice."

Vera said: "Poor darling, I was forgetting. I still don't know how it was that you and Howard were at the café tonight anyway."

Howard's eyes met Vanessa's across the room.

"We were on the beach," Vanessa said.

"At ten o'clock at night? What on earth were you on the beach for at that hour?"

"We wanted some fresh air," Howard told her.

"But why in the café?" Vera said.

"We weren't in the café, mother," Vanessa said, "not till afterwards when we saw the lights go on. We were down by the sea."

"But what an odd time to be down by the sea. You said you were going..."

"I think Vanessa's had enough for one night, Mrs Dexter," Doctor Gurney said, and Vanessa looked at him gratefully. She didn't think she would forget, not after a night's sleep, not ever, the sight of Victor lying on the floor in his own blood. Not Victor who swanked and boasted and listened to Beethoven and jazz and didn't care about anything much and who had been glad to come to Whitecliffs to look for what he called 'local talent'. Perhaps she should tell them about that, although she hadn't known what he had been up to. They never told each other. She hadn't told Vic anything about Howard... Her parents and Doctor and Mrs Gurney had gone out into the hall. Howard was next to her chair. He said: "Are you all right?"

"Yes. It was pretty horrid, wasn't it?"

"Try not to think about it. He'll be all right." He leaned to kiss her forehead.

Vanessa, her face lifted up to his, said: "Howard...?" She wanted to know if he loved her or if he was being kind.

"Yes?"

"Nothing. It doesn't matter." She couldn't very well ask.

She went with him to the hall where the others were still talking. A bell rang shrilly.

"It's the front door," Vera said. "Open it quickly, Arthur. Perhaps it's the police... Victor?"

They watched silently beneath the Venetian glass light as Arthur opened the front door. In the doorway stood a very pretty girl with auburn hair and violet eyes. The collar of her camel hair coat was turned up round her neck. She was carrying a white leather suitcase.

"I'm sorry to disturb you," she said, and her face looked tired although her lipstick was bright. "I wouldn't have, only I saw the lights and guessed you must be having a party..."

"It's not a party," Arthur said grimly. "What is it you want?"

"I'm looking for Mr Benwell's flat. I know this is the block but I'm afraid I've forgotten the number. I thought perhaps you could help me."

"There's no Mr Benwell here. I'm sorry."

"This is Shore Court, isn't it?"

"That's right. But there's no Mr Benwell."

Perhaps you don't know him. I'm sure..."

"I own the place," Arthur said, "I know everyone. You must excuse me. I'm not in the mood to..."

Howard said: "Just a minute. Benwell? Isn't that Basil's name?"

The girl smiled at him. She was very beautiful. "It's Basil I'm looking for. I know he said Shore Court, it was on all his letters."

"I'm sorry," Arthur said, "I didn't realise. It's Number Six, above this."

"Sorry for butting in," the girl said, and picked up her case.

When she'd gone Vera said: "What a funny time of night to arrive! Who do you think she is?"

"I don't know," Howard said, "but I should imagine it's Basil's wife."

Eighteen

"Elisabeth!" Basil said, peering blearily, not properly awake, into the hall. He remembered that he had been in a deep sleep when the bell rang, and that it must be some time in the middle of the night.

"Has something happened, Elisabeth? Are you all right? What time is it?"

"Nothing's happened." She looked at him, his pyjamas rumpled, his hair on end. "May I come in?"

Suddenly thoroughly awake, Basil leaned forward and took her case from her. "Elisabeth," he said, as though he had just seen her.

She followed him into the bedroom where he put on his dressing-gown. He looked round, seeing it with her eyes. "It's a bit sordid," he said.

Elisabeth said, "On the contrary. It looks very tidy for you."

"Come inside," Basil said, "there's a fire in the sitting-room I can switch on. It isn't very warm. How did you come?"

"By car."

"At this time of night?"

"I got lost once or twice."

"You never did have a sense of direction."

The sitting-room had an unlived-in look, and when Basil switched on the stove it smelled of burned dust.

"You haven't a drink, have you Basil?"

"For you? Are you all right, Elisabeth? Did you have dinner? You look cold."

"Just a little tired. If you've some whisky. The drive made me feel a bit shaky. The roads were so dark. I suppose I was nervous. I'm sorry about this; it's a stupid time to arrive. I just made up my mind and I felt I couldn't wait until the morning."

She sat curled on the hearthrug still in her coat, the red of her hair shimmering in the light.

Basil put a glass into her hands, which were twisting nervously before the pink glow of the fire, and said: "Why did you come, Elisabeth?"

"First, tell me if you're glad."

Basil sat on the very edge of the armchair, holding his glass, and watched her. "I'm so glad," he said, "that this is one of the most wonderful moments of my life. I don't know if you've come back to me. I know I don't deserve you. But I love you, Elisabeth, and with you sitting there the flat looks suddenly like home. I don't know if I shall be able to stand it if you've come to tell me there's someone else; that you want a divorce. I suppose that is what it is. You'd better tell me; don't be afraid, Elisabeth. I'll try not to make it difficult or embarrassing for you."

Elisabeth looked down at her drink, then into the fire.

"I came back because I'm going to have a baby," she said.

"But Elisabeth…"

"I know. You'll be very angry. I had a suspicion, you see, when I left you. I'd got myself all worked up and rather at the end of my tether, wondering who would support all three of us, and my idea was to go home, and if I was pregnant to get rid of it."

"You had no right…"

"I said you'd be angry. I got as far as going to see this doctor, and it was all terribly smooth and simple as long as you had the money, and that wasn't very difficult – I told father I needed a new fur coat – and two psychiatrists saw me and answered their own questions, and I had the bed booked and everything, and when the day came I just couldn't go through with it. I went to the pictures and saw the same film three times – Frank Sinatra in a night club – then I came out and cancelled the whole thing."

Basil took a sip of his drink. "I suppose it's just because of the baby you've come back," he tried to sound casual, to hide his disappointment.

"No, Basil. If it had been only because of the baby I should have come back ages ago. I waited to see; to sort things out in my own mind. I went round and round in circles and always came back to the same point."

"What was that?"

"A fundamental one. I love you. I don't know how we shall manage, what will become of us, my father won't help me any more, but I want you and I want our baby. I'm sorry that I walked out. It wasn't that I didn't love you, didn't have faith in you, you know I always have had. It was just that I was tired, terribly tired, my nerves were on edge…"

"Elisabeth, don't!" Basil said. "I can't believe, looking back, I did those things to you. I can only think I could not have been quite sane."

Elisabeth finished her drink and putting her glass on the hearth, kneeled round to face Basil. Her violet eyes opened wide.

"Tell me you want me back."

"I wrote to you."

"I know. I want you to say it." She raised a hand towards his face.

"Elisabeth, don't!" Basil drew back.

"What is it?" The violet eyes were puzzled, hurt as well as tired from driving through the night.

Basil stood up and, putting his hands in the pockets of his dressing-gown, went over to the window although he could see nothing in the black night. With his back to Elisabeth, he said: "I'm afraid I've made a hash of things, Elisabeth."

"How do you mean?"

Still not looking at her, he said: "I was fed up, desperate, and there was this girl, Honey, she was always laughing...it meant less than nothing, it was just that...well, a man can't cry, Elisabeth."

"I see," Elisabeth said.

"I suppose I've torn it properly now."

"I have to get used to the idea. It wouldn't have happened if I hadn't walked out. Or would it?"

Basil turned round. "Elisabeth!"

"I'm sorry. I know it wouldn't."

"You won't go away again now I've told you?"

Elisabeth stood up. "No, I won't go away. Only..."

"I understand. I wish it hadn't happened."

"You must give me a little time..."

"As long as you want. Only stay, Elisabeth."

He watched her take off her coat. She had a thick, white jumper over a fawn skirt.

"You don't look any different."

"I'm done up with safety-pins underneath."

"When will it be born?"

"At Christmas time."

"I'm terribly pleased, Elisabeth. I hope it will be a girl. Beautiful, like you."

"And with your brains."

"I have no brains. I had an illusion that I was capable of greatness. I suppose every man has at one time or another. I clung to my illusion too long. You needn't worry about me writing any more. I've given it up, put it all away. I am as other men. I'll look after you, Elisabeth; you and the baby. I'll make it all up to you. I promise."

"Do you mind if I go to bed?" Elisabeth said, sitting suddenly on the arm of the chair. "I must be tireder than I thought."

"Darling!" Basil said. "How thoughtless of me! That long drive, and the baby... Are you sure you're all right?"

Elisabeth smiled. "Of course."

"I'll make the other bed up. That is… I'm afraid there's only one bedroom… I understand how you feel… Perhaps…"

Elisabeth smiled. "Basil, don't. I'll help you with the bed."

Basil picked up her coat from the settee. "Those days are over. You sit down. I'll see to everything." At the door he said:

"Thank you for coming back, Elisabeth. I know I don't deserve it but you've made me terribly happy."

She looked at him unwaveringly, her eyes black-ringed pansies in moonlight.

"Don't thank me, Basil," she said. "I've only come home."

Louise, her hair loose on the pillow, her nose slightly pink, her hands encased in cotton sleeping gloves, lay in a dreamy, pleasant, half-waking state, thinking of Harry. It was not quite time to get up. She could feel the sun, up early, shining through the thin pink cotton curtains on to her eyelids. Lying there, her face was not shiny, her nose not pink, her nightdress not serviceable lawn, her hands most certainly not in gloves. She was lying, she thought smilingly, on a pillow strewn with rosebuds; naturally the sheets were bordered, a wide border, with the same; her skin was smooth, matt, one would almost suppose made-up; her hair was gold, her features, tiny, provocative, and her body, which left nothing to be desired, lay impertinently in transparent nylon; black, she thought; yes, most certainly it would be black. She had bought a nylon nightdress once, only it hadn't been black; pale blue, she remembered, and light as a dream. She had been cold all night though, and hadn't slept a wink; the next day she had given it to one of the girls in the salon and gone back to the warmth and comfort of lawn. She really wanted to think about Harry. Last night had been fun, more fun than she had had for a long time. Harry seemed to like her, he really did. She had no illusions. She knew he was a bit common, probably a thoroughly bad type, but he was interested in her, whatever his reasons. He made her feel protected, wanted, as one only felt when one was with a man, and as she hadn't felt for an awfully long time. When you were a woman on your own you couldn't just slop or dissolve into tears as married women did, you had to stand on your own feet. She was expected to look after her mother, make the decisions, be a tower of strength. It was the same at the salon. She was in charge of the girls, the one who told them what to do, chastised them, praised them, chased them up and very often advised them. Nobody ever wondered that she had no one to turn to, no one to help her with the gas bills, the burst pipe, the loose joist in the bedroom floor at home, the insurance, the payments on the television, the income tax. There was always something to worry about, and never anyone to share the worry with. It was the same in a way when something pleasant happened, something amusing or enjoyable at work. She might be bubbling over, warm with whatever it was that had happened, but there was never anyone to tell it to or share it with. Her mother was only interested in herself, and she had no real friends. By the time she had kept her excitement to herself for a few hours it had burned itself out or gone sour, or was forgotten in the necessary trivia of her daily routine. Harry had been someone to talk to. He listened to her, seemed interested in what she told him; they laughed together, joked. True, last night she had paid for the drinks but what did it matter? She hadn't laughed so much for ages. Harry had told her about his landlady, about the feuds amongst the cast of the concert party, about the pianist who was in love with the trombone who was in love with one of the stage hands. There was something else, too. Two other things, in fact, that needed thinking about. One was that Harry had kissed her. Of course, she had seen it coming, she wasn't stupid. He had been looking at her in a certain way all evening, and just before they left the 'Landscape' he had taken her hand and squeezed it, and then as they waited in the dark, country road for the bus that ran only every half hour which would take them back to Whitecliffs, he had suddenly gathered her in his arms. And because it was dark she had forgotten the too bold stripes on his suit, the over-padded shoulders, the new look of his teeth, the artificial silk of his breast-pocket handkerchief, and smelled only the tobacco and the manliness of him, and felt that she was wanted. She supposed it was the drinks, but she hadn't been at all scared, not even when he held her tightly, almost crushing her to him, and he had said, shut your eyes, Louise, and she remembered that on the films they always shut their eyes when they were being kissed. When the bus came she had felt shy and rather shaky in the light, and imagined everyone was looking at her. Harry had seemed not at all moved, but appeared to be thinking, and was quiet all the way to Whitecliffs. At the bus stop where he left her he said: "Will you meet me at the 'Landscape' on Saturday night, Louise? I've something important to ask you," and she had said, "All right, Harry," and all the way back to the flat had wondered what it could be. Could it be marriage? If this was a film that was what it would be. But this wasn't a film, it was life, and about life Louise had very few illusions. If Harry wanted to marry her it would be because she was capable of earning a good living, easily enough for two, because she could cook and sew and make a home, and he wouldn't have to worry too much about music-hall in the winter, and in the summer Southend and Clacton and Merrydown, and there would always be enough cigarettes and enough to drink. And on the other side of the coin Louise would no longer be alone, and she would have status because she had a man by her side, even though he was not her type, nothing like, in fact, and she would have someone to share things with and talk to at night, after work, and there might be something more to look forward to than the black dress and the shawl and loneliness before the television. She might even be able to persuade Harry to get a regular job and stop wearing those awful suits, and not drink quite so much. He could be quite presentable more quietly dressed; he had a good physique, and really nice hands. Her mother would live with them, of course.

Harry wouldn't mind that, he was very kind-hearted, she had noticed that… She was letting her thoughts get out of hand. Perhaps it hadn't been anything like that at all he wanted to ask her. But his tone of voice, the lingering look he gave her, what else could it be? She would have to wait until Saturday to find out, meanwhile it was pleasant to daydream; to let her imagination run on. The sound of the front door bell brought her in a moment out of her reverie. Her eyes, quickly opened, saw no rosebud pillowslip, no nylon nightie, only the pink curtains with the sun shining through, and her clothes, unglamorous, where she had left them on the chair the night before.

"There's someone at the door, Louise!"

"I know, I'm going, Mother," she called. She pulled off her sleeping gloves and struggled into the cotton, candy-striped housecoat which made it not unpleasant to get up because it was summery and pretty. She brushed her hair back with two quick strokes over her shoulders, stooping to look in to the mirror, and put her feet into her slippers.

"Who is it, Louise? Perhaps it's bad news or a registered letter."

"I haven't gone yet. I wasn't up."

"You do take a time."

Outside on the landing, fully dressed as usual in his clean stiff collar, stood Howard. Louise blushed because her hair wasn't done and she wasn't dressed.

"I thought it was the postman," she said, then: "I'm not opening up this morning, you know. I gave the keys to Victor. He asked me to change with him…"

"That's what I want to talk to you about," Howard said. "I'm sorry to disturb you, but something has happened to Victor…"

Louise wasn't able to help much. She told Howard that Victor had asked her yesterday morning if she would mind changing early duty at 'Le Casse-Croûte' with him, and she had given him the keys, thinking no more about it. It hadn't even occurred to her to ask him why. Upset and depressed by what had happened she shut the door after Howard, and turned towards the kitchen.

"You were a long time, Louise. Who was it?"

"It was Howard, mother, Mr Pennington-Dalby. Something about the café." She took the kettle off the gas stove and started to fill it with water. It was then she remembered the first night she had met Harry at the pavilion and that they had seen Victor there with that blonde girl. Harry had said at the time he knew who the girl was, but they hadn't pursued the conversation. She would dress quickly and go and see if she could find Harry. She didn't even know where he lodged, but perhaps someone at the concert party place would be able to tell her. It would be nice if she could throw some light on the situation to help Mr Dexter. Not that it would do Victor much good, but the Dexters had been so kind she would like to do something to help. Poor Victor, it made her go cold to think of it. A razor gang…ugh…

"Are you making the tea, Louise?" The voice without its teeth, was more than ever plaintive.

"I'm coming, Mother."

Nineteen

Upstairs, on his own landing, Howard found Honey dressed in pink trousers and jumper, about to ring Basil's doorbell. She had no shoes or stockings on, and her toe-nails matched her outfit.

"Good morning, Your Worship," she said, turning to him and bowing low until her long black hair almost swept the ground.

Her lipstick matched, too.

"I wouldn't go in there if I were you," Howard said, looking for his key.

"Why?"

Howard found his key. "His wife came back last night."

Honey crossed the little passage. "Elisabeth?"

"If that's her name. Pretty girl with red hair."

"That's Elisabeth." She shrugged, her face serious for just a moment. "Well, that's that." She smiled again and putting her hands in her pockets started to whistle.

Howard opened his door. "You'd better come in for a moment," he said. "I have something to tell you."

In the little sitting-room Honey said: "My word, you are a tidy one. Not like Basil."

"You were fond of Basil, weren't you?"

Honey sat on the sofa and drew her knees up to her chin. Over them her eyes were wide-looking at Howard who was lighting his pipe.

"I don't mind telling you," she said. "You're like a doctor or a…a Judge or something. I have the feeling you can see through me. I don't have to put on an act. You don't say a lot but I don't think you miss much either. I suppose I am a bit in love with Basil; he doesn't know it. There wasn't any point in saying anything. It's difficult to explain but when I was with Basil I felt different…as if life could be something else but what it is…for me at any rate…there's something about Basil, he's straight, honest… Anyway I'm glad she's come back. He needs her." She shook her hair as though dismissing Basil from her thoughts, and curled her pink toes on the cushions.

Looking at her through the haze of smoke which burst fitfully from his pipe, Howard thought, she is Eve. I have seen her in court, many times, in the theatre, on the streets. She is pure woman; a body with little soul or brain but a heart that is overflowing for mankind. She does not know it, that I understand her, pity her. She wants admiration, not pity. Pity would drown her. She knows how to keep her head above water.

"What did you want to tell me?" Honey said. "It's getting late. I have to get down to the café."

"It won't be open this morning," Howard said. "I'm afraid something has happened to Victor."

When he'd finished telling her, Honey stood up, tears were welling into her eyes. "I've no hanky," she said, and accepted the one which Howard held out. She wiped her eyes, blew her nose and put the handkerchief into her pocket. "Filthy louts!" she said. "Thank you for telling me. It's been quite a morning what with one thing and another."

Howard saw her out, and watched her go down the stairs. She didn't go right down to her own flat but stopped outside the Dexters' and rang the bell.

Arthur Dexter opened the door.

"Yes?" he said, his voice revealing the kind of night he had spent.

"I've come to see if there's anything I can do to help," Honey said.

Howard saw her go in and the door close behind her.

"Despise not any man," he said to himself, "and carp not at anything; for there is not a man that has not his hour, and there is not a thing that has not its place."

He wondered how soon the police would come, and went inside to make his breakfast.

Honey, a cup of tea in her hand, knocked on Vanessa's door. There was no reply so she opened the door softly and went in. Among the pink and white stripes, through which the sun was filtering, Vanessa slept. As Honey put the tea down by the bed she opened her eyes, then shut them again, then opened them and looked uncomprehendingly at Honey.

"What are you doing here?" she said as Honey opened the curtains and let the sun flow into the room.

"I came to see if I could help. Your mother's in rather a state this morning."

Vanessa was silent for a moment then she sat up, leaning on her elbow, and said: "Of course. It must have been that tablet that Doctor Gurney gave me to help me sleep. I didn't remember for a moment about Victor. I just had the vague sort of feeling you sometimes have when you wake up that something unpleasant has happened, and that it isn't going to be a very nice day, but I couldn't remember what or why. Have they heard anything?"

"He's all right, but they're still keeping him heavily doped because of the pain. He hasn't said anything yet."

"I was hoping it was only a nightmare. I can hardly believe it's actually happened to Victor. It's the sort of thing you read in the newspapers. It happens to other people and you say 'Tut tut, how shocking' or 'Oh, dear', and go on to read the women's page. You never actually know how it feels to have it happen to your own family, your own brother. I suppose you never can until it actually does. Poor old Vic! Did they say anything more about his eye?"

"I don't think so."

"Do you think it was just an accident, Honey? I mean do you think they were just looking for somebody to beat up, or do you think they had it in for Vic? That he got mixed up in something down here?"

"I don't know, Van. Why don't you drink your tea?"

"I feel sick."

"You'll be better if you have something. Just think how lucky it was that you found him. It might have been a lot worse."

"Yes, I suppose it might," her mind going back to the night before and Howard and the beach and the moment when he had been about to kiss her and then the horror of tripping over Victor, and the warm stickiness of Victor's blood…

"How's it going with Howard?" Honey tried to change the subject.

Vanessa looked at her, silhouetted against the bright window. She looked like an advert for something, a pin-up on a calendar.

"I wish I knew," she said. "He's awfully sort of difficult to get anywhere with. I mean…"

"You're in love with him, obviously."

Vanessa sighed. "I can't think about anything else. The trouble is he doesn't… I suppose I'm not old enough or sophisticated enough or something…he treats me as if I were a child. Honey?"

"Mmm?"

"You've had lots of boyfriends. You know how to talk to them. Tell me what to do. How can I make him take me seriously?"

Honey looked at her. Sitting up in bed, Vanessa looked almost a schoolgirl still. What advice could she give to a girl who came from another world? When she was Vanessa's age she had known for years how to get her man. It was a knowledge she could never remember not having, but even if she could put it into words it wouldn't help Vanessa. It had little to do with love, certainly nothing at all to do with marriage.

"I suggested going swimming with nothing on," Vanessa said. "He just looked shocked."

Honey smiled. "I'm not surprised. It isn't exactly you."

"Oh, you think I'm so stuck up," Vanessa said, "and when I'm with you, you make me act like it and conscious that I've been to good schools and have got clothes and can play tennis and the piano and all those things, but I don't think I wouldn't like to change, any day at all, with you."

"For what?"

"For knowing how to make men look at you like they do. I'd give anything for Howard to look at me like that. I think I'd die of happiness. Until last night I hadn't dreamed of anything else since we've been here. It seems awful talking like this with Victor lying there in hospital all cut up, but even now, you see, I can only think of Howard and how I can get him to marry me. I wish I was a man, then I could ask him."

"You could ask him," Honey said. "I don't suppose he realises…"

"I'd be making myself awfully cheap. I'd even seduce him if I knew how."

Honey smiled. How could one explain to this child what she could do, without thinking, with her eyes alone. Suddenly she felt protective, wise, as if life had given her more than it had Vanessa, like a mother to her daughter.

"I would give it time," Honey said, "sooner or later he will see it in your eyes."

Louise trailed down the side streets of Merrydown, on what she hoped was the last lap of her chase. When she had started out she had been so worried and upset about what had happened to Victor that she hadn't given a thought to the fact that Harry might be annoyed with her for coming to his digs. He hadn't told her where he lodged, except that it was somewhere in Merrydown, and it had taken her almost half the morning to find out. She had gone first to the main pavilion, in the garden of which the children's concert parties were held. The notices were outside leaning against the hedges advertising the afternoon's show, but the place had appeared deserted. She went down the long flight of stone steps and peered, her face cupped in her hands, through the glass panels of the doors; she could see nothing, the place appeared to be in uninterrupted darkness. A gardener trimming the flowerbeds looked at her curiously.

"Do you know where anyone from the concert party might be?" she asked him. "I have to find one of them. It's awfully important."

The gardener had been helpful and glad of a chat. He told her that this year's show was a sight better than last summer's, that there was one real good-looking young lady in the company, and why did people throw their ice-cream papers on the lawns when there were all them litter bins plain as plain. He then told her that with any luck she might find the caretaker if she went round to the stage door, and he might be able to help her.

The stage door was open, but nobody seemed to be about. Louise walked in, and down a dark, damp-smelling corridor. She peered into dusty dressing-rooms and musty corners. Bits of electrical equipment, old, curling advertisements and a crudely painted tree were lying about. At the end of the corridor, in a tiny room lit by a single bulb, an old man with a yellow moustache was drinking tea from a tin mug and picking a horse from the back page of a newspaper. He said 'Oh' and 'Ah' and 'Yes, Miss' and 'No, Miss', and finally admitted that he had a list somewhere with the information that she required. She waited while he finished his tea, folded his newspaper, got stiffly up, complained about his lumbago, found his glasses which had only one side-piece to them, picked up his bunch of keys and ambled off down the corridor. Not knowing whether she was supposed to wait or accompany him, she followed him down a further dark passage and up some stairs. With much selecting and rejecting, he found a key from his bunch and opened a door into a small room in which there seemed to be nothing much but a gas stove and a dressing-gown hanging behind a door. On the wall, amongst other notices, was pinned a list. The old man, peering over the tops of his glasses, ran a filthy finger down the names. "Mabel 'Enderson," he said, "Olive Campbell, she's the one what does the disappearin' for the kiddies, ah, 'ere we are, 'Arry Jessup, that's 'im, le'ssee, 51 Poet's Road, Merrydown, tha'ssit."

"I'm very grateful," Louise said, looking in her bag for half-a-crown. "Where exactly is Poet's Road?"

"Poet's Road? Well, Miss, you know the 'Penny Whistle', corner of the 'Igh Street opposight the 'arbour? Well, it's back o' there. Be'ind the 'Green Man', be'ind the 'Iron Dook' and be'ind the gas-works. Not that you wouldn't be better off, being a stranger like, to take the bus to the market place and go round by the Tudor 'ouses..."

"I'll find it," Louise said, giving him half-a-crown, "and thank you for your help."

His "Much obliged, Miss," followed her down the corridor, as did his slow and curious stare.

She asked three visitors to Merrydown, who looked at her blankly and said they were 'strangers here' themselves, before she found a coal-man who directed her reasonably sensibly to Poet's Road. The smell from the gas-works pursued her as she walked past terrace after terrace of dingy houses, some of which had cards in the window which announced greyly 'Vacancies', and some of which did not. Poet's Road was no different from Clitheroe Road, Fountayne Road and Hewitt Road, down which she had already walked. She wondered what poets had to do with it. Number Fifty-One had no card in the window, curtains with bobbles on the bottom, and an unwashed step. After she had rung twice and was really sorry that in the heat of the moment she had come, the door was opened by the ageing soubrette of the concert party who had sung 'Only a Rose' and 'Because'. She was in, or rather, half in, a pink satin dressing-gown, and had her hair in curlers. She removed the cigarette from her mouth with slightly grubby-looking, nicotine-stained fingers, and looked through half-closed eyes at Louise.

"Yes?"

"I'm sorry," Louise said, meaning she was sorry to have got her out of bed. "I'm looking for…er…for Uncle Harry. Mr Jessup, that is."

The woman turned round abruptly, gathered her dressing-gown around her until it clearly outlined her buttocks and started heavily up the stairs, her legs white above the dingy, pale blue, fluffy slippers.

" 'Arry!" Her voice was shrill from the top of the stairs. "Fer you." A door slammed, then there was silence.

Louise, her cheeks burning, wished she could go away. She waited a long time, then Harry, in the chalk-striped trousers of his grey suit, came down the stairs. His shirt was open at the neck but looked clean. She could see his prominent Adam's apple. He was surprised to see her, and looked anxious, worried. When she had told him why she had come he seemed relieved, and asked her to come in. He took her into what he called the 'front room', an overstuffed parlour with defiant-looking furniture, beige wallpaper, sporting prints and a drooping aspidistra in the fireplace above which a faded sampler said, 'Judge not lest ye be judged'.

Harry offered Louise a cigarette, then said, of course, he knew who it was her young friend was with that night they had seen them in the pavilion. It was Petal. Everyone who knew Merrydown knew Petal. She was a well-known…er…well…er…you know…everyone round here knows Petal. Worked in Merrydown Park. Why did she want to know, anyway?

Louise told him. She told him about Victor and what had happened to him, and how Howard had found him and seen this blonde girl running off with the Teddy boys and how the police were going to question them and she was anxious to do something to help. When she had finished she noticed that Harry had gone quite pale.

"You should have told me before," he said, "that that was why you wanted to know."

"How do you mean?"

"Then I wouldn't have said anything about Petal. I don't want to be mixed up."

"Don't be angry. I only want to help Victor and the police; then they can find out who did it."

"You shouldn't have interfered," Harry said, stubbing his cigarette out fiercely in the ashtray. "There's no sense getting mixed up. I'm not even sure it was Petal. As like as not it wasn't. I couldn't see very well. Did they do him bad?"

"Bad enough," Louise said. She was upset that she had made him angry. "I'd better go."

"I don't want to get mixed up," Harry said. "Don't say anything to the police about me telling you it was Petal. I don't want to get mixed up." He lit another cigarette and Louise opened the door and went out into the dark, oilclothed hall.

"I'm sorry I worried you," she said. "I shouldn't have."

"That's all right, Louise. I just don't want to get mixed up, that's all."

"Well, I'll see you on Saturday," Louise said by the coat stand.

He opened the door. "That's right," he said, although he seemed still agitated, preoccupied. "Saturday."

She wished she hadn't gone. The cheap lodging-house, the front room, the soubrette in the grubby dressing-gown, the fact that she had upset Harry, the unpleasantness of it all depressed her. Harry had looked nice though, masculine in his open-necked shirt, and not at all bad-looking. Once she got him out of his sleazy environment and showed him what a proper home could be like... Petal. She must remember the name. And worked in Merrydown Park. She hoped it would help the Dexters and Victor.

Back at Shore Court, two long, low police cars were waiting.

Twenty

Victor would not talk to the police, and neither would he talk to Doctor Gurney. To the police he said, Yes, he had gone into 'Le Casse-Croûte', no, he had not gone with a girl, yes, he had asked Louise for the keys because he wanted to borrow some records from the café. Lying there with his face, all but one eye, obscured by bandages, he did not attempt to make his story sound particularly convincing. What he invented he stuck to, and watched from his one eye while the sergeant, slowly and painstakingly, recorded what he said in his little book. It was dark, he said, and he had not seen much of his assailants; yes, he thought there were two or three of them; no, he hadn't seen any girl with them; no, he definitely would not be able to recognise any of them again; yes, he realised it was his duty to help the police, if not for his own good, that similar offences might not perpetrated upon others; yes, he realised he must tell the truth, but he was tired, he said, and he wanted to go to sleep. The sergeant buttoned up his book in his breast pocket and sighed. Victor closed his eye but opened it again to watch him plod heavily over the polished boards of the ward and out through the swing doors. That had been at ten o'clock. By two o'clock, when Doctor Gurney went to visit him, Louise had come home with her news about Petal, and the police were already investigating it. Victor repeated his story about the records.

"Know anything about a girl called Petal?" Doctor Gurney said.

Victor looked at him. "No. Do you think my eye will be all right? I've heard them whispering about it but can't catch what they say. Why do they always treat one like some low-grade moron in hospital?"

"They're going to try to save it. It might be a bit tricky because bleeding has occurred into the orbital cavity. You've got about a fifty-fifty chance of retaining the sight. About Petal. You've been seen with her, you know. In the pavilion bar. I should come clean if I were you, Vic. You aren't helping anyone. Not now that they know about Petal. The police have probably been to see her already."

"Why can't everyone mind his own business?"

Doctor Gurney stopped smiling and, leaning back in the chair by the bed on which he sat, said: "Don't you think it's time you stopped being childish, Victor? I'm afraid you're going to look a bit of a mess when you get out of here; probably for quite a while. If you aren't concerned on your own behalf you might consider your parents. Possibly you haven't considered the shock they have had. Of course, it's entirely up to you, but wouldn't it be a good idea to tell me what's been going on and exactly what you've got yourself mixed up in, before the police ferret it out for themselves?"

Victor shut his eye. Everything felt sore; his face, his arms, his hands; particularly his hands. His head ached, and with his eye closed he had the sensation that he was floating in a kind of soft, cotton-wool void. He supposed it was the effect of all the dope he had been given. It gave him a feeling of unreality. He hadn't felt real, that he was actually there, in a white hospital bed, since he had woken, properly conscious for the first time this morning. When the house-surgeon had told him what had happened and why he was there at all he hadn't at first remembered, then slowly, a small portion at a time, it had all come back. Last night and Petal; particularly Petal. When he thought about her he was filled with a curious mixture of desire, disgust and shame. The desire was for Petal, the disgust for himself, and the shame for what would be thought of him if the story came out, if Petal talked, for instance…

The evening had started well; very well, in fact. The preparations had begun earlier, as soon as he had left 'Le Casse-Croûte'. Very much a man of the world, he had realised that whatever happened Petal mustn't, as a result of the evening, become pregnant. That was most important. It did not occur to him that Petal might be capable of looking after herself. With this in mind he had set out for a chemist's shop. Not in Whitecliffs, where the dispenser at the tiny pharmacy now knew him by name, but in Merrydown itself, where the shops were many and crowded, mostly with strangers to the town. As he set out to make his purchase he smiled to himself at the old school joke of the man who set out on the same mission as himself and came home with twenty-four razor blades. After he had visited three chemists' shops he didn't think the joke so frightfully funny. In the first shop, a blonde eighteen-year-old with orange lipstick had said, "Yes, sir?" pertly and he had mumbled something and left hurriedly; in the second, an elderly woman with glasses had looked at him severely and served him with some hair tonic he hadn't wanted, and in the third, a man in a white coat had enquired what it was he wanted, and waited, eyebrows raised, wrists on the counter, for him to reply. Since he was hemmed in on the one side by an old lady with a prescription in her hand, a fat woman who couldn't take her eyes off him on the other, and the shop was full of people who seemed to be standing there hanging on his words, he had said he would call back later, and escaped. Disheartened, he went into an ice-cream parlour where he had a cold drink and a stern word with himself for his own stupidity. He made a list on a piece of paper of one or two toilet items he did not need, and the small requisite he did. He then marched into a fourth chemist's shop and thrust the list at the lad behind the counter. Without comment his package was handed to him, and he left the shop kicking himself mentally for his own stupidity in the first place.

Thus prepared, he had called for Petal at the agreed time at Merrydown Park. She had never looked more desirable. She was wearing a transparent pink blouse, beneath which he could see her underwear, and a tight black skirt. The skirt was very short, and when she bent to pick up the darts he could see her legs, in sheer stockings, well up above the knees. She had seemed neither pleased nor displeased to see him. When she had picked up her white jacket and come out from the side of the stall with it slung over her shoulders, they had walked together through the amusement park to the exit. By the winkle stand stood the group of Teddy boys. One of them said, his eyes piggy beneath lowered lids, "I've warned yer, Petal," and Petal, without looking at him, had taken Victor's arm and tossed her head. Victor said: "Warned you about what?" and Petal said, "Oh, nothing," and because she was squeezing his arm in hers and leaning the side of her body against him he had said no more about it. By the time they reached 'Le Casse-Croûte' Petal had made it obvious that she was aware of his intentions, and if one could judge by her behaviour appeared to be looking forward to it. She hadn't been taken in for a moment by the story he had told her about wanting to dance to the records, for as soon as they had gone into the front part of the café, where the self-service counter was, she had taken off her blouse and her brassière, and her breasts silhouetted in the moonlight had driven him almost crazy. Then Petal said: "Let's have some music, Vic," and he had turned to the record-player and was sorting out the records, holding them to the window and peering at them to see the titles, when he heard a scuffle behind him and somebody said: "Put your clothes on, you damned tart," and as he turned round he remembered seeing the glint of a blade and the room seemed to be full of broad-shouldered, dark suits and he caught the flash of a yellow sock before he was fighting for his life and listening to his own grunts and Petal screaming. He hadn't been scared, he remembered, only too busy hitting out to right and left, and trying to kick and butt with his head, and spit all at the same time; then there had been the sudden, unbearable pain in his eye and the light had gone on for a second, but he couldn't see anything because of the blood and that was the last he remembered until he woke up this morning. And they wanted him to tell all that to the police; not likely! It wasn't exactly that he minded the police knowing, it was only right, after all, that his attackers should be punished, but he would die of shame if the whole sordid story got to the ears of his mother and father, as it most assuredly would.

He opened his eye. Doctor Gurney was still sitting there watching him. "It was as I said," he said; "I went to borrow some records. True, I did have a drink with this girl Petal…but that was a couple of weeks ago."

"Victor," Doctor Gurney said. "The police went through your clothes. They found something that led them to suppose that you hadn't gone to 'Le Casse-Croûte' with the intention only of playing records, and that you hadn't gone there alone. I'm sorry about this, Vic. I understand how you must feel. But I rather think it all has to come out in the wash, you know."

"Oh, God," Victor said. "I wish we'd never come to this place." There was a tear in his eye. "Tell me what you would do, Doctor Gurney. What would you do if you were me?"

"I should have to know all the facts first before I could advise you," Doctor Gurney said. "If it would help you you could tell me in my professional capacity if you like."

"That means you can't go round telling everybody?"

"Not if you don't want me to."

"In that case I'd like to tell you."

"Carry on."

Victor started on his tale. With his eye shut, not looking at Doctor Gurney, he did not find it too difficult to tell him about Petal; about why he had wanted Petal; about the desperate conflict that he was constantly aware of within his own body.

At times his voice was muffled by the bandages and faded into unintelligibility as he spoke, and Doctor Gurney had to lean forward to catch his words. When he'd finished Victor opened his eye again and said "Well?" agressively.

"Well, Vic, it's not such an unusual story as you think. Every chap of your age goes through much the same emotional upset at one time or another. It's nothing whatsoever to be ashamed of."

"What about Petal?"

"Well, it's a pity about Petal. I shan't say anything at all about it, if you don't want me to, but now that the police are on her track it won't be very long before it all comes out. I'm afraid there's no chance at all of you keeping it quiet. The only thing I suggest is that you tell your story before Petal has a chance to tell hers. She may decide to embellish it with all kinds of horrible details. Her boyfriends may even invent some entirely different story for her, putting you in a much worse position than you are now. It isn't a crime, after all, Vic, to try to make love to a girl in an empty café."

"Not in the eyes of the law. It's Mother and Dad I'm thinking of."

"Don't worry too much about that. I admit it's a little embarrassing, but one tends to forget that one's parents have passed through exactly the same stage as you are passing through now; and not so very long ago. Your father was a young man once."

"Not Dad," Victor said. "He's always so right. Impeccable morals...that sort of thing... I can't imagine him ever chasing girls."

"One never can. It's the impression they give, have to give, to children. I'm afraid you'll have to face up to it, Vic. It's not the end of the world, fortunately, for you, and it won't be as bad as you think."

"Will it be all over the newspapers? I'm going up to Cambridge in October."

"We shall have to see what we can do about that."

Victor lay silent for a moment, then he said: "If I could laugh, I would."

"Why?"

"Because after all this I still haven't slept with Petal."

"I wouldn't worry too much about that. As a purely physical exercise it can be awfully disappointing."

"How do you mean?"

"Without some spiritual additive; love, tenderness, affection. It is, after all, or should be, a physical manifestation of these things. There's no happiness, Vic, in these promiscuous relations. I think you'd find them a disappointment, a snare and a delusion. They promise more than they give."

"What do you suggest? It'll be years before I can get married?"

"I don't suggest anything. It's a problem you have to solve for yourself. I'm only giving you the facts and trying to point out that your failure with Petal wasn't the disaster you think it was. She might very well have left you with some unpleasant reminder of her that it would have taken months to get rid of."

Victor groaned.

"Pain?"

"No."

"Sorry, Vic. I'm not trying to preach. I'd like to help. I'm sure you'll find things easier up at Cambridge. You'll be with others of your own age with the same problems. I'm convinced that you'll find a better solution than Petal, or a collection of Petals. You might even find yourself too busy with exams, and rowing and debates and all the other things one does find oneself busy with to worry too much."

"Sublimate my desires?" Victor said mockingly.

"I don't mean that. Down here, though, at Whitecliffs, you have too little to think of. We all have."

"You don't believe in leisure?"

"If you're mentally equipped for it. Few of us are. I accepted your father's kind offer to come down here because of Johnathon's chest condition. I can't say, though, that having accepted, because of him, I didn't become quite excited with the idea of no surgeries, no endless trail of people with their endless woes, always sick, always complaining. No jumping out of bed three or four times a week in the middle of the night, no appointments, responsibilities, panicky rings at the doorbell, telephone calls from dawn till dusk, bleeding fingers, broken legs and dislocated shoulders on the doorstep; no prescriptions to write, and no certificates and notes for work and the hospital; no work when you want to sleep, and no feeling like nothing more than a night's sleep when you have to work; and, perhaps more than anything at all, I looked forward to seeing all day and every day people who were normal, healthy, not sick in body or in mind."

"And now?" Victor said, interested.

"Now I know that we are all sick; only those who come to my surgery a little more so than those who don't. The young children playing so happily on the beach, appearing so perfect, artists' children in their beauty, have flat feet, allergic eczema, and wet their beds at night; the beautiful young models at the cocktail-parties, sculptor's work, have piles and lumbar scolioses, and the young men asthma and athlete's foot. The older men and women have arthritis and rheumatism and ulcers and indigestion and varicose veins and pains in the stomach and pains in the head, and if they're very unlucky coronary thromboses and cancer, and often they are sick, too, in their minds."

"You talk as if there are no healthy people."

"There are no perfect people. If any of us were perfect we might forget who we were; our beginning and our end. We struggle as best we can. Here in Whitecliffs I've had time to think. The conclusion I have come to is that I should be at home, doing my job, helping those I can in their struggle."

"You sound as though you have to work with your bare hands. What about penicillin and X-rays and all those new things we're always reading about?"

"Don't you think that in a hundred, in fifty years' time all these 'new' things will be ludicrous, as were the methods of doctors fifty years ago when all their pneumonias and their puerperal fevers and their diptherias hadn't a hope in hell? I believe I told your father that I regarded my work as no more vocational than that of a plumber. Perhaps I underestimated it a bit. It's a privilege, in a way, to be able to help people. I don't think we can get away from the fact that we are all responsible for each other. Speaking for myself, I shall be quite glad to get back onto my treadmill; I don't think that there's any happiness off it. In future, though, I shall put my feet down on the treads a lot more humbly. None of us can stand alone, Vic. Look at you, yesterday a strong, healthy young man, a great, arrogant stag on a mountain top, and today...well, if it hadn't been for Doctor Potts and his friends you wouldn't be here. We all have our place, Vic."

"You make life sound so serious."

"There's pleasure, too, Vic. But alone it's not enough. The party has to end; if not it becomes awfully tedious, and when the guests have gone home there has to be something else." Doctor Gurney grinned. "What I've been saying is only, I suppose, a symptom of my age. When I was eighteen I was happily anaesthetised as you are, to care, worry, responsibility and all the other horrors of maturity. Stay that way, Vic. It doesn't last so awfully long."

Vic said: "Thanks for talking to me. It makes me see things in better perspective. About Petal and all that...that I'm not the only one who ever... I suppose you wouldn't care to tell Mother and Dad for me?"

"I will if you'd like me to. I'm afraid the police will want it from you though."

"All right. All boys together, what?"

"That's the spirit."

"I say, you don't think I'll have to go through it all in court, do you? In front of all sorts of odd bods?"

"You're man enough, Victor. I shouldn't worry."

"Perhaps I shan't now. You have pointed out that there are worse things."

Doctor Gurney stood up and looked down the ward.

"Far, far worse," he said.

Twenty-one

"Pot for four," Basil said, keeping his eyes on the steaming jet of water from the still with which he was filling the large teapot. Next to him Honey reached beneath the counter and, picking up four cups and four saucers, stacked them on the tray which a woman with buck teeth held in front of her on the counter. With her left hand she stretched out for a small pink plastic bowl holding sugar lumps for four, and with her right she selected four tinny teaspoons. She took the milk jug, the teapot, now filled, and the water jug Basil had placed beside her, and put them on the woman's tray. The woman moved on, sliding her tray with her, to Doctor Gurney at the cash register.

"You needn't worry about me, you know," Honey said to Basil who had been avoiding her eyes all morning.

Basil polished the coffee urn. "How do you mean?"

"Because of Elisabeth. I understand. It didn't mean a thing to me."

"You helped me over a very sticky patch. I feel grateful. I don't like to just...well, just...now that I have Elisabeth... It seems so..."

"I told you. It didn't mean a thing to me."

"Are you sure?"

"I get bored very quickly. I like a change."

"You mean you were getting fed up with me in any case?"

"There was no one else down here."

"You're sure that's how it was? I mean I should hate to feel…"

"How else do you think?"

"It doesn't worry you at all?"

"Not at all." Honey's eyes were looking downwards to the cups she was examining for chips or stains, but which she could not see for tears. "I'm a nude," she said, "a show girl. In our business we're used to having a giggle. We think nothing of it."

" 'Having a giggle'?"

"That's what we call it. You know, just fun. Not getting involved."

"So it's quite all right?"

"I've told you. I'm looking forward to seeing your Elisabeth."

"She'll be down later."

"Is she as pretty as her photograph?"

"Prettier. You're pretty, too, Honey. In a different way."

In a different way, Honey thought, in a different way. If I lived to be a hundred, and was as beautiful as I knew how, I should never be pretty in the same way as Elisabeth Benwell is pretty. I was born in the wrong drawer.

"I'd like to buy you a present," Basil said. "I can't run to anything frightfully elaborate. Is there anything you'd like?"

"Will you give me exactly what I ask?"

"If I can afford it."

"You can afford this."

"All right."

"I'd like you to give me nothing at all. Nothing. And please, please don't thank me."

Basil looked at her. She was still looking downwards, her face almost buried in her hair, at the cups she was sorting. Basil put his hand out and removed a cup from the tray of those she passed.

"There's a chip in this one," he said gently, and removing it put it on the hatchway to the kitchen.

The café was open again. The concrete floor had been scrubbed, but there still remained soaked into its pores, the dark patch that had been Victor's blood. They all tried not to look and from behind the counter it wasn't difficult. Only when they first came in to open up, all together this time by mutual consent, Basil had looked quickly out of curiosity, and Louise and Honey, and then had quickly looked away. Vanessa, her memories of Wednesday still haunting her, had thought she might not be able to stand it again in the café, but looking at the floor it was only stained concrete and seemed to have nothing at all to do with her brother, and the café didn't look the same either, with the sunshine streaming through the window and outside the beach and the white-topped sea and the children laughing. And behind her Howard had said: "How about helping me with the ice-creams, Vanessa? There'll be a delivery soon and I really can't remember what I have left." And for about half an hour she had worked, her hands cold from the ice-boxes, beside Howard, and once she had caught him looking at her and had quickly looked away because his eyes said something she was waiting for him to say, and which he had not said. But the next moment he was discussing 'nut crunch' and 'strawberry ripple', and whether they had enough chocolate-bars for the 'six-five special', and had she not seen it for herself she might have wondered if he had ever looked at her like that at all.

Things were the same, and yet they were not the same. Outside, the sea, a hundred yards away, embraced tiny children with its bouncing foam and sent them screaming onto the wet sand, then lured them back for more. Higher up, on the dryer beach, where one or two sand-flies danced among the seaweed, the mothers and fathers and aunties and uncles and grandmas and grandads still sat and talked and knitted, or stood self-consciously in shorts and played cricket or rounders, or dug castles and boats. Or had the numbers thinned a little, and some of the mothers, sunburned and refreshed, gone back to the kitchen sink and the endless meals and the washing on Mondays, and the fathers to the machines and the buses and the Hoffman presses, and the grandmas to baby-minding, and the grandpas with their shopping bags happily to the shopping? The sun, an unfathomable, golden orb in as clear a sky as one could have wished for, shone just as brightly, but was the air as warm? Wasn't there, just recognisable, the first faintest, faintest hint of autumn in the air? The warmth just edged with a crispness, the merest edge of a notion that summer could not last for ever? The pedaloes waited down by the sea; only four of the twelve had been taken out. The man who hired them stood on his brown legs, in his woolly hat, smoking his pipe, looking towards the horizon; the deck-chair man in his black jersey sold chairs and tickets for the changing huts but leisurely; the queue outside the Corporation Café was not very long, the bare feet stood patiently on the concrete except for the odd child hopping about; on the promenade a small boy said to his friend: "You going up next term, Julian?"

In 'Le Casse-Croûte' they tried to behave as though nothing had happened to spoil their idyll. They all worked hard at their own and each other's jobs in an attempt to fill the gap left by Victor. Everything was the same in actuality: in essence it was not. Arthur came in after he had been to the hospital, but there was no, "Good morning, everyone, come along there, let's get cracking, watch your ices, Howard…"

He stood gloomily in the back kitchen and drank a cup of tea. He didn't check the stock or watch the sales, and when a customer came back complaining that the sails had come off her small boy's windmill, he didn't give her her money back. They served teas, coffees, ices, fancy-goods, everything as usual, but there was none of the customary banter, summery words, flying back and forth across the café, neither did they chat much with the customers. They kept to themselves in a tight, restrictive knot, thinking their own thoughts and unbending only to serve the boats or the candy-floss or the bottles of coca-cola. It was

Honey who kept them all going. After her quiet words with Basil in the morning she was gayer than ever. She danced into the kitchen with the empties, chaffed Howard unmercifully for his solemnity, and made them all laugh despite themselves with the bold eyes she made deliberately at all the handsome men who were in the queue. When Elisabeth arrived at four o'clock Honey was leaning across the counter, from the customers' side, and asking Doctor Gurney in dramatic tones if he knew of a cure for a broken heart, as one of the men whom she had just ogled in her best manner had turned away and looked quite cross. After that she put a cha-cha-cha on the record-player and refilled the racks with cakes, in time to the music. From the corner of her eye she watched Elisabeth watching Basil, and Basil watching Elisabeth. When she was tired she went into the back kitchen and made herself some tea. Arthur was sitting with his jacket off, and his head in his hands.

"How is Victor?"

"They can't do anything about his eye," Arthur said, "and they've left him a nice legacy in the way of scars. Don't say it might have been worse. I know. It doesn't help much."

"I wasn't going to," Honey said. "I was going to ask how many sugars you want in your tea."

"Two."

"If something like that happened to me," Honey said, "I'd be finished. My face is my fortune. My face and my… Well, what I mean is, Victor has brains and education and background and money…"

"I know you're right. You're all right. A few superficial cuts, the loss of an eye… God, I could murder them for what they've done to my son."

"An eye for an eye," Honey said.

Howard was at the sink getting fresh water for his ice-cream scoops. "Actually it doesn't mean that," he said. "It refers merely to monetary compensation for an injury done; that there should be a limit to damages paid. Of course, it's a popular misconception but the Old Testament states quite clearly..."

"Much obliged, Your Worship," Honey said, bobbing a curtsy, and even Arthur had to smile.

They locked up early. Basil walked along the promenade with Elisabeth. The sun was sitting low in the sky in a nest of pink clouds. In another half-hour the tide would be at its highest. On the small strip of beach that remained a few holiday-makers, reluctant to go home, huddled against the wall watching the sea inch up towards them. The serious swimmers were enjoying a bathe in which they did not have to wade half a mile before the water reached their waists, the children, sun-filled and happy, enjoyed their last paddle, their mothers relaxed, content that they had no supper to cook, that their fish and chips would be waiting, ready laid on a white tablecloth, with a bottle of tomato ketchup and worcester sauce to each table; their fathers, handkerchiefs knotted too late over sunburned foreheads, sat and thought or did not think. The cleaner picked up the floating papers on the promenade, leisurely emptied the bins. Elisabeth and Basil, walking along, dodged the black rubber balls on the ends of lengths of elastic of the remaining Jokari players, the chalked-out squares of the hopscotches, the women wringing out the bathing suits until the water trickled in a dark stream over the white stone and down on to the sand. They skirted children sitting in the middle of the promenade, struggling unself-consciously to fit sandals on to damp, sandy feet; they dodged round families who walked in long lines, heavily laden with bags, trailing children, homewards. They were scampered into by dogs, used as foils for children playing hide and seek, stared at for Elisabeth's good looks by the men, for her clothes by the women. They did not speak. They passed the last hut, where a man locked the door and put the key into his shorts pocket, and the point where there were no more litter bins, only a long, bare, empty stretch of stone against which the sea already slapped because it was the arm which cradled the bay, and beneath the grey water stretching out to sea they could see, just darkly visible, the black mass of the rocks. To their right a few gulls swooped plaintively over the water, to their left the chalk cliffs crumbled.

Elisabeth said: "I want you to know, Basil, now that I've seen Honey it's all right."

"How do you mean?"

"I mean I can understand how you felt; and Honey being there. She's so gay, I pretended for a moment, looking at her, I was you. I would have done the same."

"Not you, Elisabeth."

"Basil, I want to say something. You're always kind of putting me on a pedestal, accentuating, as it were, our differences. You make yourself earthy, me remote; me rich, you poor; me virtuous, you not. It's a thing you've got. You act as though I think I'm too good for you."

"You're the only one I love, Elisabeth."

"I know you love me. But there's always this feeling. I don't know whether it's because of my home or because of father's title or what it is, but somewhere, deep down, you resent me."

"You are your father's daughter."

"I am what I am," said Elisabeth. "We've never discussed this before, and I've never really been able to put it into words. But while we've been apart I've been thinking. We're pulling against each other all the time, and I think that's what's been stopping you from working, too. Until you can accept me as I am, just a woman, your wife, part of you, I don't believe we shall get anywhere."

"How do you suggest I do that?"

"Try to love me, Basil, without any reservations."

"I wasn't aware there were any. If you'd seen me down here, missing you every moment of the day, you wouldn't think so either."

"I can't put it any better than that, Basil. I have this feeling that all the time there's this thing between us. When you're working you are frustrated by the feeling that you are working to keep this Elisabeth who is richer than you; when we're out you introduce me defiantly to your friends as though you were saying this is my wife, Elisabeth; you cannot talk to her for she is not like us; when we make love I have the feeling that you handle me carefully, like old china." Elisabeth stopped walking and turned to face Basil. Against the chalky white of the cliff her hair was fiery.

"I don't want to be treated like old china," she said. "Can't you understand, Basil, I want to be dominated by you, possessed? We're all cave-women at heart. I don't want you to look at me as though any moment I might fly away or melt or disappear on my broomstick. I want to be real for you as you are real for me. Do you know how you're looking at me now?"

Basil shook his head.

"As though you can't believe your luck."

"But I can't, Elisabeth. You're so beautiful."

"You do me an injustice. Honey is beautiful. I am a woman; a woman who loves you, Basil. A woman who is going to bear your child. I am neither my father's daughter nor the unattainable customer in your book-shop. I am your wife. Only your wife." She walked along again and Basil followed her. "It's peaceful down here," Elisabeth said. "I envy you your weeks. In town it's been hot and dirty and noisy, but with the sterile, faraway feel that London has in August. You forget, amidst the dust and the traffic, that not so very many miles away the air is clean and the sea has sun sprinkled on it and is infinite, and that you can take time off to air your soul. It's very gentle here."

"About our baby. What shall we call him?"

"Who said it would be a 'him'? You're the author, invent something."

"There are several names already invented. Why don't we stick to those? Perhaps it will be a girl, beautiful like her mother."

"There you go again. Can't you think of anything, anything at all you like in me, you'd like perpetuated in our daughter? My hair will be grey before she's grown up, and my skin not the same despite what the labels on the night-creams say; what will you love in me then, Basil? You must find something for both our sakes."

"You will always be… Elisabeth."

"If I was sure of that…"

"You can be sure. How can I prove it?"

"When you tell me, I shall know."

They walked up the steep path that wound up in a gap in the cliff, and Elisabeth sat on the rough wood bench halfway to rest.

"I keep forgetting about this baby because it doesn't show," Basil said. "I'm not looking after you properly."

"I'm perfectly all right. You don't have to coddle me. The doctor says I'm a big, strong girl and should have a big, strong baby."

Back in the flat, Elisabeth put on her apron.

"I got some trout this morning," she said. "The fish is wonderful down here. I thought I'd like to do it as you like it with some of those tiny mushrooms, and you could pop out for a bottle of wine, cheap wine, but you must have wine with trout…what are you staring at?"

Basil was leaning against the window in the tiny kitchen with his arms folded and his jaw stuck forward.

"Basil, what is it?"

"Nothing."

"Then what are you looking at?"

"I'm looking at you."

"But why like that?"

Basil unfolded his arms. "If you really want to know come into the bedroom and find out." He went out of the kitchen and she heard him cross the hall and go into the bedroom.

Elisabeth hesitated for a moment. Then she took off her apron, switched off the gas under the saucepan she had put on for the trout, and followed him.

Twenty-two

"Are you sure you'll be all right?" Elisabeth said anxiously.

"Absolutely, darling. Are you sure you will? I mean all that standing around."

"I'm looking forward to it. It looked fun yesterday. Can I get you anything before I go?"

Basil, in bed, closed his eyes. "No, I shall just sleep."

"Good. I'll be back at lunchtime. I hope you'll feel better, darling."

"Don't worry, sweet."

Elisabeth, in a loose, oatmeal linen dress, looked round the bedroom in the manner of one who was about to leave but was reluctant to do so. She could find nothing to detain her. The curtains were half closed to keep the light from Basil's eyes, her own bed was made, Basil's tidy. There was water for him to drink, the newspaper to read, aspirins and cigarettes by the bed. She had swept the carpet, and dusted.

Basil, in his blue pyjamas, lay quite still. Elisabeth walked quietly out of the room and shut the door softly. He heard her let herself out of the flat. He waited until he was sure she was well on her way to 'Le Casse-Croûte' and would not be coming back for anything, before he opened his eyes. He got out of bed to open the curtains and in the full impact of the morning sun which was bright, but not yet hot, he realised that he was trembling with excitement. He showered, dressed, put on his shoes and shaved his face as carefully as if he were going to a party. When he was ready he went into the little hall, guiltily almost, on tiptoe, and opened the cupboard. The typewriter was where he had left it next to the electricity meter. He lifted it out and took it into the bedroom. Five minutes later he was sitting in front of the clean white paper he had wound into the roller, and was tipping backwards slightly in his chair. This was the moment he hated most of all. He had fiddled with the carbon, making sure it was right side up, set the margin and the indentation to his satisfaction, made sure his notebook and his pen were by his side. He lit a cigarette, burning the match longer than was necessary, then got up to find an ashtray. When he sat down again he pressed the shift lock and printed 'Chapter One'. He underlined it in red. Tipping his chair back again, he thought perhaps he ought to have one quick glance at the newspaper to put him in the mood. He got up to get it. The headlines were uninteresting; August headlines. Nothing exciting was happening on the Stock Exchange. He read a letter headed 'Why learn dead languages?' and another about the damage by seals to fishing. The women's page was all about how to make tapestry tea-cosies, and on the back page nobody he knew had given birth, married or died. He read an appeal for toys for deaf children, how to get a better mortgage, and that a leading Couturier was holding a sale of models. Short of starting on the crossword there was nothing else to detain him. He threw the newspaper on the floor and lit another cigarette from the first which he had not yet finished. The feeling that he would not this morning, not ever, be able to get started, was familiar. Today though he was not worried. Today was different. Today he was not the same Basil as he had been. He was a man complete, and because of Elisabeth. He smiled when he thought of last night, a little wistfully, for he had wasted so very many years in clinging to something he only half had, something he was not at all sure of. Last night, yesterday evening rather, he had made love to Elisabeth, for the first time since they had been married, with his mind entirely on Elisabeth and uninhibited by the fact that tomorrow he would not be able to write; without, in the back of his mind, pity for Elisabeth who was married to a failure, and pity for himself. He had made love to her for no other reason than that he loved her; he was relaxed, unaware of time and place, conscious only of his wife. For a whole night, loving and sleeping, chatting softly and idly in the dark, he had forgotten himself. He smiled when he remembered that at nine o'clock last night, lying close together in the same small bed, Elisabeth had said: "Basil, aren't you hungry? We've had no dinner. What about the trout?" And he had looked into her eyes, which were deep grey in the almost-dark, and said gently: "What about the trout?" and it had still been there, waiting patiently in the fridge at breakfast time. It must have been midnight before they got to sleep. At six, with the light already bright, he woke, conscious for the first time in years of having dreamed about nothing at all, worried about nothing at all, feared nothing at all. There was one moment, while he lay looking at the pattern made by the light through the curtains, of utter peace, then, completely unbidden, the crystals of knowledge, of work, of half-ideas, he had worried over and collected over the past years, came rushing into his mind, and for the space of one lucid moment had formed a clear, precise and recognisable picture. There seemed no doubt that he could do now, today, what he had struggled unsuccessfully for so many years to do. Looking at Elisabeth's red hair on the pillow, her breathing quiet, shadows beneath her eyes, he knew that it was something too delicate, too fragile to share, even with his wife. It was a revelation whose first and freshest telling could be only to his typewriter. He had lain there calmly, powerfully in the knowledge he possessed, and wondered how he could wangle a morning, a few hours even, on his own. He had despised himself rather for the story of the migraine and the suggestion that Elisabeth should take his place at 'Le Casse-

Croûte', especially when she had overflowed with sympathy, darling Elisabeth, but there had been nothing else he could do.

Staring at the paper, blank except for 'Chapter One', he had one moment of doubt; one fleeting moment when he wondered whether this might not be exactly as any other morning of the past few years, whether he might not sit there all morning and at the end of it have nothing at all to show, or at best a few pages of typescript which he would ultimately tear up. The moment did not last. He straightened his chair until all four legs were firmly on the ground, typed one line, hesitantly, slowly, like one scarcely able to control his hands, then lost himself in words; words which flowed so fast from the pages already written on his mind that his fingers were hardly able to keep pace with his thoughts.

He was surprised when he looked up, distracted by a noise, to find Elisabeth standing by his side.

He blinked. "Did you forget something?"

"No. Why should I have?"

"You came back."

"I came back to give you some lunch. I expected to find you in bed."

"What's the time?"

"After one."

"Are you sure?"

"Absolutely. Basil, are you all right?"

Basil stood up. His arms, his shoulders, his back, were stiff. He flexed his muscles and groaned. "Elisabeth, darling, I'm more all right than I have ever been. At least I think so." He bent to the floor and sorted through the dozen typewritten sheets that lay at all angles on the carpet. He put them in order and handed them to Elisabeth.

"Tell me quickly," he said. "I have to know."

Elisabeth put down the handbag which matched her dress and, taking the sheets of paper, sat down on the bed. Basil left the room. He couldn't bear to watch. He wandered round the sitting-room, his stomach hollow with excitement; he stared out of the window, his hands in his pockets, imagining Elisabeth reading what he had written. He felt sick. He waited five minutes, ten. He was aware of the shirt sticking to his back. He tried not to think. When it became unbearable he went back into the bedroom. She was still reading, but after a moment she lowered the sheets to her lap and looked at him. He tried to read her face.

"Don't keep me waiting, Elisabeth. I can't stand it."

"You must know, Basil. It's wonderful. Like poetry almost; but powerful. How did it happen?"

"I suppose it was because I stopped trying."

"Can you keep it up for a whole book?"

"As I feel now I could keep it up for six books. It's all there in my head. Can you go to the café again this afternoon?"

"I could. But I'm not going to. I'm not going to let you overdo it, sitting there hour after hour, like you used to, until you're stale. You can go to the café this afternoon and forget about this," she rustled the paper, "until tomorrow morning."

"But Elisabeth…"

"Don't 'but Elisabeth' me. I'm not going to let you get into a state again." She stood up and put her arms around him. "I'm very proud of you. You're capable of great things."

"If I am it's because of you."

"Basil?" She leaned away from him.

"Mm?"

"I take back what I said yesterday. I believe you do love me."

"I always have."

"Perhaps. You were afraid to show it though."

"Elisabeth, I'm hungry. What's for lunch?"

"Trout."

Basil laughed and held her very close. "I don't care. This time I'm going to have it."

Arthur said to Doctor Gurney, whom he had invited in for a drink:

"Sorry to trouble you on holiday, as it were, but I think I shall have to have some more sleeping tablets. I thought those days were past but since Victor... I seem to lie awake practically all night. I'd been feeling so much better down here, relaxed... I suppose I'm what you'd call the worrying type."

Doctor Gurney smiled. "That's about it. At home you were worrying about business, now it's Victor. Before very long you'll be lying awake because 'Le Casse-Croûte' isn't taking as much as it should be, although it's only a sideline."

"You needn't have fears about that," Arthur said. "I've decided to pack up. That's why I asked you here, and Basil and Howard. I seem to have lost interest since Victor's accident. I was only looking at myself this morning and wondering what on earth I was doing, standing there in a beach café selling refreshments to men and women in shorts and bathing suits, when I don't care a damn if they have their tea or coffee or not, or if they like it or not, or if they have to queue for it or not. I suddenly thought of my office in town and my business – a good business, all said and done – and my samples of toys, and felt terribly homesick. I want to pack up at the end of August, by which time Victor should be well enough to be moved. If I hadn't had this stupid idea of coming to Whitecliffs he wouldn't be where he is now."

"It was because of Mr Boothroyd, remember."

"Yes. Poor Willie. The shock must have sent me off balance. What's happened to Victor has brought me to my senses again. I suppose I was happier than I realised; it was, after all, my life. I can't wait to get back."

"Don't forget that being at Whitecliffs has been beneficial to you in many ways. You admit yourself you feel better, more relaxed, until the last few days, of course. I've an idea."

"What's that?"

"Have you ever thought of a cottage here? A small place for weekends. You could combine both worlds then. It seems the ideal solution."

"Not a bad idea. I'll mention it to Vera. There is just one other thing, although I don't really like to trouble you. I've a pain in my stomach, quite severe at times. Here." Arthur pointed.

"How long have you had it?"

"Well, for the past week or two. I'd been intending to mention it to you, but Victor put it out of my head."

"Eating well?" Doctor Gurney said.

Arthur said: "It's odd you should ask. Actually I don't seem to want much down here. I don't know whether it's the air… I seem to have one or two mouthfuls and feel full up." He put his hand in the waistband of his trousers: "I seem to have lost a bit of weight, too. I suppose I could do with it."

"Look," Doctor Gurney said. "Hop into the bedroom and take your things off and I'll have a look at you before Basil and Howard come."

"All right," Arthur said. "By the way, don't say anything about this to Vera. She has enough to worry about with Victor. She gets very excited."

Arthur said: "I'm sorry about the café and backing out on you all as it were. I just feel I can't carry on any longer. I thought we'd just keep going until the end of August. It gets pretty slack after then anyway."

"Don't worry about us," Basil said. He and Howard were leaning against the mantelpiece with their drinks.

Howard said: "So you're getting back again on your treadmill?"

"I suppose I am," Arthur said. "And I must admit I'm quite looking forward to it. At first I was so happy, with Whitecliffs, with the café, the easy life, but somehow it's all gone sour. In the morning I wish I were going to work, the work I know; I've done it for thirty years, after all; and in the evenings, such long evenings they seem, I find myself longing for a bit of company, a game of bridge, the odd theatre even. Quite suddenly this isn't enough. It isn't somehow me. I'm not a young man, remember, and one develops habits… I suppose I'm too old, too set in my ways for change. You see, I thought…"

"It's quite all right," Howard said. "We understand."

"I shall take it much more easy. I've learned that. Doctor Gurney here suggested something very sensible, a weekend cottage: I think that fits the bill, the best of both worlds, as it were…

"What will you both do? You're very welcome to stay on in the flats if you wish. That's the least I can do. The block is mine so you don't have to worry about that."

Howard looked at Basil. "Well?" he said, "you're the original treadmill boy. Have you had enough?"

Basil looked into his glass and swirled the whisky round gently.

"I believe the treadmills are figments of our imagination," he said. "I think we are all free to choose, to make our own decisions, if we only realised."

"Rather a *volte face*, isn't it, old boy? What's happened?"

"Several things. Personal things. I have to thank Mr Dexter for setting the ball rolling, and if he doesn't mind I'd like to stay on for a bit. I like it here. What about you, Howard? Back to the grind?"

"I don't know. I don't think you can dismiss the treadmill theory quite like that. I believe we are to a certain extent, the helpless playthings of forces greater than ourselves. You may believe that you are making your own free decisions, but how do you know they are not decisions you were intended, in the scheme of things, to make anyway?"

"I don't," Basil said. "I'm playing it by ear from now on. I've been worrying about things for the past ten years, and it hasn't got me anywhere."

"You cannot dismiss it as simply as that," Howard said. "For the moment I have no desire to go back to town and spend the rest of my life struggling to achieve something I know perfectly well I shall never now achieve."

"Isn't that rather defeatist?" Basil said. "I mean, if you think like that we may all of us just not bother at all. After all, we all know that all our struggles and endeavours and successes must end, ultimately, in only one way, whoever we are. It would be a bit silly if we all just packed up. What do you think, Mr Dexter?"

"I'm sorry," Arthur said. "I wasn't really concentrating. I was thinking about Victor. You must forgive me. What will happen, Howard, if they find his attackers?"

"I'm sure they will," Howard said. "The girl, Petal, will give them away eventually, without a doubt. They'll be charged with causing grievous bodily harm and may get anything from three months' to three years' imprisonment."

"I wish I was the Judge," Arthur said. "I'd make them sorry."

"What is it makes them capable of such acts?" Basil said.

Howard put down his glass. "I don't know. Sometimes I think we make too many excuses today; bad homes, unsettled homes, unsettled times, lack of family life, love and care. Of course, these environmental considerations may be something to do with it, but once the offenders hear about them they begin to feel sorry for themselves, and we may even be helping them to believe themselves incapable of any other behaviour."

"We're back to free will," Basil said. "Are you saying that we are what we are despite our parentage, upbringing, environment and all that? That there is no original sin?"

"As I said," Howard said, "I still have a very open mind about it all."

Arthur said: "I believe the mistake we make is to discuss all this too much. I think perhaps it would be better if we just got on with our work. That's what I shall do as soon as I get home.

I'm going to ask Vera to make some tea for you chaps. Or would you rather have another whisky?"

Howard, Basil and Doctor Gurney all held out their glasses.

Getting undressed, Doctor Gurney said to his wife: "How do you feel about going back, Mary?"

"I shall be glad. It's been very nice here, but I feel a bit of a fraud. We were doing something useful at home."

"You complained enough about the bells and phone and the useless foreign helps and the disturbed nights and the stupidity of some of the patients."

"I know. I suppose I was overtired. It's a nice life though. Apart from being useful it's never boring, is it? I mean we never have time to work ourselves up into neuroses over things, do we?"

"I'm glad you feel that way about it. I shall be glad to get back. We shall just have to organise ourselves better. What are you smiling at?"

"You."

"Why? Apart from the fact that I have no trousers on?"

"Because we're always saying we must organise ourselves better, but in our business I don't think it's possible. There isn't the help available today; people cannot be expected to be ill in prescribed hours, and four children need quite a bit of looking after."

"You're absolutely right. We have to face it. Are you willing to go back on those terms?"

"Yes. What about you?"

"Completely. Mary?"

"Yes?"

"I shouldn't be at all surprised if Arthur Dexter had a carcinoma of the stomach. I'm having him investigated tomorrow."

"No!"

"Yes. Ironical, isn't it? He came down here because he was scared of dropping dead from a coronary thrombosis."

"It just shows you," Mary said, getting into bed.

"What?"

"You can't run away, can you?"

Doctor Gurney turned out the light. "No," he said, "I don't think you can."

Twenty-three

Vanessa sat on the floor in Howard's flat listening to Chopin. She was wearing a full, pink, pleated terylene skirt and a sleeveless pink jumper, and she was thinking. She was thinking that she would be happy to spend her whole life just as she was now, with Howard sitting behind her where she could not see him but was very much aware of his presence, and among the things that were Howard: his pipe and books, his journals and his stack of records. She hadn't seen very much of him since the night they had found Victor at 'Le Casse-Croûte'; they had exchanged the odd word at the café, met at her father's flat, but when there were always people there, and smiled to each other on the stairs. She was ashamed and yet not ashamed that she had engineered the situation she was now in. Since the night, one she would always remember because of its horrible ending, that Howard had taken her to the 'Landscape', although he had been very kind and gentle to her when they talked, the conversation had been on a strictly impersonal level, and he had not asked her to come out with him again. She had been content to wait, sure that as time went by he would feel the same about her as she did about him. Each day as she stood near to him in 'Le Casse-Croûte' she had said a little prayer. When her father had started talking about packing up, leaving Whitecliffs and going home, she had decided that it was necessary to do more than pray. That morning in the café she had told Howard she was going to see Victor after dinner and asked him if he would like to come with her. "I'm sure Victor would like to see you," she said.

"I didn't think he was allowed visitors, apart from the family," Howard said.

"From today. Just one at a time. I thought you might like to go first, before the others."

"Indeed I will," Howard said. "I'll call for you after dinner."

It had been as simple as that.

Victor said: "Ah, my two heroes!" when he saw them coming towards his bed, and when they'd sat down on the chairs the nurse provided, he said, "The police have just phoned through. They've rounded up my boy-friends. Petal squeaked."

"Aren't you glad, Vic?" Vanessa said.

"I don't care much either way. I'm a one-eyed monster for life, and that's that. What will happen to them, Howard?"

"Imprisonment, I presume."

"Petal, too?"

"Not if she can convince the jury she had nothing to do with it, was completely ignorant of what they had in mind."

Victor smiled. "Petal wouldn't like it in jug."

"I doubt if that consideration would sway the jury."

Victor said: "I haven't thanked you, Howard, for saving my miserable life. I'd shake your hand if I could. It's jolly awkward without hands, you know; you'd be surprised."

Howard said: "It was just fortunate that we happened to be around at the right moment."

"That's putting it mildly. Although what you two were doing on the beach at that time of night I shudder to think."

Vanessa blushed. "She's quite pretty when she blushes, isn't she, Howard?" Victor said.

"Shut up, Vic," Vanessa said. She could feel her cheeks burning.

"I hope you're going to ask me to be best man if I don't look too grotesque and frighten all the bridesmaids."

Vanessa couldn't look at Howard. "You know we're going home as soon as you're fit," she said to Victor.

"Suits me. I shall have plenty to remember Whitecliffs by."

"Do you still hurt?"

"A little. There's a bod in the end bed in a really bad way though..."

After ten minutes a nurse told them they had to go. They said goodbye to Victor, and Howard moved off towards the doors.

"Van!" Victor whispered.

She turned back to the bed. "Well?"

"Sorry about that. It looked as if it was in the bag. You're dead nuts keen on him, aren't you?"

Vanessa nodded.

"Good luck. Although I must say Cliff's more your type."

She went to join Howard who was waiting for her by the door.

There was a brisk wind blowing in from the sea, and it was too cold to walk. When Howard said: "I was going to listen to some records, would you care to join me?" Vanessa said, "Yes." Had he not asked her she would have asked herself. As far as Howard was concerned she had no pride left. She watched him select a pipe and light it, search through his stack of records, move about the room heavily, purposefully. They discussed Victor, some interesting cases Howard had had, Whitecliffs and the café. After that they were silent, listening to the crystal trills of a Chopin nocturne. Vanessa, sitting on the floor, had the feeling that if nothing was said tonight it would never be said. She swallowed, felt herself start to tremble, then said: "You know I'm in love with you, don't you, Howard?"

There was silence for a long moment, nothing but a melody in a minor key haunting the room. Vanessa was afraid to turn round, then Howard said: "It did occur to me."

It's up to him now, Vanessa thought. I've said it. I can't sink any lower. Perhaps I was stupid, terribly stupid, but I've said it now. She waited. Behind her she heard Howard get up and turn off the record-player. The quiet seemed to have weight and body.

Howard sat down in the armchair opposite the one against which she was leaning. She stared straight ahead, not daring to look at him.

"Vanessa, do you know how old I am?"

"I suppose about forty."

"Forty-three. More than twice your age and old enough to be your father."

Vanessa waited. She was conscious of her own breathing.

Howard said: "When you are in your prime I shall be an old man."

Vanessa turned her head towards him slowly, daring to hope.

"Does that mean…?"

"It doesn't mean anything really."

"I thought…perhaps…"

Howard leaned forward and looked at her. "Vanessa," he said, and his voice was gentle, "it would be so easy for me to be in love with you. You're so pretty, sweet, young…"

"A child, you mean," Vanessa said indignantly looking up to face him then sitting back on her heels. "But I'm not, Howard, I'm not…"

"That's not what I meant, Vanessa. What I'm trying to say is that I'm more than fond of you, and it would take very little effort on my part to love you very much, to ask you to marry me. Don't you think I could be happy with you as my wife? Couldn't any man?"

"Well?" Vanessa's face was tilting up towards him, her voice barely audible.

Howard picked up his pipe again and, standing up, went over to the window.

"Well, one day, Vanessa, the honeymoon would be over. You'd wake up one morning to find yourself married to a middle-aged man with a paunch, a bald patch growing larger week by week, and an income that was not very adequate. You'd still be young, Vanessa, very young, probably in your early twenties, and you'd look at your friends with their slim, handsome husbands with full crops of hair, with youth and enthusiasm and time on their sides, and above all with hope."

"You talk as though you have one foot in the grave."

"Perhaps I haven't made myself clear. When you're young, Vanessa, at the foot of the mountain, as you are, you have the excitement of the climb ahead of you; some days you'll get on fast, on others not so fast, but always you'll have the strength and enthusiasm to pull yourself to the top if only to see what lies on the other side. At eighteen it might be anything, anything at all. But you see, Vanessa, I've reached the top of the mountain; I can see what's on the other side and it isn't particularly exciting. If I married you I'd be taking away from you the most exhilarating years of your life: the years of striving, fighting, hoping, surging forward, upward, perhaps even to the stars. It wouldn't work, Vanessa. It simply wouldn't work."

"I wouldn't want the stars, Howard, if I had you."

"You think you don't, but you must. At eighteen we are all unreasonable enough to imagine that we are going to make the world conform to our dreams. When you reach the age, the age of maturity and reason, you realise you haven't a hope in hell of altering the world; that it is you who have to conform to it."

"I only know I love you."

"I wish I could accept your love. It's not so simple. It's common for girls of your age to fall in love with men of my age. We're always very flattered. You admire our sophistication, our knowledge of the world, our smooth manners, the fact that we are masters of the situation at parties, in restaurants, in all aspects of social life. An older man knows how to treat women, you say, to make her feel loved, wanted. But shouldn't we by now, Vanessa? Wouldn't it be surprising if a bachelor of over forty were not an expert in flattery? Hasn't he had enough practice? But you see, Vanessa, these qualities which at eighteen seem so desirable and not to be found in your contemporaries, this sophistication, this man-of-the-worldliness are not qualities at all. They are a veneer a man acquires with very little trouble, and when you come to touch it, it crumbles. The fact that a man knows all the best night-clubs and exactly how much to tip the head waiter won't help you at all when your child is crying in the night, when you're sick and need comforting, when you've no help and the housework is piling up, when you're despondent and depressed and things seem to be going wrong."

"But if that man loves you?"

"It takes more than love. It needs tenderness and affection and tolerance to meet the vicissitudes of married life, and these are things which must be planted like a seed and which must grow. Beside them, those other things which make girls like you believe themselves in love with men like me, look awfully insignificant."

"Are you trying to say that just because a man is forty-three he is incapable of showing tenderness and affection?"

"Not at all. But marriage, the kind of marriage you are still young enough to make, needs roots planted in fertile soil, mutual roots. My roots have withered long ago. I've formed convictions, habits. I know which things are important to me, which not: it's too late to change. When you marry you will decide these things together with your husband, so that the same things are important to both of you; you will have the same set of values. If you haven't you're doomed. A marriage like any other edifice must have foundations, Vanessa."

"Suppose I agreed with what you said but was willing to slide gently down the other side of the mountain with you? Suppose I expected nothing, other than to love you?"

"Love cannot live in a vacuum. Nothing can. It has to be fed, watered."

"What does all that mean to us, to me?" Vanessa said.

Howard leaned against the window-sill. "It means that everything we should be doing together and for the first time I shall have done before. I should be stealing from you something it's impossible to replace, your youth, your hopes, your dreams. They are very necessary. And there's another thing; you won't think it important but I promise you it is. I'm not earning a remarkable living and I don't suppose I ever shall. I have accustomed myself to the idea that I shall never be a rich man, and have folded away my dreams of costly possessions together with my hopes of an outstanding career at the bar. You have been brought up surrounded by everything that money can buy."

"I wouldn't mind not having any, Howard."

"It doesn't matter not having any money when you're young. When you're old it's not so good. While I've been at Whitecliffs I've come to terms with the situation. I've thought extremely carefully, and have come to the conclusion that although I would have accepted gladly all the things I was going to buy had there been gold on the top of my mountain, I have perhaps discovered something more worth while. I'm going to stay in Whitecliffs, Vanessa. There's more honesty. You don't have to smile at people who might be influential, give lunch to solicitors you hate the sight of, mouth pity to those for whom you have no pity, see the latest play by the best bad playwright of the year so that you can hold your own att cocktail-parties, say in one hundred words what could be said in ten, join clubs not because you want to but because you must, ask old so-and-so out to dinner because old so-and-so asked you. It's not just that I want to be different, that I don't want to conform; believe me, Vanessa, it's easier to conform. It's just that I'm fed up with all the hypocrisy we have to live with."

"Outside is a lonely place, Howard."

"What's that you said?"

"It's from a poem I once read."

"I'd rather be lonely than wallow in all that dirt. I can't thank your father enough for helping me to get sufficiently far away from it all for me to see."

"What is there for you down here?"

"Fresh air for the mind and the spirit. I'll find something to do. You see, Vanessa, you wouldn't want to be married to a crank."

"Don't sling mud at yourself. I think you're a very fine person."

"It has taken me more than forty years to decide how I will come down the other side of the mountain. I couldn't let you decide while you are still on the nursery slopes, going up."

"I'm sorry I made myself so cheap."

Howard left the window, and going over to Vanessa took her hands and pulled her up. When she was facing him he said: "You've paid me the biggest compliment I've ever had. You have everything, Vanessa, a girl could wish for, brains, beauty, youth, and you offer it all to me. Nothing you ever did, Vanessa, could make you cheap."

Vanessa looked into his eyes. "I think we could be happy, Howard."

"I wouldn't do it, Vanessa. Someone else could give you so much more. Moonlight and roses, Vanessa."

"I don't want moonlight and roses, Howard!" Vanessa raised her voice.

Howard moved away from his pipe. "You wouldn't want to marry someone who doesn't love you." He didn't look at her.

"That's not what you said before."

"I say it now."

"It isn't true."

"It's true."

"You talk about hypocrisy. Prove that you don't love me, prove it!"

"The onus of proof is on you. You made the allegation that I do."

Vanessa picked up a cushion from the chair and threw it across the room at him. He didn't move when it hit him. "Stop being so confoundedly pompous! 'Onus of proof'! We're discussing love. Love!"

"Don't shout, Vanessa, the walls are thin."

"All right, I won't," and Vanessa lowered her voice. "I won't shout and I won't throw a cushion again. That was childish. Will you do one thing for me, Howard? Just one?"

"What is it, Vanessa?"

"Promise to do it?"

"If I can."

"You can."

"All right."

"Kiss me."

He looked steadily at her across the room. "Of course, Vanessa."

She came across to him and lifted her face. Howard took her head in his hands and bending, kissed her forehead.

"Not like that, Howard." She put her arms round his neck and drawing him down to her pressed her lips on his. She was offering everything but he did not answer. Vanessa dropped her arms and moved away. She didn't look at him.

"I'd better go. Thanks for the Chopin."

He followed her down the little hallway and opened the door for her.

"Good night, Howard." Her voice was flat, defeated.

"Good night, Vanessa."

When she had gone he went back into the little sitting-room and played the last few minutes of the nocturne they had been listening to. When it had finished he removed the record, put it into its sleeve and then, on its own, in a drawer. He knew that it would be some time before he played it again. When he did he knew that the familiar melody would be irrevocably linked with the image of a girl in pink who had lifted her face so trustfully to his own. With what was an effort, for Howard, he picked up his pipe, refilled it, then clenching it hard in his teeth, took Nietzsche's *Antichrist* from the bookcase and began to read at the place he had marked with a toffee paper.

Twenty-four

On Saturday morning as Louise went into the hairdresser's, after a sleepless night during which she had decided to take the plunge and have her hair cut off, Vera came out. They met on the rubber mat in the doorway of the shop and Vera, a chiffon scarf over her newly-set hair, nodded, mumbled, "Good morning," and hurried off down the High Street. Louise stared after her. There was something funny about Mrs Dexter this morning. It wasn't just the fact that Maison Barbara had made her hair too blue, almost violet, in fact, nor that they had given her a wave on her forehead almost deep enough to sail a boat in. No, there was something else, Louise thought, and then she realised: Vera looked as if she had been crying. That was odd, and it accounted for the fact that Vera had not stopped to speak to her. There was nothing she could do now. She turned towards the glass door of the shop and, pushing it open, stepped into the embracing warmth and perfume of Drene shampoo and setting lotion for the transformation with which she was going to dazzle Harry.

In front of the shop at a semi-circular desk a girl, her hair in tight sausage-curls, busy filing her nails, said "Yes?" and blew on her fingertips to remove the debris. Louise didn't answer. They could at least give her a clean overall, she thought, and teach her to say "Good morning, madam." My goodness, two weeks in my salon and I'd make something of her. Not a bad looking little girl if she was taught to make up properly and took that disagreeable expression off her face. No stockings, too, and those grubby toes hanging out of her sandals. Dear, dear, some people have no idea at all.

"You gottanerpointment?" the girl said. This time she looked at Louise.

"Yes. For eleven thirty."

The girl flickered a lazy eye over the appointment book. "Pat!" she yelled into the back of the shop. A girl with a pony-tail, looking no more than fifteen, slouched out of a cubicle.

"Shampoo'n set, Pat."

"I'm having it cut," Louise said. "Your manageress is going to do it for me."

"Number three," the girl at the desk said, "and tell Mrs B. Has anyone been out for the doughnuts?"

"I'll go in a jiff," Pat said, and Louise followed her into a cubicle in which there was hair on the floor and soap in the basin.

Vera made her way down the High Street. She passed the baker's with its congress tarts, the wool shop with its knitting patterns, the men's shop with its khaki-coloured shorts hanging in rows outside. She neither noticed them nor made odious comparisons with the shops to which she was accustomed. She walked slowly and looked straight ahead. It was true she had been crying and she had good reason to cry. The world of Vera Dexter had come apart at the seams. Nothing had gone right, she thought, since Willie Boothroyd's death, and now it seemed that nothing ever would. Victor had been bad enough, but that she had been able to share with Arthur; this last shock was something with which she was quite alone. It almost wasn't fair. It had come so suddenly, too. She had been tidying up the flat this morning in her dressing-gown, so that it was straight before the daily woman came, when the bell rang. Vanessa and Arthur were at the café and she was by herself. She had opened the front door expecting to see Mrs Jessell and had found Doctor Gurney in the hall.

"Arthur's gone," Vera said. "He went a long time ago."

"I know. I wanted to speak to you. May I come in?"

"Of course. It's not about Victor? He's all right?"

"Victor's getting along nicely, yes."

In the sitting-room, Vera sat nervously on the arm of the chair and watched Doctor Gurney, who stood by the window.

"Did you know Arthur hadn't been feeling well?"

"He said once or twice he had stomach-ache. There's nothing wrong with Arthur, is there?"

"I'm afraid there is. We had him X-rayed yesterday at the hospital."

"He didn't tell me," Vera said, not because it mattered but because she was suddenly nervous.

The doorbell rang. "That will be Mrs Jessell. Excuse me while I let her in." She fussed with Mrs Jessell for a moment telling her to be sure and wash the insides of the windows, not to forget the light-fitting and to do some potatoes for lunch. When she could think of nothing more to say she said: "Don't forget to put some vinegar in the water when you polish the furniture," and went back to Doctor Gurney.

"I am afraid your husband is not very well," Doctor Gurney said.

"But he's been so much better down here," Vera said, "sleeping better, good-tempered; of course, he hasn't been eating much but the change of air I thought…" She wanted to talk – to keep on talking. She felt that if she kept talking, anything at all, just to stop Doctor Gurney saying what she felt sure he was going to say. She could suddenly think of nothing else she could say. She fiddled with the satin tie of her dressing-gown.

"I'm afraid the X-rays showed a growth in his stomach."

"A growth? You mean…"

Doctor Gurney nodded. "Of course, one can't be certain, but I believe there's very little doubt. The surgeon who examined him and saw the X-rays said an operation could be attempted. I don't think though that it will help your husband very much."

Vera stared. The pale grey curtains she had paid so much a yard for and had had so expertly made at Maple's, the olive tapestry furniture, the dark grey carpet, the misted walls, all seemed unreal, or was it unimportant?

"Of course, we must take him to London," she said. "...another opinion..." That was what Arthur would say.

"I'm afraid it isn't going to help very much."

"Does Arthur know?"

"No. That's why I came. He mustn't get to know either. In a man of your husband's temperament it would be more than unkind to let him guess."

Vera took out her handkerchief. "I don't think I've the temperament." She began to cry and Doctor Gurney watched her.

"Everything was so good," she said, "and first Victor, now Arthur. It's so sudden. My husband, Arthur, has..."

"Cancer," Doctor Gurney said. "It isn't a pretty name and it isn't a pretty complaint, but I'm afraid you have to face it and you have to face it alone. I've told Arthur he has a stomach ulcer, and he was satisfied with that explanation of his pain. It's up to you to make bearable what remains of his life. To make sure he doesn't know what lies ahead. You have to act a part, and you have to learn your lines so well that Arthur never finds out you are acting. If you take my advice, you'll tell nobody else at all, nobody. That way your husband will never know."

"I don't know if I'm strong enough."

"Mrs Dexter, you have to be. All your married life your husband has been there for you to lean on. Now he has to lean on you. You mustn't let him down."

Vera rubbed his eyes. "I wish we'd never come to this wretched place. Arthur, too, sees now how stupid it was. I wish poor Willie Boothroyd hadn't died like that and upset Arthur. I wish we'd never left London. I shouldn't have listened..."

"It would have made no difference to your husband, Mrs Dexter."

"Perhaps if he'd gone to someone when he first had the pain..."

"He's only had it for a week or two. These things grow very rapidly. You may take my word for it that nothing more could be done than will be done."

"I can't believe it. I just can't believe it. How long...?"

Doctor Gurney shrugged. "Three months, six months, a year at the outside. I'll do everything I can to help."

Vera stood up. "I made an appointment at the local hairdresser. I couldn't get up to town this week because of Victor. I must just cancel it."

"Because of Arthur?"

Vera nodded.

"Then don't. I expect he knows you're going. He'll wonder why. I know it's difficult, but you must try to carry on as usual. Exactly as usual."

"Exactly as usual," Vera said, and put away her handkerchief. "I'll try."

Doctor Gurney went back to his own flat before going down to the café.

"Did you tell her?" Mary said. She was sitting in the kitchen beside Jonathon's high-chair, feeding him from a bowl.

Doctor Gurney nodded.

"What did she say?"

"She cried."

"So would anyone."

"We weep for ourselves," Doctor Gurney said. "That's all we're capable of."

"I feel sorry for the old girl, silly as she is."

"What about Arthur?"

"For Arthur? What can one feel?"

"What can one feel?" Doctor Gurney said, and kissed his wife and son on their heads.

Vera was nearly at the end of the High Street. They had given her a terrible shampoo at Maison Barbara, and the girl had let water run down her neck. Her hair had been crimped and pinned until it was almost unrecognisable as her own. On any other day but this she would have been furious, indignant, hurrying home to comb it out, to make herself look normal. She was not hurrying. Her hair seemed unimportant. She did not care.

Two men were standing outside the Estate Agents' office.

"Vera!"

"Arthur!" she said. "I thought you were at the café."

"I was. I took half an hour off because Mr Parker here had something interesting to show me. You remember I told you about buying a cottage here for weekends? Well, the very thing has just cropped up. I knew you'd be coming past about this time so I waited for you. It's a bungalow really; I've just been to see it. It's pink-washed with a blue-tiled roof, three bedrooms, gets the sun all day, centrally heated, beautifully built; I'm quite excited. Mr Parker has the key; we can go and see it again straight away. I know you'll love it. There's a properly fitted kitchen; it's only been built about a year, and do you know what I like best?"

"No," Vera said.

"There's a greenhouse in the garden with a grapevine. Very young, of course, isn't it, Mr Parker?"

Mr Parker nodded. "Naturally, Mr Dexter." He looked at Vera. "In five years from now," he said, "Mr Dexter will have some of the finest grapes in Whitecliffs."

"In five years?" Vera said.

"Five to seven."

"Sounds good, doesn't it?" Arthur said.

Vera looked at him. "It sounds very good indeed."

On the beach, Vanessa and Cliff sat glumly side by side throwing stones into the water.

"I knew there was something wrong," Cliff said, "from your letter. That's why I came down to see what was going on."

"There's nothing wrong," Vanessa said unconvincingly and for the umpteenth time.

"Of course there is. You haven't even kissed me yet."

"There hasn't exactly been the opportunity." Vanessa had been standing at the fancy-goods window soon after lunch when someone had asked if they had any 'pretty girls' for sale. She had looked up to find Cliff leaning against the counter. She had managed a smile and glanced quickly towards Howard. He was busy serving ice-cream.

"I came down to see how you were," Cliff said. "I've been missing you."

"I'm fine," Vanessa said. She had forgotten how young he looked.

"I have to go back tonight. I came down on the bike. Can you get away for a bit?"

"I don't think so. We're one short. I wrote to you about Victor."

"Yes, you wrote about Victor all right. I'm sorry. I would have liked to see him, but I don't think there will be time."

"Have you had any lunch?"

"Yes, on the road. I didn't come for lunch, Van. I came to see you. You're looking prettier than ever."

She sold a bucket and a tin of bubbles to a small boy. Cliff disappeared. In a moment he was back again fiddling with the windmills on the counter.

"Your father says it's all right. They can manage without you."

"All right then," Vanessa said unenthusiastically. "I'll be with you in a second."

She had forgotten that Cliff was so tall. Tall and thin. His hands, strong-looking and the only part of him that was suntanned, seemed to be stuck on at the end of his gangling arms. They walked across the beach in between sand-castles and over people's legs and bodies, and beach bags, and rivers dug by the children, and jumped over the breakwater. There was a stretch of beach with not many people because it was rocky, and they sat down. Neither of them said anything for a moment, but the silence was awkward and then they both started talking together.

"Carry on," Cliff said.

"I was only going to ask how the Anatomy's going," Vanessa said.

"Fine. Just fine. What have you been doing?"

Vanessa told him. She told him about Whitecliffs and about Victor and about Honey and Basil and Elisabeth, and about Louise and her mother, and about the Gurneys.

"Who was the chap serving the ice-cream?" Cliff said.

"That was Howard. I forgot about him."

She felt Cliff looking at her. "You've changed, Van. I shouldn't have let you come."

"I didn't want to come, did I?"

"No."

They drew meaningless pictures on the sand with bits of stick. They talked about what Cliff had been doing in London, about his friends, his work, his exams. Vanessa thought about Howard.

"Do you realise, Cliff," she said, "that the sea will still be here just the same, doing exactly the same as it is now, thousands of years after we're dead?"

Cliff laughed at her serious tones. "I wouldn't worry about that," he said. "Besides, I'm too busy worrying about my

Anatomy. The quicker I get through that the quicker I can carry on and we can get married."

She had said nothing, and that was when they had started throwing stones into the water.

Vanessa watched Cliff's stones scudding across the surface and out to sea and her own plop dully, a few yards only, into the water.

"I suppose I might have guessed really," Cliff said, squinting into the sun at a stone he had thrown.

"Guessed what?"

"That it was all up."

"How do you mean?"

"Us." He waited for Vanessa to contradict him, but she was silent. He stood up dusting the sand from his clothes. "I might as well be getting back. There's no point driving back in the dark for…nothing."

Vanessa flung her last stone and stood up beside him.

"I'll see you off."

Cliff's motor-bike was parked along the top promenade among the gleaming rows of cars waiting warmly in the sun for their owners who had gone down to the beach. They walked to it in silence. From the saddle-bag Cliff took a thick pullover and a pair of goggles.

"It gets quite chilly when you're going along," he said.

Vanessa watched him struggling clumsily into it as men do. He wound his college scarf round his neck and straddled the bike.

"Well, Van…?"

She watched him manoeuvre the bike out into the road. The sun was shining through his hair and outlining the bones on his face. He trod hard on the starter, then again. The engine burst into sound then throbbed steadily in the warm air. Cliff was looking at her, waiting. For the first time she met his gaze unfalteringly. She said nothing but gathering her skirt round her slid on to the passenger seat behind him. He made no comment but throttled up and, looking both ways, spluttered off along the sea road.

Vanessa leaned her head against his back. "I've been such a fool," she said, but didn't know if he could hear.

Cliff turned his head half sideways.

"Where are we going?" he yelled.

Vanessa put both arms round his neck. "Up the mountain," she said, "together."

Twenty-five

On Saturday evening while Louise, in her flat downstairs, was sitting before the mirror preparing herself to meet Harry at the 'Landscape', Vera and Arthur were relaxing in their sitting-room, after an early supper, with cups of coffee, discussing their cottage. It was a rather one-sided discussion. Arthur, who had the details before him on a typed sheet from the Estate Agents, was enthusing about its charm, its modernity, its southerly aspect. Vera was saying yes and no at appropriate moments and watching him. She was thinking. But she was not thinking about the polished boards throughout, the modern floor heating, or the waste disposal unit in the kitchen; nor indeed was she thinking about 'Castellamare', the cottage upon which Arthur had already paid a deposit, at all. Vera was thinking about herself. About herself and Arthur. The remarks he was making about the immersion heater, the double windows, the tiled roof, were going over her head. She scarcely heard them. She was looking at her husband and she was thinking that it was probably the first time in twenty-odd years that she had done so; properly that was. She had, of course, been aware of him. Aware of him as the years went gently by, losing his hair from where it had grown abundantly round his forehead as Vic's did, losing the slim figure which had been his as a young man, growing stouter and, or so it seemed, shorter. She remembered when he had lost the four teeth in the front which were now replaced with a small plate, but when had the firm line that had been his jaw disappeared? When had his hands grown middle-aged, his hair turned completely grey? She could not remember. Surprisingly, suddenly and startlingly, in the little sitting-room of the flat at Whitecliffs, Vera Dexter decided that she loved her husband. Or was it that she had just grown used to him, as one grew used to a home, a pet one was fond of, a favourite coat, and did not want to lose him? He was still talking enthusiastically about the cottage. When they were first married, she remembered, they used to talk about nothing. When was it that they had become silent in each other's company unless there was 'something' to discuss? Their home, or furnishings, or help for it; their children and their problems which varied through the years from suspected measles to examination worries and what to Vera and Arthur were undesirable friendships; Arthur's business, prospering or, in years that were not so good, a little shaky; Vera's health; holiday plans; new cars; new maids; new acquaintances. When there was something to talk about they talked. When there wasn't Arthur buried himself behind a newspaper or they watched the television or asked people in for bridge and made busy, happy noises. Vera shut her eyes and tried to imagine how it would be without Arthur. She couldn't. Arthur had always been there. There had always been Arthur to make the arrangements, deal with people and problems, pay the bills, cope with the children when they got extraordinary, extravagant ideas. She admitted to herself what she had never troubled to think about because it had not been necessary. Arthur had been a good husband. A thought suddenly occurred to her which with new found courage she picked up and examined. There was no doubt that Arthur had been a good husband; had she been a good wife? If her conscience was capable of blushing it was blushing now. There was no doubt about the answer to her question, the answer was no. True she had made a home for him, a nice home, a smoothly run, luxurious home, entertained friends, brought up Victor and

Vanessa, but what had she done for Arthur, for Arthur himself? Had she loved him, cherished him, been a companion to him through the years? She knew she had not. They were strangers. She had no idea what he thought about, nor when he was thinking it. And what of the other thing? The thing that for many years now they had not discussed, and which long, long ago Arthur had ceased to ask for. There was only one answer to the question she had put to herself; there could be only one. She had not been a good wife. A housekeeper, yes. A wife, no. Even now, when Doctor Gurney had given Arthur so little time to live, what was she worrying about? Not that Arthur was ill and must suffer, suffer most probably until he would be glad to die, but she was worrying about herself, what she would do without him, when for eighteen years, since the twins were born, Arthur had had to do without her. These thoughts did not come easily to Vera who was unaccustomed to self-analysis, nor did they come altogether suddenly. They had started as a vague awareness on the afternoon that she had taken Vanessa's place at 'Le Casse-Croûto' while Vanessa went to Walmer with Howard.

She had taken over the tea-urn as they thought that would be easiest for her, and from her place, standing on the wooden slats behind the long counter, she had been able to watch Arthur. It was a new and different Arthur, an Arthur she did not know. Mrs Boil, the washer-up, said: "Isn't 'e lovely Mrs Dexter the way 'e talks to the kiddies and asks after me veins reglar and sees I don't stop on me feet too long?" And Charlie, the old man who slowly and arthritically kept the tables wiped and the floor swept in the garden, pointed a knotted finger towards her husband and said: "Your husband and me have a grand talk every morning over a cuppa. Course I was born and bred round these parts and a good many changes I've seen, but these days not everyone wants to listen…" And Arthur himself. With his sleeves rolled up, he smiled, laughed, chivvied the customers, patted the children on the head. Vera was amazed. It was a side of him she had never seen, didn't know existed. Arthur in charge. At home, of course, she was always in charge. She said where they were going, what they were doing, who they were entertaining, or what they were to buy, how much it would cost. Arthur either agreed or disagreed, in which case they had an argument which she usually won. Perhaps if she had visited him more at his office she might have seen this other, this different Arthur, but he had never encouraged it, and for her part she had never wanted particularly to go. "Mr Dexter, should we take some more cornets out of stock? They're going awfully fast." "Mr Dexter, this lady has lost her deposit token." "Mr Dexter, can you make up a 'Casse-Croûte' Sundae? I've all these trays to do." A 'Casse-Croûte' Sundae! Arthur! And there he was happily in the kitchen fiddling around with ice-cream and nuts and burnt almonds and chocolate sauce, when at home she didn't remember the last time he had been in the kitchen, had never even, as far as she could remember, made himself a cup of tea. But then, of course, she hadn't wanted him to. When they had staff it wasn't necessary, nor was it his place, and when they hadn't Vera preferred to do it herself or with Vanessa. Her kitchen at home was formicaed and chromiumed down to the last detail, shiningly surgical, and she didn't want Arthur blundering about and leaving saucepans not washed up and tea-leaves and drips on the silvery draining-board. But more than she was surprised at the domestic things he was capable of doing, she was surprised at his happiness. Arthur was smiling, laughing, sparkling almost. At home he sat behind his newspaper and grunted, or sat behind his cards and called. Sometimes he talked tersely into the telephone, answered the children's questions in monosyllables, agreed gruffly to something Vera had suggested. Usually he was silent, unless they had friends round in which case he discussed the news or the stock market until it was time for bridge. Watching him, Vera could not believe that this was Arthur with whom she had lived for so many years. She watched him cheerfully empty the bucket of drips from under the tea-urn, slap Basil on the back at some funny remark made by a customer, put his arm round Honey. She had seen a stranger, a laughable, lovable stranger. That was the night of Victor's accident, the night they had rushed so apprehensively to the hospital, the night Mary Gurney had made tea for them all on their return. Two days later, when they had heard the true story of what Victor had been doing in 'Le Casse-Croûte' so late at night, Vera and Arthur had come closer together than they had been for years. They had just got into bed. Vera said:

"It's so terrible, Arthur. One doesn't realise the children are old enough to…well, you know…and with some frightful girl he picked up on the beach… I would never have believed it of Victor."

"We know nothing of what's going on in their minds. They act a little play; a sort of façade for our benefit. We don't really know them at all, Victor and Vanessa."

"Perhaps we haven't tried to know them."

"Don't let's delude ourselves, Vera; we never will. Eighteen cannot talk to middle age. It's a different language. You can make a guess, of course, but by the time you get to our age you've forgotten all the clues."

"We aren't all that old, Arthur."

"I feel we are. That was until we came to Whitecliffs. What is it they say about ill winds? If poor Willie hadn't died I would never have come here. I would have stayed at home, the office by ten, home by six, Saturday morning in bed, drinks on Sunday, the same old routine and barely knowing I was alive. Look at me now. Face in the sun every morning, telling the time by the tide… I feel almost like a young man."

"But you want to get home?"

"I do, Vera, yes. But it'll be different now. I've broken away long enough to get a sense of proportion about things. It's not such a bad business, mine, and I really enjoy it. I'd just got stuck in this treadmill thing, and forgotten there was anything else in life."

"Such as?"

"Well, six-five specials, bath buns, buckets and spades."

"They don't seem all that important to me."

"They're more important than you think, Vera. You probably won't admit it, but I think that being down here has done you good as well. You seem more relaxed, easier…you even have some colour in your face…and I don't mean Elizabeth Arden."

"What about our poor little Victor? If we hadn't come here…"

"Are you trying to tell me that what happened to Victor is my fault?"

"No, Arthur. But…"

"I believe you are. It's unfair, Vera. You know I'd give anything not to have had this happen to Victor. It won't be very pleasant for him – scarred and with the sight of only one eye. Sometimes I think you regard me as a sort of machine useful only for handing out the money. You forget that I have feelings, although you did your best to stifle them years ago. When I think of Victor I could cry. It's taken away any heart I had for anything. Does that surprise you? I'm not a stone, you know. I don't only eat and sleep and work. I have feelings…not that you've ever considered them. Do you think I would have wanted to come to Whitecliffs if I'd known this was going to happen to Victor? I know that if we hadn't come it mightn't have happened, but then if it hadn't been for Willie dying we mightn't have come…you can't foresee these things. It hardly makes me feel any better about Victor, though, to know that you're really holding me to blame."

For the first time in eighteen years Vera said into the darkness:

"I'm sorry, Arthur. It was unfair of me."

Arthur was so surprised he said nothing; just lay there looking at the scrap of moonlight that crept round the side of the curtain. He wondered what had come over Vera.

"Perhaps we should have talked to them more about… about…well, you know," Vera said.

"Prehaps someone should have talked to us more."

Vera stared into the darkness, her cheeks burning.

There was a slight noise in the room.

"Are you crying?" Arthur said.

"A little."

"What about?"

"Us, Victor."

"You can't put back the clock."

"I suppose you can't," Vera said, and wished suddenly that there wasn't such an unbridgeable gap between the two single beds.

Now, listening to Arthur rambling on like an excited schoolboy about the cottage she knew he would not have very long to enjoy, Vera yearned with a longing she did not know she was capable of for every one of the lost years which had taken them step by step farther apart. If, at home, Arthur was taciturn it was she who made him so; if he never discussed his business affairs with her it was because years ago she had made it clear that she was uninterested; if they avoided physical contact it was because that was the way she wanted it. She realised that she now had everything she wanted, but with the prospect of losing Arthur it had all turned sour.

"I suppose you'll enjoy yourself furnishing it," Arthur said.

"What's that?"

"Furnishing. The cottage. Curtains and carpets and things."

Vera stared at him. She hadn't thought of that. Previously nothing would have delighted her more than to tour the shops to furnish a brand-new little seaside house. Now she didn't know if she could do it. She had to do it; cloud grey for the walls, pink for the chairs, yes, and a cottagey print for the bedroom…knowing all the time that it would be for nothing, she wouldn't keep it, of course, after… It was going to be awfully difficult. She had an idea.

"Why couldn't we keep this flat on?"

"It's not really homey. Besides, I want a garden and there's the grapevine."

The grapevine.

"Of course I don't suppose we should come every weekend. Not in the winter, at any rate. There's wistaria by the front door. Tiny of course as yet. The frame's there for it to climb up though."

Wistaria.

"You see, if we hadn't come to Whitecliffs I would never have thought of this cottage idea. One must make decisions. You see, good comes out of everything."

Good comes out of everything. Vera looked at him. Why has it got to be just when he is so happy, she thought. Why haven't I bothered to see that he was happy before? I never knew he could be like this. I never thought about it.

"I can hardly wait until next summer when we're settled in."

Vera looked away so that he would not see the tears in her eyes.

"You do like the cottage, don't you, Vera?"

The doorbell rang. Relieved, Vera stood up. "I'll see who's at the door."

On the landing stood Honey. She was wearing a navy blue linen suit and had a white coat over her shoulders. She was carrying her make-up case. "Can I see Mr Dexter?" She followed Vera into the sitting-room.

"I'm sorry to walk out on you, Mr Dexter," Honey said, "but I have to leave."

"What is it, Honey?" Arthur said.

Honey's eyes were sparkling. "Well, I met this man," she said. "He owns a big hotel not far from here and he's something to do with the BBC. He's going to give me a spot in his show. Singing. His name's Terence. Are you awfully cross?"

"Not a bit," Arthur said. "We're packing up soon anyway. We shall miss you."

"You're sweet," Honey said. "You really are." She crossed the room and bending, kissed Arthur on the top of his head. "Isn't he a poppet, Mrs Dexter?"

"Yes," Vera said, and Arthur looked at her.

When Honey had gone they went together over to the window which looked onto the front of the block.

Downstairs was a red sports car in which was a good-looking, grey-haired man wearing a signet ring, and Honey's luggage. He reached across to open the door for Honey, and started the engine. Arthur and Vera watched until they had disappeared in a welter of exhaust along the sea-front.

"Farmyard morals!" Vera said.

Arthur looked at her and the look said: Victor.

"Oh, God," Vera said, "I shall have to remember."

"I don't suppose," Arthur said, "that they'll be able to do such a good job on him that we shall ever be able to forget."

Twenty-six

In the bar of the 'Landscape' Louise waited for Harry. She sat at a little table from where she could watch the door. With her left hand she clasped the small glass in which was a gin and orange she had barely touched, and with her right she patted the hair at frequent intervals which felt so light, so odd upon her head. She had enjoyed her morning at the hairdresser's. Watching the manageress like a hawk she had told her where it should be long, where short, where thinned, where tapered. Louise knew more about hair than did this woman who called herself a hairdresser, and with whom the local inhabitants were apparently well satisfied; she ignored the sighs and glares with which her instructions were obeyed. When it had been cut she suffered in silence while the sloppy Pat shampooed her hair looking anywhere but at what she was doing, chiefly at her own face in the mirror, while the water dripped down Louise's neck or into her eyes. After applying the brightening rinse Louise had asked for, she brought her, sopping, up from the basin and, not bothering to put a dry towel round her neck, shambled off to call the manageress again. They had no rollers with which to set her hair; had never heard of them. Louise painstakingly showed them how to make rolls of cotton-wool round which the strands of hair could be wound. She practically set it herself, and when they went away to find a hair-net for her she heard them muttering about her outside. She didn't care. There were two heats on the dryer – unbearably hot or icy cold. Louise read a magazine two years old – Winter Sports edition – and suffered. When she was pronounced dry by Pat who came in chewing the remainder of her 'elevenses', she said she would comb it out herself. The result was pleasing. She paid the bill, gave tips to compensate for the trouble she had caused, and went home.

Her mother said: "Louise, what have you done? Your hair was the best thing about you."

"Thank you, Mother," Louise said, and went into the bedroom. Her mother hobbled in after her and watched her as she sat before the mirror.

"You're not eighteen, you know."

"Forty-three next birthday."

"Why have you gone all kittenish?"

"A change. I was fed up with that bun."

"You've had it long enough. Don't know what you wanted to mess about with it for. Tinted it, too, haven't you?"

"A rinse."

"Waste of money. Who'll notice? It's not as if you were young enough to..."

Louise got up and walked past her mother into the kitchen to see to the lunch. Her mother was wrong. Quite wrong. She would have quite a shock if she knew she was young enough to... Harry obviously thought she was anyway. The day didn't go quickly enough.

When it was seven o'clock she put on the blue dress she knew suited her, and ranged all the make-up she possessed on the top of the dressing-table. When she had finished she knew she had done a good and expert job. With the material at her disposal she knew it was not possible to do better. With her pots, her bottles, her pencils, her brushes and her newly cut hair she had created an illusion of beauty. She knew it was unimportant, but she had been in the world of beauty for long enough to know that it helped. By the scared look on her mother's face she could tell she had succeeded.

"You've met someone, Louise! A man's been paying attention to you. You wouldn't get yourself up like that just for the cinema."

Louise said: "Don't be ridiculous, Mother," and waited until Miss Price came to sit with her mother before she left.

In the 'Landscape', the eyes of the men dispelled any doubts she had left. She had been accustomed to them sliding over her unremarkable appearance as though she were one of themselves. Tonight they had registered 'woman', and lingered if only for a moment.

Harry had said eight o'clock. It was half-past. She would give him until nine. An hour was long enough to wait for any man, even if they were as few and far between as they were in Louise's life. One could only stoop so low...and she was stooping low, she knew, with Harry. She didn't care. She knew there must be something else, but life as it was with nothing but work and life with mother and few friends and the cinema on Fridays...was that him?... No. She had butterflies in her stomach for a moment. She repeated to herself what her mother had told her. She was not eighteen. What a silly way to behave! It was jolly in the bar; seaside and holiday conversation on all sides; sounds bred of Manchester and Liverpool as well as local accents. The men wore open-necked shirts as they held their pints; the girls were bare-legged, sun-tanned, laughing. She wondered whether he was perhaps angry with her for going to his digs, and wouldn't come at all.

When he did come in she didn't see him until he was standing by the table.

"Hallo, Louise." He looked nervous and kept glancing over his shoulder.

"Hallo, Harry."

She waited for him to comment on her changed appearance. He got himself a drink and sat down next to her. He appeared not to have noticed and she felt a small pall of disappointment.

"I'm sorry about Thursday," Louise said, "barging in on you like that. I wouldn't have dreamed of it only everyone was so worried about Victor and I wanted to help."

"That's all right," Harry said vaguely, as though he didn't know what she meant. Then, as though he had suddenly remembered something, he looked straight at Louise, gave her the full benefit of his false-toothed smile and took her hand.

She had to admit to herself it was not unpleasant, and did not take it away.

"Louise?"

"Yes?" Louise held her breath.

Harry hesitated. "What have you been doing with yourself since Thursday?"

"Nothing much. Busy at the café." She told him how Victor was progressing, about Basil's wife coming back to him, about some amusing things that had happened at 'Le Casse-Croûte', about an argument she had had with her mother. Harry listened, nodding from time to time, then he got up to get them each another drink. The bar was getting crowded. Harry was tall, she could see his head above all the other men round the bar. He sat down again with the drinks.

"Louise?" He took a handkerchief from his breast-pocket and patted his forehead. It was getting warm in the bar.

"Yes?" She wished he would say it and get it over. He was making her nervous. When Johnny had proposed (was it really so many years ago?) there had been no hesitation, none at all. They had been in the officers' mess when the order had come over the loud-speakers to 'Scramble' and that had meant Germany and the night sky for Johnny, and it had taken him a second to say, "Marry me, Lulu," and even less for her to say, "Yes, Johnny," as their eyes met, and then his lips had touched hers so quickly she might have dreamt it, and he had said: "Until I get back, my love," and made for the door to which the other boys were running, and she had said: "Come back safely, my darling!" but he had already gone.

"I hope you won't mind my asking you this," Harry said.

Louise shook her head and waited.

"You see, we haven't known each other very long, but I feel that I've known you longer, that we understand one another, Louise…"

Listening, she knew that it sounded like a bit from a second feature film. She sighed and remembered she was forty-three and couldn't afford to be so choosy.

"…I wouldn't ask you, Louise, if it wasn't desperate, a matter almost, you might say, of life and death, only…"

What was he talking about? His face was quite flushed and the perspiration gathering again on his forehead.

Louise sat back and held tightly to her glass with both hands.

"Harry," she said, "What is it you want to ask me?"

He dabbed at his forehead. "Well, it's like this, Louise…"

"Wouldn't it be better if you came straight to the point?"

He tipped his glass to his lips. It was empty but the action appeared to give him courage.

"Can you lend me five hundred pounds, Louise?"

Louise sat back in her chair. As well as her feeling of shame and disappointment she felt a kind of relief. There was something she had to know.

"What makes you think I have five hundred pounds, Harry?"

"Well, I know those sea-front flats aren't cheap, and you told me you had a good job and you must've been puttin' a bit by each week and you aren't as young as you were, so I reckoned by now…"

"I'm sorry," Louise said.

"Wait till I tell you how it is."

"I don't want to know. You've made a mistake. I couldn't lend you sixpence."

"I thought you liked me, Louise," he said reproachfully, his smile forcing itself back over his teeth.

Louise stood up. "You were wrong about that, too. You must excuse me."

In the 'Ladies' she shut her eyes and leaned against the wash-basin.

"Feelin' queer, love?"

A brassy blonde breathed smoke and port into her face.

"I'm all right." She washed her hands although they did not need washing. The towel was grubby and someone had left lipstick on it. When she got back to the bar Harry had gone. She ordered a double whisky and sat down again. Something inside her whispered a warning about mixing drinks. She didn't care. That was that, she thought; absolutely and positively that. She watched a girl with short hair and beautiful legs make bedroom eyes at the good-looking man she was with. Their gazes did not falter. I've seen too many films, Louise thought, and not looked long enough, not frankly enough, in the mirror. How stupid of me to have my hair cut! The scissors can do nothing to the years. She looked away from the girl she had been watching and down into her drink. In the amber of the whisky she saw a black dress and a lilac shawl. Wearing them was an old lady sitting before a fire. She could not see the old lady's face, but she knew it was her own. She drank the whisky to destroy the image.

"Louise!" a man's voice said beside her. "It is Louise, isn't it? I hardly recognised you."

"Hallo, Howard," Louise said.

"May I join you or were you…?"

"No. You can sit down if you like."

Howard put down his glass on the little table and sat down opposite Louise.

"You look extremely nice. You've done something to your hair. I had to look twice."

Louise was on the last sip of her whisky. She said nothing.

"It suits you. It makes you look a great deal younger."

"I'm forty-three." Louise emphasised the words.

"The same age as I."

"It's different for you, you're a man." Howard looked up at the bitterness in her voice.

Louise said: "Bachelor! What a gay, romantic sound – a whirl of gaiety and girl friends. Now think of the word they use for me."

Howard was silent.

"Spinster!" Louise said. "Dead wood. Pitiable. Laughable."

"Louise," Howard said, and his voice was gentle. "What's the matter?"

"I suppose I'm a little drunk," Louise said, "and saying what's on my mind for a change. I'll be sorry tomorrow."

"Shall I get you another?" Howard said.

"You're not shocked?"

"It looks as if we both need it tonight."

"You, too?"

"Me, too," Howard said. He took out his pipe and bit on it as he did in moments of agitation. Earlier in the day he had watched Cliff, a young god, call at the café for Vanessa. He had concentrated on his ice-creams, trying not to watch. He had looked up as they strode down to the beach, young limb by young limb, Vanessa's sweet face serious. Later still, from the back kitchen where he had been fetching fresh supplies of ice-cream, he had watched them linger by the motor-bike, had seen them drive noisily off, noticed Vanessa's head go down against Cliff's back and wondered whether he hadn't been unwise. He hadn't realised that Vanessa had hit him so hard. There were many things he wished. He wished he were twenty years younger; he wished he were beginning again at the start of his dream; he wished he could, with a good conscience, have opened his arms to Vanessa who was the sweetest, freshest, most desirable thing he had ever had offered to him. Above all he wished to eradicate the image of her which formed itself every time he shut his eyes. For this reason, as well as one which had been at the back of his mind for a long time, he had come to the 'Landscape'.

Howard fetched two double whiskies from the bar and set them down on the table. They drank in silence for a while, listening and not listening to the hum and sudden throb of noise around them. When Howard looked across at Louise he was surprised to see tears rolling down her face and into her glass.

"Louise, what is it?"

"I'm sorry. The drink most probably. I can't remember when I last shed tears. When one is the head of the family one can't afford to. I thought for one moment tonight...but I was wrong. I suppose it was the disappointment. I'm sorry if I'm embarrassing you although with the gin and whisky I can't say I really care. I don't care about anything at the moment. I'm just having a good wallow."

"Would it help if you told me?"

Louise looked at him, her face gentle, and damp with tears, the new hairstyle disarranged. Because she didn't care her face had lost its usual tense look, was animated... "I don't want you to feel sorry for me."

"I'm too busy tonight feeling sorry for myself."

"All right. It was like this..."

Louise told Howard about Harry. She told him more. She told him about her mother, about when her father had been alive. She told him about Johnny. When she had finished, when the whole of her life was in his lap, Howard told Louise about himself. About his hopes and dreams about Vanessa. When neither of them had any more to say they were silent. Howard looked at his watch.

"Ten more minutes."

"I like it here," Louise said. "The place has a friendly atmosphere."

"How strange you should say that!" Howard said.

"Why strange?"

"I'm thinking of buying the 'Landscape'."

"Buying it?"

"Yes. The man that owns it is selling up. I'm not going back to London, to the pretence, the deceit, the back-scratching, the lies. I'm going to run this road-house and at least be honest with myself."

"Men have it all ways," Louise said. "You signal to the driver of your treadmill; he stops it for a moment, you pick up your briefcase and umbrella and get off. Thanks to Mr Dexter I got off, too. In a few weeks, though, I shall be back at my reception desk and 'Yes, Modoming' and 'No, Modoming' to those sickening women until they say, 'She's a bit past it, poor dear', and present me with free perms for life and get somebody younger, smarter." She shrugged. "I have to live, and there's Mother..."

"Time, if you please, gentlemen!" the bartender called.

Howard said: "I've got the car. I'll run you home."

They were silent on the journey. Outside Shore Court Louise said: "I'm sorry I made such an exhibition of myself. Will you forget it?"

"Our souls need airing occasionally. Please don't worry. Louise?"

She was powdering her face in the moonlight. She knew her mother would be waiting up and she did not want her to see she had been crying.

"Yes?"

"Louise, I shall need a partner for the 'Landscape'. I suppose you wouldn't by any chance be interested...?"

"Are you serious?"

"Louise, I talked to you tonight as I don't remember talking to anybody. It was so easy. We seem to be on the same wavelength somehow."

"You mean...?"

"I mean, for the moment, that you could help me run the place. I don't know much about the domestic side of things. Of course your mother would live there, too. Later perhaps... Well, we could see how we got on with each other."

Louise said, "To smell the fresh air every day, and not the perfume, the setting lotion, the high-class sin. You'd better wait until the morning, Howard. You may think better of it."

Howard said: "Louise, I think it's time you stopped underestimating yourself. I know it's your mother's fault, but you're a woman, Louise, and given a chance..."

"Yes?"

"You'll take a chance with me?"

Louise ran her fingers through the hair that felt soft and light and free. She bent back her head and laughed, her teeth shining, her eyes steadily on Howard's.

"I'll take a chance."

Twenty-seven

In November, the more exposed, less populated English seasides die quiet deaths. In the High Streets the shops are back to a barely pulsating normal; to Cheddar cheese, to endless chats over small purchases with the local inhabitants. The telephone does not ring with imperious orders, the shop is empty, only Grandma Spillikins sits on the solitary chair; the remaining tins of paté, asparagus and other delicacies are put into store until the next hopeful August. The business at the twopenny library improves with each fall of the barometer and at the 'Tea Shoppe', steamy with heat, replete villagers are reluctant to leave the table and totter down a High Street which has quite forgotten its tempting tables outside the shops of rubber sand-shoes, biff-bats and plastic boats. In echoing boarding-houses recuperating landladies are setting profits against losses, imaging new paint in Number Four, new curtains certainly in Six...or will they do another year? Those three from Bridlington were nice...but never again that dreadful child from, where was it?...near Edinburgh? No, that was that nice inoffensive couple with the baby; she hadn't regretted letting her into the kitchen with her tins, such a tidy little person...and the rent in the bedspread in Number Two was a shame – that careless London couple...and lying in bed till ten.

In Whitecliffs, only the wind moaned down the empty streets. On the promenade, 'Le Casse-Croûte' and the

Corporation Café shuttered, empty, sat amicably silent, battles fought and won, waiting stoically for the sea that would lash icily at them before the winter was out, the snow that would lie impartially on their roofs. Summer, brief as it was, had picked up its colours and gone. The red, yellow and orange of the pedalo boats, the blue of the sky, the green of the sea, the brown bodies of the children, their bathing suits in many colours, their beach-balls, their kites, their buckets and spades; the colours and the voices. The sand stretched greyly silent down to the sea that met the grey sky. The gulls circled looking for food.

Across the empty beach, across the hard, flat winter sands which knew neither flagged castles built by pudgy fingers nor carefreely paced cricket pitches, a man, head bent, walked slowly with a stick. Huddled into his thick tweed coat, his collar up, his hat down, his face nearly as grey as the sea and the sand, he walked a few paces, battling against the wind, then glanced up with, was it fondness? at the closed face of 'Le Casse-Croûte'. His progress across the bay was slow; painfully slow. Outside there was the wind, cutting round his face, his ankles, threatening at times to blow him over, and within the pain. The pain. That was something he had been thinking about. It was two months now since they had operated on him for his ulcer, but the pain had not only not got better, it had become worse, much worse. He would have to speak to Doctor Gurney about it when they went back to town. The local chap who was looking after him at 'Castellamare' was all right, of course, nice young chap in a way, but he couldn't talk to him as he could to Doctor Gurney. The young man, pompous rather, not very long qualified, talked to him as if he were a child, an idiot almost, he hadn't the humanity...funny, Doctor Gurney had once said he might as well have been a plumber; had changed his mind though after Whitecliffs; realised he was made for medicine, medicine for him; he understood people in all their horridness. This young chap now hardly remembered your name. He would walk to the far rocks, black, slime-covered, where the beach huts, white and chilly-looking, ended, he had promised Vera… Vera now! She was a different person if anyone was. If he wasn't back before twelve as he'd promised, she'd be down to the beach in her crepe-soled brogues and her warm stockings, a scarf round the grey hair that was no longer blue but soft, silvery, and her cheeks pink from the wind, and woolly gloves, and she wouldn't turn up her nose at the sand as though it were something dirty but would stride across it towards him and take his arm, and her voice would be gentle, tender almost, as it had never been, and she would tell him off for being too long, getting cold, as if he were precious to her, as he knew he never had been, for all those years until Willie Boothroyd… Willie Boothroyd. Perhaps he was the only one who had really cared. Polly Boothroyd was talking already of marrying again and going to South America. He wondered if Vera…? No, he was sure she wouldn't, not so soon at any rate. Once he might have thought so, but not now. Not now. She listened for his every move in the night, was ready with a drink, his pills, a water-bottle. Not that he had any intention of dying for years and years anyway; not now that he was taking things easily, had 'Castellamare' for weekends, the healing air of Whitecliffs. As soon as he was feeling properly fit from this operation he would be back in the City, but gently, much more gently; oh, he had learned a lot! And they talked even, he and Vera – had got back again into the old way of talking about 'nothing'. When the pain in his stomach was bad and he had to do something to take his mind off it, before the pills worked, they switched on the fire in the bedroom from which they could hear the wind sweeping the shore and the sea battering against it, and they'd talk. They'd talk of Victor, now with eye-shade and stick, and scars on his face, cutting a dash at Cambridge, his shame forgotten, a kind of hero, not denying the stories that circulated through the colleges about how he received his injuries, only when the girls fell at his feet, stepping warily… Vanessa, now officially engaged to Cliff, waiting patiently, contentedly, as, having passed his Anatomy, he waded painstakingly through rivers of Pathology, Medicine and Surgery. They talked of Basil, now the blue-eyed boy of his publishers; Elisabeth waiting for their baby; of Howard philosophising happily, nightly, from the other side of the bar at the 'Landscape'; of Louise, his ring on her finger, watching him with love. Often, when the pain was bad, the efficient, sterile, young doctor had been with his efficient, sterile syringe, and they were waiting for the drug to work, they talked of themselves. They rolled back the carpet of their married life and discussed the times before the twins were born, their early months together, or they rolled it down and talked of the happy summer at Whitecliffs. They never trod on the years in between. When the pain grew less and the effect of the drug greater, Arthur would talk of 'Castellamare' and how lucky they were to have thought of it and found it, and of their happiness and of the vine in the greenhouse and of the grapes they would have, and how Vanessa and Cliff could bring their children for holidays by the sea, and, whenever he did, Vera's face would be turned towards the fire or she would busy herself with something or other in the bedroom.

Behind him on the sand was the firm imprint of his footsteps, and beside them the line of holes left by his stick. Ahead the beach lay smooth and the rocks seemed very far away, and was it that the wind was colder today? Perhaps he would walk only until he was level with 'Le Casse-Croûte' and then turn back. That had been a joke, that had. But a good one. Arthur Dexter running a beach café. He had surprised them all. He had surprised himself. But he had had the courage to get off his treadmill, hadn't he? He had been off it too long. A month, two perhaps, Doctor Gurney said, and he would be back at the office, but this time it would be different. He would run his life, he would not allow life to run him. He looked up towards the promenade. He was level now with 'Le Casse-Croûte'. By the shutters that hid the ice-cream counter stood a girl; a girl in a duffle-coat and trousers. For a moment she was motionless, her hands in her pockets, looking out to sea. Then she saw him and she was all arms and legs and black hair flying, running across the sands towards him.

"Mr Dexter! Mr Dexter!" She was excited, breathless from the wind.

"Honey!" Arthur said as she stopped in front of him. "What are *you* doing here?"

Honey didn't answer. She was staring at him. Staring at the greyish-yellow skin, the accentuated cheek-bones, the sunken eyes. The wind whistled round them. Suddenly Arthur understood. Looking at Honey's face as she gazed into his own, he understood why he was not getting better as quickly as he had hoped; why the pains in his stomach were becoming worse; why his son and daughter could not look into his eyes; why, when he talked about the vine in the greenhouse of 'Castellamare', Vera stared into the fire. How stupid he had been!

"You're ill," Honey said.

"I had an operation," Arthur said. "I'm getting better now. What's been happening to you?"

"I'll tell you," Honey said. "I just came back to say goodbye to 'Le Casse-Croûte'. To Whitecliffs. I didn't expect to see you."

"Shall we walk along?" Arthur said. "It's too cold to stand."

Honey took his arm, and he was glad of her support as they walked back across the sand.

"Of course I've been a fool," Honey said. "I always am where men are concerned. Terence looked after me very nicely, but this broadcasting thing just never came off. It was always next week, and when next week came, the week after that. Honestly, Mr Dexter, I don't think he had anything to do with the BBC after all."

Battling with the wind, Arthur smiled at her naïveté.

"So I'm going back to Jimmy," Honey said, "and back to the show. It was lovely of you to get me away and I must say I enjoyed it. The café was fun, but I suppose you've got to go back to work some time. You can't stay away for ever. That's life."

Arthur, frail, finding the walking difficult, looked out to the unquiet and inexorable sea. “Life is a gift, Honey,” he said slowly. “And we should not look gift horses in the mouth.”

ROSEMARY FRIEDMAN

GOLDEN BOY

This is one of Rosemary Friedman's best-loved novels. Freddie Lomax is a slick, work-driven city executive, popular and sociable, other eyes always drawn to the magnetic field of his charm. Utterly without warning he is given two hours to clear his desk at the bank and he finds himself joining the ranks of the middle-aged unemployed. His confidence that a new job will appear proves unfounded, and with all the time he now spends at home his marriage to Jane begins to suffer…until, when he thinks he can go no lower, he discovers that he is not the only one with problems and he applies his talents to a last attempt to save his relationship.

'What a story! What a storyteller!' *Daily Mail*

LIFE SITUATION

Oscar John has it all: a successful author, he has been married happily for sixteen years. But then everything changes when he meets Marie-Céleste, an elegant French doctor. When his sexual curiosity turns into passion and an all-consuming love, he is completely unprepared…

Rosemary Friedman

Patients of a Saint

The doctor's practice, first introduced in *No White Coat* and again in *Love on My List,* is expanding. He finds himself buckling under the strain of an increased workload and the demands of his exuberant twins. His wife, Sylvia, persuades him to take a much-needed break and he realises that it is time to find an assistant.

This proves to be a difficult task, but once he has found the right man, the doctor has more time to devote to individual patients and to his family.

Into this busy environment arrives the doctor's alluring cousin Caroline. On a study visit from the US, she invites herself to stay for six months – a situation which causes much chaos and hilarity.

Proofs of Affection

One year in the life of a London Jewish family at a time of great change: Sydney Shelton's business is not doing too well these days, but he has provided for his future and his worries are not about trade but about his own health and his children, now young adults. Sydney's wife Kitty knows how ill he is – but they cannot talk about it. The children openly flout tradition and go against his wishes. What will happen to them if he dies?

With a light satirical touch and great sensitivity, Rosemary Friedman explores the tensions and deeper feelings of a traditional family facing the pressures of change in a non-religious society. A thoughtful and moving novel.

ROSEMARY FRIEDMAN

ROSE OF JERICHO

Kitty's husband Sydney is dead, and eighteen months later she is still struggling to come to terms with his death. She takes comfort in the lives of her children, and the full comedy and crises of Kitty's circle of family and friends vividly unfold. On a package holiday to Israel, in between awe-inspiring visits to the Dead Sea and the dramatic desert, she gets to know Maurice Morgenthau, reserved New Yorker and survivor of the Nazi concentration camps. The friendship between them grows and Maurice helps Kitty gain a new sense of perspective on her life. In turn Kitty helps Maurice tell his harrowing story of survival for the first time.

TO LIVE IN PEACE

This novel pursues the story of widow Kitty Sheldon from Rosemary Friedman's delightful earlier novels *Proofs of Affection* and *Rose of Jericho*. Kitty has watched her beloved husband die, and her children grow to adulthood. She takes security from her role as family matriarch, but now her north London Jewish community is rife with dispute about the recent Israeli invasion of Lebanon. At the invitation of her gentlemanly suitor, Holocaust survivor Maurice Morgenthau, Kitty visits New York – where she learns to please herself and in so doing learns to *discover* herself too.

OTHER TITLES BY ROSEMARY FRIEDMAN AVAILABLE DIRECT FROM HOUSE OF STRATUS

Quantity		£	$(US)	$(CAN)	€
	The Commonplace Day	6.99	11.50	15.99	11.50
	An Eligible Man	6.99	11.50	15.99	11.50
	The Fraternity	6.99	11.50	15.99	11.50
	The General Practice	6.99	11.50	15.99	11.50
	Golden Boy	6.99	11.50	15.99	11.50
	Intensive Care	10.99	17.99	26.95	18.00
	The Life Situation	6.99	11.50	15.99	11.50
	Long Hot Summer	6.99	11.50	15.99	11.50
	Love on My List	6.99	11.50	15.99	11.50
	A Loving Mistress	6.99	11.50	15.99	11.50
	No White Coat	6.99	11.50	15.99	11.50
	Patients of a Saint	6.99	11.50	15.99	11.50
	Practice Makes Perfect	6.99	11.50	15.99	11.50
	Proofs of Affection	6.99	11.50	15.99	11.50
	Rose of Jericho	6.99	11.50	15.99	11.50
	A Second Wife	6.99	11.50	15.99	11.50
	To Live in Peace	6.99	11.50	15.99	11.50
	Vintage	6.99	11.50	15.99	11.50

ALL HOUSE OF STRATUS BOOKS ARE AVAILABLE FROM GOOD BOOKSHOPS OR DIRECT FROM THE PUBLISHER:

Internet: **www.houseofstratus.com** including author interviews, reviews, features.

Email: **sales@houseofstratus.com** please quote author, title, and credit card details.

Hotline: UK ONLY: 0800 169 1780, please quote author, title and credit card details.
INTERNATIONAL: +44 (0) 20 7494 6400, please quote author, title, and credit card details.

Send to: **House of Stratus Sales Department**
24c Old Burlington Street
London
W1X 1RL
UK

Please allow for postage costs charged per order plus an amount per book as set out in the tables below:

	£(Sterling)	$(US)	$(CAN)	€(Euros)
Cost per order				
UK	2.00	3.00	4.50	3.30
Europe	3.00	4.50	6.75	5.00
North America	3.00	4.50	6.75	5.00
Rest of World	3.00	4.50	6.75	5.00
Additional cost per book				
UK	0.50	0.75	1.15	0.85
Europe	1.00	1.50	2.30	1.70
North America	2.00	3.00	4.60	3.40
Rest of World	2.50	3.75	5.75	4.25

PLEASE SEND CHEQUE, POSTAL ORDER (STERLING ONLY), EUROCHEQUE, OR INTERNATIONAL MONEY ORDER (PLEASE CIRCLE METHOD OF PAYMENT YOU WISH TO USE)
MAKE PAYABLE TO: STRATUS HOLDINGS plc

Cost of book(s): ______ Example: 3 x books at £6.99 each: £20.97
Cost of order: ______ Example: £2.00 (Delivery to UK address)
Additional cost per book: ______ Example: 3 x £0.50: £1.50
Order total including postage: ______ Example: £24.47

Please tick currency you wish to use and add total amount of order:

☐ £ (Sterling) ☐ $ (US) ☐ $ (CAN) ☐ € (EUROS)

VISA, MASTERCARD, SWITCH, AMEX, SOLO, JCB:

☐☐☐☐☐☐☐☐☐☐☐☐☐☐☐☐☐☐☐

Issue number (Switch only):

☐☐☐

Start Date: ☐☐/☐☐

Expiry Date: ☐☐/☐☐

Signature: ______

NAME: ______

ADDRESS: ______

______

POSTCODE: ______

Please allow 28 days for delivery.

Prices subject to change without notice.
Please tick box if you do not wish to receive any additional information. ☐